BEAUTY TO THE HIGHEST BIDDER

Roselind Arden had much to offer a man. Youth. Beauty. Grace. And noble blood.

What she demanded in return was simple. Wealth. Enough to repair her family's shattered finances and insure her beloved younger brother's future.

One man in England fit her bill beyond all doubt—icy and elegant Reginald Darnley, with the vastest fortune in the realm and a huge desire to add Roselind to his possessions.

Thus, at the height of the season at Bath, the bargain was struck—and only then did Roselind learn the hideous secret of her promised husband's past ... and the price she had to pay....

The Montague Scandal

THE MONTAGUE SCANDAL

A Regency Romance

by
Judith Harkness

For my parents,
who made the writing of this book possible.

Print ISBN: 978-0-7867-5506-6
eISBN: 978-0-7867-5507-3

Distributed by Argo Navis Author Services

Distributed by
Argo Navis Author Services
www.argonavisdigital.com

The
Montague
Scandal

1

It had been a wet spring. All of England, and the south in particular, had seen a number of those strong slanting shower storms for which that Season is so justly renowned, and though the rough weather had at last cleared off to make way for a sparkling June, the roads had suffered greatly.

This state of affairs must be expected to have taken its toll on the swarm of stately carriages making their way toward Bath for the start of the summer season. Sir Walter Chumley's chaise, bearing the baronet and his lady, together with their daughter, the lovely Miss Clarissa Chumley, had been only an hour out of London when it was forced to draw up to allow for the disentanglement of a farmer's dray from the wheels of an elegant black phaeton. Already a large crowd had gathered to gawk at the spectacle. A dozen other vehicles had been similarly immobilized, exciting a stream of jeering remarks from the onlookers. As a young know-all observed to his father (in something less than elegant language), it was clear that even these fashionable chariots were powerless against the elements.

"All right for you to talk, lad," came the blunt retort, "but

Jenkins, he'll have the devil to pay, with all them victuals scattered here and yon about the road, and his cart done to smithereens."

The farmer Jenkins did indeed look dismayed. He stood off to the side surveying the damage to his vehicle and livelihood, while the fine dasher who had caused it all was arguing in the middle of the road with another gentleman.

Lady Chumley emitted an impatient snort. She was not a woman accustomed to being kept waiting, either in the highway or anywhere else. It was abhorrent and unpardonable that the wife of Sir Walter Chumley should be incommoded in this abominable manner.

"Do get out and see what all the fuss is about," she commanded the baronet. That docile gentleman complied, as was his habit when ordered to perform any service by his better half. He proceeded to walk about the tangled and overturned vehicles and to discuss the matter at some length with some other of the onlookers, hoping to be of service in any way which would neither muddy his boots nor entail any real exertion. That proving impossible, he ensconced himself beside a young man of vaguely familiar aspect, who likewise appeared to be immersed in the spectacle. The crowd's attention had now turned to the argument under way between the two dandies in the middle of the road.

"Why," exclaimed Sir Walter, in genial amazement, "it is Darnley!"

"Yes," said the young fellow next to him, a tall, coltish youth with enormous gray eyes and a mop of thick wavy hair which had the effect of making him look both sensitive and younger than his twenty years. "It was his phaeton caused the accident. Devil of a row they're having!"

"Who is the other man, do you know?"

The youth shook his head. "Drove up a moment ago in that chaise." He gestured at a closed carriage by the side of the road, of the type hired by travelers who did not possess their own means of conveyance. "Seems to be holding out pretty well against Darnley, though!"

The youth looked with some pleasure at the spectacle of the two men arguing. Fiery words were being thrown about, mostly on the part of Reginald Darnley, a swarthy black-haired gentleman dressed in an immaculately tailored dark brown riding coat, over which was thrown a greatcoat, the innumerable capes of which only enhanced the impressive width of his shoulders.

"By Jove!" he was crying now in an exasperated tone very unlike his usual voice. "I don't give a brass farthing *what* you said, you impudent jackanapes! What gives you the right to come blustering in and interfere? If you do not move off this instant, I shall have your hide, I promise you! What d'you think, that we have all the day to sit about while you send off for a smithy from town, who very likely won't be here till dawn, and then shall certainly not have the proper tools about him and be forced to retrace his steps? We, I suppose, are meanwhile expected to make a picnic of it. Perhaps we should have dancing bears, and send for the gypsies, so as toregale ourselves the better!" Darnley's face composed itself into a sardonic smile.

The other gentleman only smiled in quiet amusement. He was very tall and slender, with a complexion tanned to a shade more nearly resembling brass than bronze. A shock of sun-lit wheat-colored hair and a pair of piercing humorous blue eyes set off the fine aristocratic features of his countenance. He was dressed in a traveling coat of plain design that had evidently seen better days; his hessians were worn, though of beautiful leather that hugged the lines of his slim, muscular calves. Something in his carriage and in the quiet assurance with which he regarded Reginald Darnley belied the shabbiness of his garb.

"I only," he said now, in a quiet, well-bred voice, "asked you to wait. If you wish to enjoy yourself while you do so, sir, it is entirely up to you." A hiss of approval rose in the crowd. Darnley looked furiously about him.

"The smithy shall certainly be here before dawn. Before midnight, even, I should think. It may be no concern of yours, as your own vehicle appears to be undamaged, but perhaps you will not mind this little inconvenience to yourself, since this poor fellow here"—gesturing at the astounded farmer—"has lost not merely half an hour of his time but all his livelihood as well."

Darnley was enraged. A blood vessel stood out on the strong broad olive brow, his lips twisted into a sneer, and he drawled, "Of course, you will wait too? I should hate to think you had gone to so much trouble not to see the outcome of your noble intentions. But then, I suppose you have nothing better to do."

The other gentleman merely bowed and smiled, and was about to walk away when a commanding voice sounded a few yards away.

"Hold! Hold, sir!" cried Lady Chumley, descending out of her carriage with all the dignity of a battleship under full sail. She stood, huffing a little from the exertion, her immense purple-satin-swathed bosom heaving from emotion. Immediately the titters which had risen in the crowd on the heels of the last exchange ceased. All eyes were upon her.

"I suppose you do not know who this gentleman is, young man?" she demanded of the blond gentleman in the voice of one used to brook no argument. "It is Reginald Darnley you address so lightly, sir! Reginald Darnley you use so ill! Intimate of the prince, no less!"

If she had meant to terrify the young man with these words, Lady Chumley was sorely disappointed. Instead of the expression of awed obedience she expected, she saw with some confusion that the impudent laughing expression he had first leveled at her was suddenly replaced with a frigid stare. The gentleman certainly looked astonished, but the surprise did not appear to be having the proper effect. The laughing blue eyes turned instantly hard, and cold as ice.

"Is that so?" he inquired quietly, gazing at Darnley.

"You may take my word for it," replied that gentleman with a sneer.

"I did not hope for such a stroke of good fortune," said the other, so softly that even those members of the crowd nearest him had to crane their necks to catch his words.

"What, what?" demanded Lady Chumley, feeling somehow that she had lost control of the situation.

The blond man's expression had returned to its normal good humor. Bowing civilly to Lady Chumley, he remarked, "I only said, madam, that I never expected to be so fortunate as to make the acquaintance of so consequential a figure as Mr. Darnley— and yourself, of course—on a mere journey of forty miles."

Something in his tone of sarcasm struck Lady Chumley as grossly impertinent, but before she could open her mouth, he continued in a wonderfully respectful tone of voice, "Still, I think even the prince himself would not mind waiting half an hour for the sake of a poor fellow whose cart he had overturned. My man has gone to fetch the smithy, and will be back at any moment.

We shall shortly be able to resume our travels without much inconvenience."

"Hear, Eliza," interjected the mild voice of Sir Walter Chumley, "we might as well make the best of it. Man's got every right on his side—" An icy glare from his wife cut short the further elaboration of his thoughts. Sir Walter shrugged meekly and turned back to the young fellow at his side. "My wife abhors being contradicted," he apologized.

The young man smiled. "Oh, yes," replied he sympathetically, "women are the devil. My sister is just the same way."

"That so?" demanded Sir Walter with interest. The idea that there could be two dragons of the cut of Lady Chumley had never occurred to him.

"Yes, indeed. Rosie's the very devil if she don't get her way! Puts up an enormous fuss when she's crossed—though, to be fair, she's awfully sweet most of the time."

The baronet's smile faded. Sweetness was certainly not one of his wife's outstanding qualities. Any thought that there might be some grounds for mutual commiseration here was swept away.

"Oh, indeed. Sweet."

"Yes. She's just having her come-out this season, as a matter of fact. At Bath. That's why I'm on my way there. I've just come from school, you know, and I'm to meet her at Bath."

"Ah, indeed. And where are you in school, young man?"

"Eton, though as a matter of fact I've finished now. I go up to Oxford in the fall term."

"Do you indeed?" Sir Walter's face took on a dreamy expression. He was harking back to the years when he himself had been enrolled at that splendid institution, the days before he had ever heard of Lady Chumley.

"Which college?"

"Balliol. It's where my father went, you know. I should have preferred Christ Church, but it was impossible. I think I shan't stay long, in any case."

"No? Why not, if I may ask? Great mistake to leave university before one's time, you know. Great mistake! If I were you, I should stay as long as possible. When once you're out, you know, there's no going back. Oh, yes, you should undoubtedly not leave."

"Well, I had thought," said the young man, "that I should like to take up farming."

"Farming?" inquired the baronet, looking very much surprised. The young fellow did not in the least look like a farmer. Rather like a poet, or perhaps a philosopher. And in any case, he was dressed in a natty sort of green Bath superfine coat, evidently a bit too big in the shoulders and short in the arms, but looking quite new and expensive, and rather swank. It did not at all resemble the garb of a farmer.

The fellow nodded. "It's quite the coming thing, you know. In my father's time there were always agents and people of that sort to look after everything, and I suppose it is really still expected of one. But I have been doing a bit of reading about the subject of innovative agricultural methods. Look here." The youth dived into a pocket and extracted a much-folded and -perused manual, a sort of pamphlet, which he handed to the elderly man. "It tells all about how our agrarian methods should be reformed. We waste heaps of land, not to mention labor, with our antiquated systems. Mr. Fox spoke several times before Parliament on the subject."

Sir Walter glanced at the manual in his hand. Besides being rather untidy, it seemed to be full of extremely technical language, and reeked of liberal politics. Sir Walter, though himself attracted to the style and thought of Mr. Fox, dared not even mention that name at home, his wife being of the opinion that any system which threatened her present comfortable position did not deserve the time of day.

"I wonder Fox has time for anything," said the baronet, fingering the manual tentatively, "what with all the goings-on in France."

"Oh, you mean about Boney and all that," replied the young man. "As a matter of fact, my uncle's just returned from France. I shall be hearing all about it very shortly—he and my aunt have taken charge of us since Father died."

"Your uncle is in the army, then?"

The young man's nod was interrupted by the loud utterance of Sir Walter's name. He was being summoned back from his pleasant little holiday from his wife. Apologetically he turned to take his leave. It was the devil, always being bossed about in this fashion.

"Oh, by the by," he said, remembering, "name's Chumley—Sir Walter."

"Oh, yes, how do you do?" The young man bowed politely, retrieving his manual. "Mine's Arden. Albert Arden."

An astounded look came over the baronet's face. "By Jupiter! Not the Earl of Iseleigh's son?"

"Yes, but now father is dead, and so I am the Earl of Iseleigh. Rather peculiar, ain't it?" The young man grinned.

"Dear me! Eliza will never forgive me! To think I have been talking this long time to the Earl of Iseleigh without knowing it!"

"Sir Walter!" came his wife's voice again. He hurriedly took his leave, expressing the hope of seeing his young friend again at Bath, and once more apologizing for the fate which made him rush off in this undignified manner.

The crowd was by now beginning to thin out. The blacksmith, having arrived some while ago, had finished the repairs to the farmer's dray and was now assisting Mr. Darnley's tiger in putting right the upended phaeton. The mysterious blond gentleman stood a little way from these proceedings, engaged in conversation with the farmer. Lord Iseleigh, watching, was amazed to see the gentleman extract a fat purse from his coat and hand the farmer three gold pieces. The farmer, himself too amazed at having been treated with any degree of justice by the "haristocracy," could hardly contain himself at this fresh evidence of a change in the nature of the world's order. He seemed ready and willing to go down upon all fours and kiss the boots of the marvelous peculiar fellow who seemed to want to make him rich.

But the blond gentleman was too quick for him. Having performed his little charity so inconspicuously that no one but Lord Iseleigh, who had been watching him particularly, had noticed it, he jumped back into his chaise, and in a moment was being driven away. Shortly thereafter, all the carriages, including Lord Iseleigh's little curricle and the Chumley chaise, had disappeared in the direction of Bath.

2

Lady Agatha Banforth leaned back against the carriage pillows and sighed. The Great Southern Highway was in no better repair than the London Road. Even the elegant indigo chaise in which she traveled with her niece, with its golden arms emblazoned upon the side, its modern accoutrements and team of powerful grays, had been forced to put up at Wells while a broken wheel was repaired. The delay had caused a journey of eight hours to be extended to twelve, and would result in their arriving in Pulteney Street much later than planned. Lady Agatha doubted they would be at Bath much before nightfall. Her husband and Bertie, she hoped, would have dined ahead of them.

Lady Agatha leaned over to adjust a moleskin rug which had been thrown across her niece's lap. Lady Roselind Arden had been sleeping for an hour. Her pretty little head, with its mass of glossy dark waves, was thrown back against the pillows, and the huge gray eyes were closed in sleep. For a moment Lady Agatha gazed at the young lady, biting her lip absently. Then she leaned back herself and tried to concentrate her attention on the passing panorama of fields and hedgerows laid out like a neat patchwork quilt in the dappled light and shade of the late afternoon.

But her thoughts were elsewhere. After a few minutes, restless and aching from the constant jogging of the carriage, Lady Agatha reached toward a little bag which contained her needlework. As she did so, a letter fell out from one of the side pockets. Frowning, she picked it up, and leaving the work untouched in her lap, commenced to read. The letter was from her husband, General Desmund Banforth, and was postmarked Alsace. It was dated April 10, 1814.

> My beloved wife [it began],
>
> I could not wait for a more convenient time to reply to your last letter, received this morning just as we were on the point of quitting camp. It was so rushed, so unlike in every way your usual style, that I understood at once how upset you must be. How unhappy I am that I cannot be at your side in this difficult time, and even the thought that we shall be reunited ere two months are up has no power to soothe me.
>
> I know not how to begin, nor what words to use to express my great sympathy for your darling niece and nephew! You know I never liked their father, though he was your brother, too, and everything that was ever yours I have tried to love. But Iseleigh was ever a vain and selfish knave, more in love with his immediate comfort than afraid of the disgrace he might bring on himself or his family. It is not much cause of astonishment to me to know that he ran through all his

fortune with profligacy and waste; and yet I am very sorry for it! How unkind that two innocent young people should pay the price for his foolishness! I had rather a hundred times over have seen him live worse and yet leave his heir some dignity, though it were only in his death.

Poor Bertie! I received a letter from him only last week, in which he boasted of all his plans for Windham, and of the vast improvements which will be made through what he calls "agrarian reform." To think there will be no more Windham, nor any Scottish estates, nor even, I suppose, lands left in the West Indies! I boil when I think of it, and yet I shall not pursue this vein any longer. It only gives you more pain than you already feel, I know.

Of course I shall not say anything to Bertie, if you think I ought not. I do not understand your reasoning on this point, but as ever shall obey your wishes. As to Roselind—what can I say! Your suspicions fill me with amazement. Why should a young lady risk everything in order to save her brother? If it were possible, I could conceive of it; but what can she do? Marry very well indeed, I suppose. But there is no one rich enough in England to save Bertie's fortune, and still be solvent, except perhaps Darnley. But if I were you, my love, I should leave off all these dreadful imaginings of yours, and only proceed calmly until I see you next, which will, God will it, be soon enough even for your impatient

Desmund Banforth

Lady Agatha read through the entirety of this letter, and then read it once again. She smiled a little just at first because of her husband's tone, which was so very like him she could almost see him spring to life before her. And yet his masculine disinclination to believe anything dreadful could not really comfort her much. The more she read, the more she frowned, and each time a certain line caught her up. "There is no one rich enough," she murmured to herself out loud, "to save Bertie, except perhaps Darnley." At last she folded up the letter and put it away, taking up her needlework again.

But the intricate pattern of leaves and grass and flowers could not hold her attention. Every moment her mild hazel eyes wandered up from their task to gaze bemusedly at the sleeping figure seated across from her. It was easy to tell when Lady Agatha was preoccupied, for she had a nervous habit of biting her lip, and now her lip was half chewed away, and the handsome lines of her face creased in worry. Lady Agatha was one of those women who, though never beautiful, have so much inner animation, so much quiet intelligence, and such a natural elegance of aspect and manner that they are always accounted beauties by those who know them. Her softness and her gentle nature inspired love in everyone, even in some who would never have admitted to admiring softness and gentleness. But at this moment Lady Agatha was thinking only of one human being.

"Poor child!" she murmured to herself, gazing at her niece's innocent sleeping face. "To think you never had anything from your father, save neglect, and now you are destined to have nothing but unhappiness from his death! And yet, heaven help me, I shall do everything I know how to do to save you from your own generosity. I shall not let you throw away *your* young life, only because your father chose to throw away his own!"

But Lady Agatha's thought was broken off, for her niece began to stir, and then sat up, and with a happy, sleepy smile inquired if she had been dead to the world for very long.

"Not above an hour, my dear," replied her aunt. "But I am afraid this carriage makes a poor bed."

"A wonderful one, Aggie!" protested Roselind with a little laugh, which had a gay, unaffected sound that was very charming. "I was so tired, I could have slept upon the very ground!"

And then a slight frown crossed the young lady's face, but was immediately replaced by a smile once more. Roselind gazed out of the window and said nothing for a little, and though she appeared to be watching the passing trees and farms with every sign of interest, Lady Agatha knew her thoughts were elsewhere. How often in the past months had not she seen that same flickering little look of unhappiness, and how many times had it not been smoothed away, by the greatest effort of will, into a smile!

"There is the beacon light!" exclaimed Roselind in a moment. "I think we are getting near to Bath, for it is my signpost. In a little while we shall see Bertie!" And now Roselind really did look happy, for she had not seen her brother since Christmas, and he was dearer to her than the whole world.

Within an hour the carriage was making its way into the outskirts of the city. The sounds and smells of the open country gave way to the cries of muffin men, newsmen, and milkmen. Flower girls bawled at every corner, the scent of roasting chestnuts mingled with the stronger odor of horses and smoke, and the streets were full of carriages, carts, and people hurrying to and fro on foot. An old man passed them, carrying a long implement for lighting the streetlamps, and the gay spectacle of a city lighting up its windows for the evening replaced the peaceful hush of the countryside in the lowering dusk. The sights animated Roselind as much as they did Lady Agatha, who had been away from her city too long. Nearly a year had gone by since she had left to undertake the care of her young niece in Devonshire, where the chief seat of the earl, her brother, was. With much anticipation she watched for the familiar streets and landmarks.

The carriage trundled slowly over the cobblestone streets of the ancient city, past the massive portal of St. James Cathedral, through Union Passage and Cheap Street, past the Pump Rooms and the Lower Assembly Room, and at last ascended the hill to a modern part of town in which lay Pulteney Street and Laura Place. It drew up eventually before a large, stately house of Bath stone, constructed in the currently fashionable neo-Grecian mode, with a small marble portico supported by six Ionic columns. Almost before the horses had come to a halt the front door was thrown open, and down the steps flew Lord Iseleigh.

The young man's cheeks were flushed with excitement, his eyes sparkled, his whole slender frame seemed to quiver beneath the bottle-green coat with its oversized shoulders and the sleeves which exposed his bony wrists and large slender hands. He thrust open the door of the carriage, hardly waiting for the liveried footman to climb down from his perch.

"Rosie!" he cried, his deep voice cracking into a tenor sound.

The young lady was not long in climbing down. In an instant she had jumped out, and was buried in her brother's embrace. Her whole face had lighted up at the sight of him, giving her pretty, regular little features, her huge soft gray eyes, and the full mouth with its peculiarly placed mole, just at the corner of her bottom lip, an animation and youth which made her delightful to look at. She, too, was slender, and though below the average height, possessed of a pert elegance of carriage which made her seem taller. Her entire manner was one of ingenuous enthusiasm and pleasure. Gone was the solemn gaze she had worn for nearly six months, gone the pensive wrinkling of her pretty brow, the troubled expression which had come over her, at private moments, since the fateful day some months before when she had received a piece of news which had muddied the peaceful waters of her young life. In this instant she was transformed by the sight of her darling Bertie, of his dear slender, awkward frame, the adoration which shone in his eyes and made him, a moment after embracing her as if his whole life depended on it, stand back with a new solemnity and look down at her.

There was something changed in him. Lady Agatha, helped down the next moment by the footman, and General Banforth, who had come out to receive them and stood now on the marble step watching this scene of reunion with kindly amusement, noticed it also. Albert Arden was going up to Oxford in the fall term. The fact had very recently descended over him like a rather frightening, wonderful light. He was no longer a boy, but a man. He held himself with a new self-conscious dignity, and his gray eyes held an expression of gravity, as if everything depended upon his maintaining a serious, appraising view of life. He remembered himself as quickly now as he had forgotten, in that moment of utter joy, to walk slowly, his head a little to one side, his hands behind his back, as he had seen some of his older friends do. He stood back now and regarded his sister with an air of fatherly concern.

"You are not too tired from the journey?" he inquired gravely. "I was awfully worried about you."

Roselind was not sure whether to laugh outright or cry at this strange grown-up fellow before her. She chose to reply, in an equally serious tone. "We were put down at Wells with a broken wheel, and forced to stay there four hours. What *have* you got on, Bertie?" The question escaped her before she could suppress it. She giggled, and gave him a push with her little pointed fingers.

Bertie looked taken aback. "Why, it is a new riding coat I had made up specially! Don't you approve of it?" He looked down with a puzzled expression to survey the possible flaws in this handsome new getup.

"It seems a little short in the sleeve," remarked Lady Agatha with a smile. "But ever so handsome—quite *à la mode*, to be sure!" she added hurriedly.

Lady Agatha cast an amused, knowing look at her husband, who came down the steps, arms outstretched, to greet her. General Banforth was a man of five and fifty years, still vigorous, with a strong, proud bearing and a face that had grown more handsome with the years. He had been much decorated during his long years of service to the king, and the many medals which dotted the scarlet coat of his uniform belied the genial, good-humored expression in his eyes and the mild manner which had made him much beloved by his regiments. He had married Lady Agatha some six years before, causing a tumult in society, for she was a lady twenty years his junior, and handsome enough to have won almost any man she had chosen—though none, as she was fond of saying, who could have made her more happy. Lady Agatha was tall, like her brother and her nephew, with fine expressive hazel eyes and a mass of pale red hair. She had a low melodious voice and a manner born of a true feeling for people, which made her a great favorite in society and lent her a natural dignity seldom found in fashionable women.

There passed between husband and wife, without a word, messages of complex and profound recognition. Who can say what two people, deeply in love, and separated for a period of eleven months, cannot read in each other's eyes on first being re-united? Their moment of intimacy, though brief, was recognized by the young people, who, a little embarrassed to be the chief reasons for their aunt and uncle's restraint, quickly found an ex-cuse to go inside, where a moment later they were joined by their aunt and uncle. A great commotion followed, what with footmen carrying in trunks and portmanteaus, the relegation of certain pieces of luggage to certain apartments, the necessary inspec-tion of the rooms and appointments, and a great many anecdotes recounted about Napoleon's confinement to Elba, the final term at Eton, and the events of the last months in Devonshire. Only one subject went unmentioned, though it was certainly in every-one save Bertie's mind: the tragic fate of the Iseleigh fortunes. A penetrating look from General Banforth across the dinner table to his wife spoke of his concern. Her answering glance, full of warnings, reassurances, and little nods, told him she understood. Roselind, deep in the business of pressing partridge, pies, and every sort of delicacy on her brother, while listening attentively to his accounts of Mr. Fox's latest speech before the House of Lords, had certainly not forgotten what had made her lie awake for so many nights.

It was not until late, when the young people had retired to their own apartments, that Lady Agatha could contrive to find her husband alone.

"And so, my love," said the general, standing before the mantel in the library, after recounting the events in France which had led up to the victory over Bonaparte, "I suppose you have other things on your mind besides the movements of the English army. Tell me, what is worrying you now? I hoped you had put to rest those fears about Rosie racing off with a rich husband she would not love. She seems content as a kitten to me. No doubt she has forgotten anything of the kind, if it was ever in her head."

Lady Agatha Banforth frowned. She was sitting in an over-stuffed chair near a pair of French windows which opened out into a small inner garden full of flowering trees and the sounds of a summer night.

"I have no idea what is in her head! It is like trying to guess what is in the head of a kitten, exactly as you say. She *seems* cheerful enough—perhaps too cheerful. I do not trust it. I wonder sometimes if I have not invented the whole thing."

General Banforth raised an eyebrow. "Well, then, perhaps you have! What makes you think all these peculiar thoughts, eh?"

"Something . . . something purely instinctive," replied his wife, gazing abstractedly into space. "A woman's intuition."

"Ah! Your innuendos once again. I hoped my influence would make you as blunt and practical-minded as myself. Your innuendos will leave you no peace, Aggie, if you insist on tormenting yourself with 'em. Better forget the whole damned business."

"I can't. Indeed, I wish I could! I have been imagining all sorts of awful things."

General Banforth moved to a sofa near his wife, and sighing, sank down. He wore the expression his adjutant knew as the one preceding any long and harried session of planning maneuvers.

"Since you won't forget them, then, perhaps you had better

drag them all out into the plain light of day and have a good look. Now, what is the greatest worry?"

"That Rosie will not confide in me. She has always told me everything, and suddenly she's become as deep as the ocean. I have no notion anymore what she thinks or how she feels. There is always that sweet, open face looking at me whenever I come upon her, but something . . . something has closed behind her eyes. I have the sensation sometimes that when I happen to walk into a room, she has pinned an entirely new person onto herself, so as not to worry me. It is only by chance, you know—merest chance—that I discovered about all this at all."

"Indeed? How was that? I had thought you were the first to know."

"No, no ... I suppose I never mentioned it in my letters. I happened to go into the agent's office one day, to see about some accounts for the housekeeper, and while I was waiting for Mr. Sharpe, I happened to look down and saw a letter from Iseleigh's solicitor lying on the desk."

"Not particularly noteworthy—I suppose Sharpe and the lawyer have done a good deal of conferring since your brother's death."

"Yes, but this letter was addressed to Lady Roselind Arden. I thought perhaps it was some mistake, that it was meant for me, and so, picking it up, I just glanced at the contents to be sure. What I saw, even at first, brought me up cold. Rosie, who had never once given a sign that anything distressed her, must have known of the disaster for some time! She had been conferring with the lawyer, pleading with him to keep the matter a secret between them, at least till the end of the summer. This letter was evidently in response to one of her own. It agreed to do as she had asked, and to hold off selling any part of the estates for four months, till she should, as the lawyer put it, 'have come to her own terms.' Mr. Sharpe was in the secret as well."

"And then, of course, you spoke to her?" General Banforth was frowning.

"Not immediately, no. I waited for her to confide in me herself, but after a week, when she had said nothing, I contrived to open the subject myself. She was all surprise, all chagrin, that I had found out. Indeed, I felt rather like a horrible spy. She begged me not to tell Bertie, which, naturally, I agreed to do. She would say nothing against her father, though of course she must have felt great condemnation of his behavior, and only begged to be allowed her four months of grace. Try as I might, I could not extract from her any hint of what she intended doing. Her only words were, 'I think there may be some solution. I know not what, but I feel it!' How could I respond? And what could I think, save that she had some scheme of her own. A young lady of her position has not many routes open to her in such a case—she may marry, or use her own money. Roselind has fifty thousand pounds of her own, left her by her mother, but not ten times that much would suffice to save her brother's fortune!"

"No." General Banforth stood up, and moving to the windows, gazed out into the warm summer night. He passed his hand across his brow and said wearily, "Poor child! She loves him so!"

A hard look replaced Lady Agatha's normally soft expression. "And no wonder! Who else, while Iseleigh was off gallivanting in town, with his wine and his gaming, his dinners, routs, and balls—who else was there for her to love? He is everything to her—the whole world. I believe if her death would help him be one whit happier, she would not hesitate to die for him! She has the devotion of a completely innocent creature, and yet . . . and yet it is as though somehow, in some mysterious way, a new woman has been born beneath that guileless child's face. I feel it—I can't help it! She could not have done as much as she has already, without an inner strength of purpose so far unknown to her. It is as though a strong steel wire, slender but quite definitely there, had been inserted into her. I wonder, not what would she do for Bertie, but what would she *not* do?"

The question hung in the air between them for a moment.

Lady Agatha broke the silence with a soft reply to her own question.

"I think ... I am certain she would marry to save him."

General Banforth's strong pragmatic sense sounded in the room like a reassuring rumble. "What good will that do, my dear? There is no one in England rich enough to help her, save the prince ... and perhaps Reginald Darnley."

"Yes," replied Lady Agatha Banforth softly, "and Reginald Darnley. *He* is quite rich enough!"

3

The opening assembly was in full swing. Richard Nash's lower rooms were packed to overflowing with fashionable humanity, some dancing to the merry lilt of an *eccossaise*, some laughing and conversing in little clusters, some seated about the tables on the outskirts of the dance floor which had been set up for the purpose. Through one door in the gallery, preparations for a late supper could be glimpsed, while another gave into an enormous card room where ladies and gentlemen were already immersed in baccarat and whist. Masses of flowers were banked in every corner, and in the heavy perfumed air which hung about the bare shoulders of the ladies like a soft cloak, hundreds of candles glimmered in a fairy-tale effect. It was a splendid occasion by any standard. *The Tattler* had announced that no fewer than three royal dukes had abandoned Brighton for the season. Not since the sad occasion of Roderick Montague's flight from England had so many consequential figures gathered at Bath.

Roselind Arden, her cheeks flushed from the exercise of dancing, her eyes shining with an almost unnatural excitement, had inspired a great deal of comment on coming into the room. Her name and title were well-known. She was the daughter of the deceased Earl of Iseleigh, the noted Corinthian, a man considered by some a vain roué, but by most of the world a dashing and elegant leader of the ton. It was known, too, that she had been living in seclusion in the country most of her life, and if some had suspected that her come-out had been delayed to prolong the humiliation of exposing a homely girl to the Polite World, their speculations were now proved fruitless. As little as she resembled the proud tall beauties in vogue at the moment, her small, pretty figure and lovely animated countenance had drawn the attention of nearly every man in the room. Her feet in their little lilac satin slippers seemed to fly over the marble floor. Her slender arms and throat, the guileless smile of genuine pleasure on her lips, the effortless way in which she executed the intricate steps of the country dance, laughing across at her brother as she went, were like a breath of fresh air amid the lacquered beauties around her. One gentleman in particular, his deeply bronzed complexion set off by a pair of fine expressive blue eyes, seemed unable to tear his eyes away from her. He stood against a pillar at one side of the dance floor, one elegantly swathed gray arm resting on his hip, and an expression of happy admiration giving his handsome features a very appealing look.

Roselind had been aware of him for half an hour. The peculiar sensation in the small of her back would not go away, no matter how she endeavored to ignore it. She allowed her eyes to wander toward him now; and quickly, as if a pail of cold water had been hurled in her face, she turned away again. Her cheeks were flushed. A hot, prickling sensation was climbing up her throat. His eyes had met hers with an impudent, amused look, which, however, could not disguise his admiration. Never before had

Roselind seen anything like him. He was certainly the handsomest man she had ever glimpsed.

Nevertheless, she did not let herself look back. A small, strong voice spoke inside of her, delivering, as it were, a lecture. "I do not like the look in his eyes," it said. "It is very impudent, and not at all what I think he should look like." Just what he *should* look like was a question for the moment ignored. "He looks rather frivolous," the voice continued. "I do not like frivolous gentlemen. They are apt to be very charming and very selfish, like my father." The monologue was kept up in this vein for some minutes, but without any notable success. Each time Roselind reached the end of the line, from which position she had no choice but to look at him, she found her eyes wandering almost unconsciously to where he stood. At last, as if to purge herself of fascination, she demanded of her brother, next time the movements of the dance brought them together, if he knew who the gentleman was.

Lord Iseleigh's gaze followed his sister's. To her astonishment, a happy exclamation of surprise escaped his lips.

"Why! That is the fellow!" he cried. For a moment he forgot to keep on dancing, standing quite still, so that his sister was forced to take his arm to avoid their being run into by the other dancers.

"What fellow, Bertie?" she asked impatiently when they had rejoined the dance.

"The fellow I saw in the road yesterday! The one who gave Darnley the set-down."

Roselind had heard nothing of Darnley, or of any set-down administered to him. She demanded to be enlightened on the subject.

"Oh, I forgot, I never told you, Rosie!" he replied. "We were delayed yesterday, no more than an hour out of London, by an accident. It was a phaeton collided with a farmer's dray, and the fellow's produce was all over the road, and his cart nearly wrecked. It was Darnley's phaeton, as I soon discovered, and that fellow there jumped down from his chaise to help. I think Darnley would have been happy to continue along as soon as possible, but this fellow would have none of it! Made him send for a smithy, and pay the piper good and proper. I never saw such wrath in all my life! You should have seen Darnley's face when he looked about to see a perfect stranger lecturing him on the subject of his duty."

"I am sure Mr. Darnley did not intend running off and leaving the farmer," said Roselind somewhat primly.

"Oh, I shouldn't be so sure if I was you! He looked dashed mad to be delayed for half an hour! But that fellow there, quiet as you please, only smiled at him the more and told him, in so many words, to mind his manners."

Roselind turned to look at the gentleman with new interest. He seemed to smile and bow. She looked away again quickly.

"I should be ever so glad to make his acquaintance," Bertie was saying. "But look now . . ." He frowned. "He is got up so different, I hardly know him."

"What do you mean?"

"Why, when I saw him before, he was dressed so plain I nearly thought he had not enough ready to get himself a new pair of boots. But tonight he is quite the dandy. Well, I suppose it is just his way."

Roselind had been distracted by another thought. The subject of the stranger's attire seemed to lose its fascination for her.

"Do you think," she said quite carelessly, "that Mr. Darnley is at Bath?"

"Oh, I suppose so," replied Bertie, not much interested. "He was coming in this direction. Oh, yes, there I see him—he is conversing with the old hag who was lecturing us all in the highway." Bertie's indecorous speech was accompanied by a gesture in the direction of a group of people standing a little to one side of a row of potted palms.

Lady Chumley, her immense bosom swathed in a gown of black lace, appeared to be lecturing Reginald Darnley in an intimate manner, throwing back her head from time to time to let out a bellow of laughter. Lord Chumley, at her side, was immersed in a perusal of his slippers, which he interrupted now to cast one anguished glance at his wife, while the lovely flaxen-haired creature standing a little behind her mama was gazing in rapt admiration at the gentleman. Mr. Darnley's face, being turned in the opposite direction, was invisible, but his broad shoulders in their exquisitely fitting black evening coat lifted now and then as if in laughter. Roselind stared at the group for an instant, so immersed in the spectacle that she never noticed the fair-haired gentleman following her gaze.

"Oh, dash it!" exclaimed Bertie. "He is disappearing! I am determined to make his acquaintance sometime."

Roselind turned back to her brother. "Who are those people, do you know?" she inquired.

"The gentleman is Sir Walter Chumley—we had quite a pleasant chat while watching the proceedings. The great fat one is his wife, Lady Chumley, and I suppose that is their daughter."

"She is exceedingly pretty," said Roselind, biting her lip.

"Do you think so?" Bertie turned to look with some interest. "Yes, I suppose she is. But not my type, you know. Rather too fragile-looking for my taste."

Roselind looked at him in surprise. She had started to say "I never dreamt that you ..." but cut herself short.

"Lud!" cried Mrs. Hogarth, her usually piercing voice raised even louder than usual so as to be heard above the din of voices and music. "I never saw such a gathering in all my life! I am exceeding fond of balls, are not you, brother?"

General Banforth scowled. He had been dismayed to see his sister bearing down upon him through the crowd, for he had forgotten that she was coming to Bath this season. Mrs. Hogarth was a thin, nervous-looking woman much given to getting herself up in wild combinations of color and ornament, which made her resemble some exotic tropical bird more than the mother of four grown daughters. Tonight she had decked herself out in a breathtaking display of crimsons, purples, and apricots, and through her scanty orange locks was threaded a ribbon the shade of a peach, which bobbed and wagged as she spoke. The air of constant motion about her was further increased by a fan, which she continually batted in front of her face, stopping only now and then to lift a gilt lorgnette to her sharp eyes.

"I do not suppose," she continued to shriek, "there has been such a splendid array of figures at Bath these many years! It is quite sad, quite pathetic indeed, what has happened to Bath of late! I am convinced it was all due to that dreadful Montague scandal. No one wished to be associated with the place anymore! I do not wonder, I swear, for it was such a devastating affair."

Mrs. Hogarth had two loves in life. The first was shopping, and the second speculating about the affairs of others. Oblivious to the expressions on her companions' faces, she prattled on. "No, no! It was too dreadful, to be sure. *I* should not have liked to be here at the time. I have not been at Bath these five years. Indeed, I should not have come at all, were it not that Prinney was taken ill. Brighton is too awfully dull when he has the gout. I do not wonder everyone is come here. Do you know ... I am sure you will never guess! Only a moment ago I saw Georgina Devonshire! And just now, as I was coming to meet you, who do you suppose nearly ran me down? None other than Reginald Darnley!"

Mrs. Hogarth stared triumphantly at her brother and Lady Agatha.

"Well, that is wonderful indeed," rumbled General Banforth, wondering if his sister expected him to turn a cartwheel at the news. Lady Agatha, however, seemed more interested.

"Is that true, Clara? I do not see him." Her eye swept over the crowd and fastened at last on an elegant broad back.

"Oh, yes!" cried Mrs. Hogarth. "It is quite true! What a fine thing for you dear Roselind, to have such a gathering of figures for her come-out! Lud, she is looking very well this evening!" The lorgnette lifted to take in the sight of Lady Roselind dancing with a tall horse-faced officer in the red tunic of the Guards.

"A perfect jewel!" declared the general, turning an affectionate eye in that direction. "My word! How those little feet do fly about! I do not believe she ever touches ground."

"Tell me," said Lady Agatha, turning to her sister-in-law. "Do you know whether Darnley is intimate with the Chumleys?"

Mrs. Hogarth emitted a snort of disdain. "I should hope not, my dear! I hope Reginald Darnley has no great love for *that* overbearing female! Such a snob as she is, too! Why, one would never think, to hear her go on, that she was plain Miss Brown before she married Sir Walter! Plain Miss Brown, and now she pretends to have married beneath her, always talking of her family as if it had been something quite grand!"

Mrs. Hogarth herself had made a foolish match when she had been young, and delighted in nothing so much, now, as disdaining the marriages of her acquaintances.

"But Clarissa is perfectly lovely," said Lady Agatha thoughtfully.

"She is well enough to look at, my dear, but the poor creature has not a brain in her head! Quite a dim-witted little thing, to be sure. I am certain Darnley could not have any interest in her. Why, he is so witty and quick himself, such a nonesuch in every way! The most admired gentleman in London. I wonder," continued Mrs. Hogarth vexedly, staring at the group, "what he can find to say to them for such a great while. Why, he is leading Clarissa onto the floor! It is beyond everything!"

"Not beyond everything at all," put in the general in his gruff, amiable voice. "I did not know Darnley had so much sense. Miss Chumley is a perfect delight to look at."

"But quite hen-brained, I assure you! No, no, I am sure there is some mistake!"

Mrs. Hogarth was most provoked. Louisa Chumley had been her great friend at school, and as her friend, Mrs. Hogarth considered it her right to be also her worst enemy. She could not conscience the daughter of her friend getting the best catch in the whole kingdom when she had gotten only an officer and three younger sons for her own darling girls.

A thought struck her.

"Was not Darnley a great intimate of your brother's, my dear?" she inquired sweetly of Lady Agatha.

Her sister-in-law replied that that was what she believed.

"Then I suppose Roselind must have met him once or twice?

Poor child—secluded in the country as she was, I suppose she has not much acquaintance among gentlemen. It is a great pity . . . well, I don't suppose ... it would be a very great thing, you know," she said in a significant tone, "for your dear niece to make a great match."

Lady Agatha looked startled indeed. She shot an astonished look at her sister-in-law, but Mrs. Hogarth had taken on a new expression. She seemed to have lost interest in the subject altogether, and commenced immediately to ask after young Lord Iseleigh.

"Such a delightful young man!" she exclaimed. "I suppose he will very soon be making all the young ladies' hearts tremble! To think he was only a schoolboy not six months ago! And now an earl, and an Oxford man to top it all!"

The earl and the Oxford man so much admired by his uncle's sister was at that moment engaged in a most delightful conversation on a similar topic. Having sought out, and at last found, the blond dasher he had been longing to meet, having ascertained that his name was Grey, and that his eyes did indeed resemble the color of cobalt—a substance Lord Iseleigh had come to know and love through the rigors of an otherwise unnoteworthy course in chemistry—Bertie was currently immersed in interrogating that gentleman on the ins and outs of university life. Mr. Grey, it seemed, besides being equal to a dressing-down of London's most awesome nonpareil, was also a graduate of that famed institution. While he had attended Christ Church College rather than Balliol, he seemed well-versed in the articles which would best facilitate the smooth entrance of a young man into any one of the colleges.

"Never mind the dandies and the snobs," he had advised the

earl, "only stick to your own ideas and you'll soon find a group of compatible spirits. Oxford's full of men who have nothing better to do than satirize their colleagues. Pay them no heed, stick to your studies, and engage in whatever sports you like best."

"I suppose you were there a great while ago," murmured Bertie tentatively. "Things may have changed a good deal."

Mr. Grey put back his head and roared—a delightful, friendly kind of roar which made a fellow feel included in the amusement. It was not the sort of laughter, which Bertie had had a taste of from his father's friends, that made you feel ridiculous.

"Do I look such an old codger as all that?" inquired Mr. Grey solemnly. "I only came down from Oxford five years ago, you know. Things haven't changed much there in a hundred years, and I suppose they're not likely to do so in five."

Five years, while not quite representing an age to Lord Iseleigh, seemed long enough to justify his suspicions that Mr. Grey, well-versed in the subject so far as it went, might not be quite up to scratch on the details of behavior currently fashionable at Oxford.

"Well, in any event," said Bertie, "I shall probably not stay there long."

One blond eyebrow shot up.

"Why on earth not?"

"I should like to go into agriculture. We have a great lot of land, you know—in Devonshire and Scotland, besides my father's estates in the West Indies—and I've been doing a bit of studying up on farming methods. The old ways waste enormous quantities of land and labor, besides doing the owner a great deal of harm from losses due to fires and flood."

A new kind of respect was in the blond gentleman's eyes.

"Yes, yes—you mean you have taken to Mr. Fox's theories, do you? I am of your mind completely. These innovative methods are far preferable to the old feudal ones. Gives the farmers self-respect, and makes them feel a part of the whole scheme, instead of simply like cogs in the machinery. But one mustn't abandon one's education, you know."

"I can't see what good," interposed Bertie somewhat peevishly, "all that Latin and Greek will be to a farmer."

"Well, well . . . it's only four years, ain't it? Not much time to spend improving one's mind. After all, it goes to rack and ruin soon enough in any case."

Mr. Grey's attention was suddenly distracted by something else. The good humor which had formerly been in his eyes gave way to a chilling look. Surprised, Bertie followed his new friend's gaze, and perceived him to be watching Reginald Darnley, who was just leading Miss Clarissa Chumley off the dance floor.

"Do you know that gentleman?" Mr. Grey inquired in a cold voice.

"Darnley? Why, everyone knows him! I was astounded you did not, when that accident occurred yesterday! He is accounted the richest man in England, and a famous nonesuch. Intimate of the prince, and all that. Father was a merchant—vastly wealthy—made it in the Indies, I believe. But surely you've heard of him?"

Mr. Grey replied that he had not hitherto had the pleasure, and looking, Bertie judged, as though that particular term had been chosen more from civility than sincerity.

"But I have been away from England these five years," explained Mr. Grey. "I do not believe your Darnley fellow was then quite so much talked of."

"Oh, really? I was of the opinion Darnley had always been the beaux' beau. But where have you been all this time?"

"In India," replied Mr. Grey with a smile. "And otherwise traveling."

"Oh, I hope you are not a merchant!" exclaimed Bertie, hoping he had not made a faux pas when he had mentioned Reginald Darnley's heritage.

But Mr. Grey only smiled. "No ... I was only traveling on a personal matter."

Bertie would have liked to inquire further into this adventure, for the Orient, and especially India, had ever held a great attraction for him, but something in the other's expression made him hold back. For the briefest second, something like a haunted look had come into those piercing blue eyes, the full, almost beautiful mouth had formed itself into a hard line, and the insouciant amusement had deserted Mr. Grey. But in a moment he was his old self.

"And who is that young lady Darnley is dancing with?" he asked.

Bertie looked. "It is Miss Chumley, I think."

Mr. Grey was silent for a moment, seemingly immersed in thought.

"You said you knew *of* him," he remarked after a moment. "But do you actually know Mr. Darnley?"

Bertie would rather have discussed some other topic, but seeing that his companion was bent on learning more about London's darling, he volunteered what he knew.

"He was a great friend of my father's," he said. "I only met him once or twice, when he came to Devonshire for a hunting party. Aside from being much admired by the ladies, and a great sportsman, I know nothing of him. There was the business of Roderick Montague, of course—but that was a great while ago."

"What business was that?" inquired Mr. Grey.

"Oh, I hardly remember. I was still in short pants, you know. I believe Montague—he was the heir to the Duke of Hamilton— lost a great deal of money at cards, and having used up all his own income, he signed away a deed to some of his father's lands, as a guarantee against payment. The matter came to light, the duke was outraged—nearly disinherited him, I believe—and in the end, Montague fled the country, disavowing his claim to the dukedom, and all his fortune. I believe he died not long ago, quite derelict and riddled with malaria. Anyhow, it seems Darnley was his great friend, and when he saw how it was going with Montague, he managed to secure the incriminating document and paid it off. He went about for a great while vouching for the honor of his friend. Quite the hero he was for some time."

"How very strange," said Mr. Grey, "that a man who would go to such lengths for a dishonorable duke's son should begrudge half an hour to a farmer whose livelihood he had just destroyed."

Bertie shrugged. "It is strange, isn't it? But then, Darnley always was a great one for buttering up the aristocracy. My father used to say that he would never have Darnley for a friend if he weren't an earl. Dashed peculiar some people are, don't you think?"

Mr. Grey smiled thoughtfully.

"Dashed peculiar," he agreed.

         ━   ━

The doors to the supper room opened at ten o'clock. By the time the Banforths began to go toward them, a great crowd had already gathered in the entrance. The smooth flow of the guests inside was inhibited by the necessity of greeting everyone who had not yet been spoken to that evening, and in the crush of satin gowns, waving fans, and cries of recognition, Roselind could not for the moment descry her brother. She had glimpsed him once, in conversation with the blond gentleman who had caused her so much distress at the commencement of the ball, but now Bertie was nowhere to be seen. And Roselind, whose mind had been occupied elsewhere for the past hour, had lost nearly all her interest in fair-haired gentlemen with tanned complexions and impudent expressions of amusement.

She barely heard her aunt murmur, as they began to move forward, "My dear, I see you have torn your hem."

Roselind looked down in chagrin. There, indeed, was a great rent in the hem of her lilac silk, and around it, a scuff mark. The horse-faced officer she had danced with earlier, a gentleman by the name of Edison or Edington, had been so immersed in recounting a number of adventures he had had with a horse named Gad-About and a friend named Smythe that he had trod twice on her slipper. He seemed to have done greater harm than that.

"Oh, dear!" she exclaimed. "It is my best frock!"

"Never mind," replied Lady Agatha, "we shall soon set it to rights. Come along, let us just go into the ladies' sitting room and have it mended."

But Roselind did not like tearing her aunt away from her friends, and insisted on going alone. The sitting room was easily found, and a buxom young maid soon repaired the damage with the deftness of experienced hands. Still immersed in thought, Roselind made her way out, and was just turning into the passage which led out toward the ballroom when a deep masculine voice sounded behind her. For an instant Roselind stood frozen to the ground. But when she turned around, it was to see the imposing figure of Reginald Darnley bearing down upon her.

"Lady Roselind," he murmured, almost as though he had been speaking to himself, as he came up beside her. Bowing, he stood gazing down at her with his impenetrable black eyes. Though not much above the average in height, the breadth of his shoulders and the commanding way in which he held himself made Darnley seem larger than life.

Roselind took in her breath. "Oh!" was all she could mutter at first, and then a somewhat awkward, "Mr. Darnley!"

"You remember me, then?" he drawled, the strong lines of his mouth hinting at a smile.

"Remember you! Of course I do! You came to Windham with my father several times—"

"And you were nothing but a soggy little duckling then. But now you have grown into a swan."

Roselind blushed, and tried to avoid his eyes, which seemed to be threatening to eat her up alive. But Darnley would not let her escape. He held her with his gaze, and then, as if that were not enough, he lifted her hand to his lips, and held it, before he actually kissed it, a full minute in his own strong broad fingers. It seemed an eternity to Roselind, and another eternity while she felt the warmth of his mouth pressed against her flesh. She was half in agony, and half in rapture. She knew not where to look, nor how to behave, but certainly there had never been such a willing victim as she was. As quickly as Darnley had grasped her hand, he let it go again. It fell to Roselind's side with a strange, empty little thud, and she met his eyes.

"A very swan," drawled Darnley again with a slight smile. "I wonder ... are you here for the whole season?"

"Yes," muttered Roselind, thinking that she had never felt so inadequate to what was demanded of her, "I am here with my aunt and uncle—it is my come-out."

"Ah! Well, then, I suppose your calendar is quite filled up. I had hoped—but there, it is no doubt impossible!—that you might spare me an hour or two to drive you about the town."

"I ... I should be very happy if you would!" exclaimed Roselind with no trace of the coldness or restraint which any seasoned lady would have shown in such a situation. "I should like nothing half so well!"

"Indeed?" Darnley smiled at her in amusement. "Well, then perhaps tomorrow would not be too soon? I have got a very nice conveyance, it was made up for me by Hingam. I think you might like it, your ladyship."

"I am sure I shall!"

"Well, then, shall we say eleven o'clock? Or do you stay abed in the morning?"

"I am always up early," replied Roselind very eagerly, "for in the country, you know, the morning is always the best time."

"Yes, of course." Darnley smiled. *"La belle campagne.* Well, then, shall we say eleven o'clock?" And brushing her hand once more against his lips, but with none of the intensity which had accompanied his first conquest of that little appendage, he disappeared into the crowd.

Roselind watched him walk away, taking in the number of admiring looks he inspired in the ladies he passed, and, it must be admitted, not at all displeased to see one or two curious gazes directed at herself.

Before she could even collect her emotions enough to pro-ceed on her own way, Roselind saw her brother coming toward her. At his side was the gentleman she had seen earlier, the one Bertie had spoken of so admiringly. "Rosie!" he cried. "This is Mr. Grey—the one I told you about."

Mr. Grey smiled and bowed. He made no move to kiss her hand, but gazed down at her with his insouciant expression. Rose-lind was amazed to find that she no longer flushed at their look. Though taller than Mr. Darnley, and handsomer by far in regu-larity of feature, Mr. Grey had not the other's presence. Roselind found herself gazing quite easily at him, and censoring, before he had spoken three sentences, the untoward easiness of his man-ner. With every look and word he seemed to take liberties with taste and sense, giving the effect of a perfectly frivolous character.

"So you are the Lady Roselind," he said, "about whom I have heard so much from your adoring brother." He seemed to have forgotten they had already exchanged enough, in significant looks, to make them familiar to each other.

"Mr. Grey is just come back from India!" exclaimed Bertie. "He has been telling me a great deal about Oxford, and knows all about Mr. Fox."

"Indeed?" said Roselind.

Mr. Grey bowed, with an impudent expression. "Oh, yes." He smiled. "I am a great believer in the fellow's ingeniousness. Not but what I pay much heed to all these political gentlemen. Most wearisome, you know, to have to follow all their endless talks before Parliament."

The sentiment sounded so exactly like one her father might have expressed that Roselind was forced to look again to be sure Lord Iseleigh had not come alive again suddenly. Mr. Grey took out an elegant little inlaid snuffbox and proffered a pinch of it to the end of his aquiline nose, sniffing delicately. The sneeze which ensued was muffled by a beautiful damask handkerchief, which, having served its purpose, was stuffed back into an elegant gray sleeve. The three of them moved toward the doors of the supper room, which had by now been cleared. They found the Banforths quite easily, seated around a large round table. Already at the table were Lady Agatha, the general, and Mrs. Hogarth. One or two others, whom Roselind did not recognize, were there as well, conversing with a small, brilliant creature in emerald green, whom Roselind knew to be the Duchess of Devonshire.

"Little jewel!" cried Georgina Devonshire, her small, diamond-cluttered hands waving about in the air as she reached up to kiss Roselind's cheek.

Mr. Grey was introduced around and seated himself, to Roselind's displeasure, at her left. Mrs. Hogarth, on the young lady's other side, commenced instantly to question him.

"Mr. Grey!" she shrieked. "Grey? I have some acquaintance at Lancashire by the name. You are not related to the Osborne Greys, are you? A very fine family. Mr. Osborne Grey keeps three carriages. A splendid house! I am sure they must have thirty servants indoors alone!"

"How fortunate for your friends, ma'am," said Mr. Grey. "But they are no relations of mine."

"No? What a pity! Are you from Lancashire?"

Mr. Grey was smiling widely. "No, indeed, ma'am."

"How sad for you! Where do you come from, then? But I see you are quite bronzed! Perhaps you are come back from the West Indies?"

"From India. I have not settled on a place to live as yet. I only returned a fortnight ago."

Mrs. Hogarth was nonplussed. She only wished to know Mr. Grey's particulars—his income, and his family, where he lived, and if he was likely to prove a social advantage for her.

"Well," she said a little vexedly, "you must have some family in England!"

"Must I?" inquired Mr. Grey. He looked ready to burst out laughing. "If I must, then, I shall tell you that I have family, and that they live at Lancashire. But it will all be a falsehood, merely to please you."

Mrs. Hogarth did not know which way to turn. The fellow seemed bent on teasing her. He was irritatingly like her brother in that. She determined to try once more. In a coquettish wheezing voice reserved for prying out bits of useful information from unwilling subjects, she inquired as to his profession. "You do not have lands, I take it. Then you must be a merchant?"

"No, no, I am not a merchant. Everyone seems bent on making me one, so perhaps in the end I shall have to give up my indigent life and turn useful. But I am not—nor ever have been—a merchant. In fact, I am just what you see—a plain fellow given to leading a lazy kind of life, with the one object of my existence being amusement. A most unnoteworthy business, I assure you, but one which serves me very well."

Here Bertie could not restrain himself.

"Why, you know that is not true, Grey!" he cried from across the table. Lady Agatha looked up. She had been conversing with the duchess.

"Grey is a dreadful liar," Bertie rushed on, a little red in the face. "He ain't at all what he claims to be. Why, only yesterday he showed himself for a perfect hero, stopping a great caravan full of consequential figures to make sure a poor farmer did not get cheated out of his livelihood."

"Is this true?" demanded the duchess, turning her eyes interestedly upon the gentleman. Mr. Grey seemed displeased at his young friend's speech.

"Not a whit of it," he replied, smiling impudently. "Lord Iseleigh seems bent on making me a saint, when in fact I am nothing of the kind. I only saw we would all be waiting hours if no one stepped in to interfere, and as everyone else was busy dashing about like mad in circles, I only endeavored to expedite the affair. Hero! I was only sick of being kept waiting in the middle of a dusty road."

Bertie looked disconcerted. "Well," he ventured, "he that as it may, Grey here did not flinch at telling Reginald Darnley his duty. Gave him a perfect lecture on allowing the poor farmer to be let off without a cart and with his livelihood scattered about the highway."

A hiss sounded from the area of Mrs. Hogarth. "Lectured Darnley!" she sniffed. Turning to Roselind, she murmured rather loudly, "What an impudent fellow! I do not like him a bit."

Roselind would have liked to agree, but restrained herself out of common civility.

The Duchess of Devonshire was vastly amused by this narration.

"Mon Dieu!" she cried in mock horror. "You did not do anything so foolish, I hope? Darnley does not like being lectured, you know. I should think it would have made him *quite* cross!"

Mr. Grey smiled. "It apparently had that effect."

"Our Reginald is a most delightful addition to society," said the duchess, who was herself on intimate terms with the gentleman, "but I should not have the courage to cross him!"

Roselind could contain herself no longer. "Nor was there

probably any reason to. I am sure I have never met a more courteous nor a more civil gentleman in my life!"

This little declaration was made rather softly, but with so much warmth and earnestness that everyone at the table looked in Roselind's direction. She herself, surprised at her own words, subsided instantly with a flush. Her eyes wandered almost against her will to a part of the room where Mr. Darnley was seated with the Chumleys. At that moment he looked up, and catching her eye, smiled. A prickling sensation, not altogether unpleasurable, rose on her neck. That slender structure had been much taxed this evening.

Mr. Grey seemed weary of the subject, and having cast one hard, curious glance at the young lady on his right, turned to speak to Lady Agatha. Mrs. Hogarth was eager to vent her views on the gentleman.

"A most impudent man!" she declared again, not quite so low as Roselind might have wished. "I do not wonder but he is one of these odious fortune-hunters who are forever hanging about in places where there are young girls of good family. I should be most particularly careful, my dear, if I were you! You are especially vulnerable, you know, without any parent to protect you."

Roselind glanced once more at Mr. Grey. While she found his manner both impertinent and distasteful, while she thought him frivolous and ill-mannered, she could not persuade herself that he was just the sort of undesirable character that her uncle's sister seemed to think. "No," she thought. "He is only a vain, egocentric man without any thought to the concerns of others. I only hope he will not disappoint Bertie horribly, for I see how fallen his expression is. A hero, indeed!"

"Do you know," she inquired out loud of Mrs. Hogarth a

moment later, "whether Mr. Darnley intends staying at Bath the whole season?"

In point of fact, Mrs. Hogarth was acquainted with that nonpareil not at all. She existed on the nebulous fringes of the very society which revolved around the Darnleys and Brummels, but liking to delude herself and others that she was more intimate with them than she was, she readily replied, "Oh, I should think so, my dear. Prinney is ill, you know, and when that happens, Brighton is not at all what it should be. Yes, yes, I suppose he will be here for the whole three months—it is very like. If I were you, I should be very civil to him, my dear." Mrs. Hogarth's tone took on a confidential quality. "He is a great prize, you know! Rich as Croesus, and as amiable as you please. Why, he has always been most agreeable to *me*—a great favorite of mine; you know."

Roselind did not think to doubt the older woman's words. Assuming Mrs. Hogarth to be the expert on Mr. Darnley's affairs which she claimed, she questioned her closely, but with as much subtlety as she could. At last, having heard a great deal about the gentleman's virtues, she murmured, "I am to go out driving with him tomorrow."

Mrs. Hogarth was all pleased astonishment.

"How delightful!" she cried. "Why did not you mention it sooner? Darnley has a most elegant kind of phaeton, you know. Oh, I am very pleased indeed, Roselind, very pleased indeed!" She shot one victorious glance across the room at her friend Lady Chumley, who, however, was too busy complimenting Reginald Darnley on his good sense in sitting with them to notice.

4

"I hope you do not intend standing in front of the window all day long in such glorious weather," remarked Lady Agatha to her niece, looking up from her letter-writing.

Roselind gave a little start and turned around. She had been so lost in thought that she had forgotten she was not alone. The day was indeed a glorious one—one of those softly breezy, brilliantly clear days which sometimes come between the lingering chill of a late winter and the advent of stifling heat. It had not been of the weather, however, that Lady Roselind Arden had been thinking. For some few minutes she had been stationed before the bow window, staring stubbornly out at the groups of ladies and gentlemen walking, and the occasional nurse with her charges in tow for a morning constitutional. She had long ago given up the attempt to read a novel, running back and forth to the window every minute to gaze down at the street below, hoping to see Mr. Darnley's black phaeton drawing into view. She had been dressed since nine o'clock; it was now approaching one. The pretty lilac walking costume which had looked so fresh in the morning was beginning to wilt and wrinkle in the front.

It was impossible that Mr. Darnley had mistaken the day—or was it? Roselind considered the matter, recollecting exactly the expression that had been on his face when he had made the appointment. "I shall call for you at eleven o'clock," he had said. But eleven o'clock was long since past, and no word, no message, had been sent to excuse his absence. He was in every way so much the gentleman that Roselind could not imagine his neglecting so elementary a civility as sending a servant to explain his delay. Perhaps something had occurred to detain him, something he had not foreseen, and which had left him without the means to convey a message. "That must have been the case," she told herself, yet not believing, even as she did so, the truth of what she said. "He must have been called upon to perform some favor for someone ... or perhaps he was taken ill." But if he had been taken ill, she was sure he would have contacted her. No, no, it must have been some piece of business impossible to overlook. Roselind tried to imagine the complexities of Mr. Darnley's life, the innumerable arrangements which must be made daily, the overseeing of so many houses and estates. It was very likely he had been kept away on business.

"What I had better do," said Roselind's stubborn inner voice, "is to engage in some activity which will take my mind away from this." So saying, she moved to the little inlaid desk where her aunt was working, with several dozen cards of invitation spread out around her.

"Is there no way I can be of help, Aggie?" she inquired, aimlessly picking up a card and reading it.

"No ... no, thank you, my love. I am nearly finished. I only wanted to get all the invitations off as soon as possible. I do so abhor being informed of a ball without sufficient notice. One wants time to plan one's agenda and to go to the dressmaker's. There is nothing so abominable as to receive a card only a day or two before the event, as is always the case with Lady Jersey. She delights, I am convinced, in giving costume balls which everyone besides herself must attend in plain dress, as a result of being invited too late."

Lady Agatha bit the tip of her pen and gazed into space. "I think we shall have orchids and peonies for flowers. That will be very pretty, don't you agree? And early supper will be six courses, with perhaps partridge and a rack of mutton, and of course ices, and Mattilda's wonderful turtle soup, and for late supper, I should think, a lobster salad and cold viands. I must get Buxton to open up the pavilion this week, for we have not used it in ever so long. It needs airing, I'll warrant, and . . ." Suddenly Lady Agatha stopped. She followed her niece's passage to the other side of the room with a sharp eye, frowned, and then re-sumed her chatty tone.

"And I am afraid one or two of the glass doors needs repair. The chandeliers are dreadfully dirty, too. They must come down." Lady Agatha made a note on a page in front of her, already cov-ered with similar memoranda.

"I think, you know," she continued, now looking very hard at Roselind's back, where she was standing beside a little table and fingering a small porcelain figure, "that Lord and Lady Arbuth-notte will certainly come over from Ireland for your come-out. Three weeks is not too little notice, do you think, my dear?"

Roselind murmured that she supposed it was sufficient.

"Good, for I wrote to them this morning. Lady Arbuthnotte was a great friend of your mother's, you know. She would never wish to miss your presentation." Lady Agatha made a quick mental calculation. "Three hundred guests for a certainty, and perhaps another seventy-five. We will just fill the ballroom. I do hope it is good weather, for then we shall have a marquee outside, and dancing in the fresh air. Hadn't you better think about a gown? There is a wonderful woman in Bath, Madame Renault, who can make you as good a dress as any you could get in town."

Roselind made a great attempt to be interested. "I remember you took me to her last year when I was visiting you," she remarked. "A funny, talky little creature, is she not? With tight ringlets and a knowing manner?"

"That is Madame Renault! Ringlets and a knowing manner." Agatha Banforth laughed. "She had a shop in Paris before the war, and when her husband died, she abandoned her native land to come over and teach the poor English how to dress. She approaches everyone as if they were babies, or at least dim-witted children. I think she has no faith in anyone save herself—but what a wonder she is with her hands! I took her an old gauze slip once, good for nothing, and she made me out of it my most coveted frock—the gold-and-white one, do you remember?"

"Did she indeed?" Roselind, her aunt noticed with pleasure, was beginning to show signs of interest. "I thought you had had that made up in London!"

"No, indeed. It is all Madame Renault's work. I think," said Lady Agatha, regarding her niece with her head cocked a little to one side and a thoughtful expression in her hazel eyes, "I think we shall have to solicit her advice on your presentation frock. I am torn between ivory silk—perhaps crepe de chine, with some sort of petticoat, silver, I think—and the very shade you are wearing. It is exactly the color of the blossoms in the garden, and quite the most becoming thing I ever saw you in."

Roselind looked down at her walking costume. The sight brought her back to her old worries. For a moment her lovely young aunt's voice, and simply her presence, had taken her out of herself. There was something so peaceful, so reassuring about Lady Agatha. She always seemed to smell faintly of lavender water. Even her apartments were permeated by the same aroma. There was an aura about her rather like a garden in summer, and whatever room she entered instantly became a kind of sanctuary. Her voice, low and beautifully modulated, her graceful, easy manner, and the elegance which, though unconscious, seemed to lift everyone else about her into its spell, all reminded Roselind of the faint memories she had of her mother. The Countess Iseleigh had died when she had been only a small child, but Roselind still cherished the memory of those great gray eyes and the graceful dark head bending over to wish her good night.

Suddenly Roselind longed to rush to her aunt, to throw herself into her arms and unburden her heart. So many months, so many sleepless nights had passed when she had longed to do the same thing, only holding back for fear Lady Agatha would contrive to muddle her plans. Roselind loved her aunt, loved her all the more for wishing to protect her, but her ambitions now were outside the realm of personal happiness, or even peace. Tranquillity, if it was to be hers, would come when and if she could save her darling brother. Dear Bertie—he was so much dearer to her than herself! The thought, conjuring up as it did an image of his face, his awkward new manliness and irrepressible joy in life, gave her a burst of new courage. Almost unconsciously her back straightened, her shoulders braced themselves, and she seemed to breathe more evenly.

"I think," said Roselind, smiling brightly, "that I should like ivory and silver—I never had a gown of silver before. And I shall wear Mother's pearl-and-diamond necklace, and the little tiara."

"The tiara will go very well," agreed Agatha Banforth. And then suddenly she demanded, "Why do you suppose Darnley is not come?"

Roselind crumpled. "I have no idea. I suppose . . . perhaps he was detained on business."

"Reginald Darnley is a collector," Lady Agatha said slowly, gazing absently into space.

Roselind looked up in surprise. "A collector?"

"Yes. He collects exotic pieces of statuary, obscure Chinese vases, rare miniatures—and above all, I believe, people. He has successfully collected some of the greatest names in Europe as his friends. I imagine he would like to add something to his collection."

"Why, whatever do you mean, Aggie?" asked Roselind.

Her aunt gave her a hard look, and then, as quickly as she had opened the subject, it was closed. "Nothing, dearest, nothing at all. I was only thinking out loud. Let us go out into the pavilion and see what must be done for your ball, shall we?"

The pavilion lay at the back of the mansion, jutting out into a large courtyard of formal gardens and walks. It had been constructed some twenty years ago by the third Earl of Iseleigh, when pavilions had been fashionable at Bath, and when all the world had taken its cue for what was fashionable and what was not from a handful of tonish men and women of which Lady Agatha's father had been one. Though long in disuse—for neither Agatha Banforth nor her husband was much given to entertaining on a grand scale—it was still quite beautiful, the few repairs needing to be made being of a minor nature. The structure was octagonal, with every side save the one which joined it to the main house fashioned out of myriad partitions of glass. Four immense crystal chandeliers hung down from a domed ceiling amply covered with plaster reliefs of garlands, birds, and wild beasts. It was, by the current standard, out-of-date and strangely symmetrical. The Adam brothers, who had built it, were considered *outré* in this age of Chinese wall hangings, campaign furniture, and garish colors. A craze for the furnishings and fashions of Greece and Rome had overtaken England by storm, so that an average English sitting room resembled a Peloponnesian campsite more than a place for ladies and gentlemen to converse in the leisure of home and the comfort of modern convenience.

"I am so fond of Adam." Lady Agatha sighed, gazing up at the pastel ceiling. "I suppose your uncle's sister will say we are dreadfully out-of-date not to have this whole place torn down and put up a Chinese pleasure palace! Oh, well . . . Help me, Rosie, will you? I only want to move this old tapestry from the door." Together, and lifting a good deal of dust in the process, they removed the ancient tapestry to a less cumbersome position.

"I think it will be a perfectly splendid ball!" exclaimed Agatha Banforth, standing back.

Roselind, too, was gazing about her. The huge pavilion seemed to come to life in her mind's eye, filled with elegant women in satin and jewels and gentleman looking quite dashing in back-and-white evening costumes or the scarlet tunics of officers. The ball was three weeks away. Would it, she wondered, signal the end of an age of splendor for a family which had for hundreds of years led the kingdom in fashion as well as government, in grace as well as loyalty? Would the first Earl of Iseleigh, granted lands in the time of King John, be repaid for his courage by a fortune wasted in profligacy; would those lands, so dearly won, be auctioned off to merchants and rich shopkeepers, parceled into bits, and destroyed? A vision of Windham came into her mind. Graceful, lovely Windham, the earldom's chief country seat. Its noble expanse, the deer park and ornamental waters—would they all be dispersed in another ten years' time? Last night—for the first time in how long?—she had lain awake, not with just this awful image, but with another, a brighter. Reginald Darnley had approached her himself. His name had sounded in her mind like a wonderful warning, an omen of what she might, what she *must* do. But he had taken the first step! Until she had seen his face, until she had heard the wonderfully powerful quality of his voice, the idea that she might be in a position to really do something had been only a dream, a hope she had longed for rather than cherished. Until that moment, her greatest expectation—for she *had* had expectations—had been that she might meet and marry some properly eligible gentleman, someone whose fortune was secure enough so that she could give all her own income, her fifty thousand pounds, to Bertie. But even fifty thousand pounds, great sum though it seemed, could not, as she had known, have done much to help him. Still, it might have saved the manor house and some of the grounds; it might have kept the wolf from the door a little longer, and saved Bertie for a few years from the humiliation of penury.

But now! Now it seemed (or at least it had seemed, for a little) as though more could have been given him. Surely Darnley, an old friend of her father's, would have been eager to help them? He was so vastly wealthy, so she had heard, that such a sacrifice, a sacrifice made by choice, of course, and out of love, would mean very little to him. Reginald Darnley, as everyone knew, could buy

and sell whole kingdoms. What would the matter of a mere earldom have meant to him?

Losing herself deeper and deeper in the matter, Roselind
barely heard the butler, Buxton, come to the door and announce
a visitor. Her aunt moved up the little flight of stairs into the
main house, turning about for only an instant to look back.

"Are you coming, Rosie?" she asked gently. "It is Georgina
Devonshire, I think."

Her grace was already seated in the morning room when
Roselind and her aunt went in. The duchess rose at once to meet
them.

"I was just passing by, my dear Agatha, and could not resist
coming in to have a look at you! Why, my dear," she said, turning to Roselind, who had followed Lady Agatha into the room,
"I never thought I should find *you* at home! Why are you not
abroad, walking and tempting all the young men on such a glorious day?" The duchess seemed to demand no reply, for she
prattled right along, her little gloved hands gesturing quickly in
the air as she spoke, her brilliant green eyes alive with laughter.
"There! But I know what you young girls are! Always liking to
break hearts, right and left! I shall make no demands on you,
Agatha, dear, I only came in for a moment. I was about to send
you a card in any case, for Thursday next, when I am giving a
little soiree—nothing grand, mind you, only one or two friends."

Lady Agatha smiled. She had heard of Georgina Devonshire's
"one or two friends." They usually consisted of three or four hundred, for dinner and dancing, and cards and drinking of champagne until dawn. They were not the sort of entertainment Lady
Agatha liked to attend, but then, Georgina was an amusing soul,

and one did not go about snubbing duchesses, no matter how impractical the size of their entertainments.

"We should be delighted, I'm sure," she murmured.

"Splendid!" Georgina Devonshire clapped her gloved hands with a child's pleasure. "It is too dreadfully dull, I think, when one's particular friends cannot attend these things. What is the point, I always say? Only to have a little good conversation, to be civil and merry, and drink as much champagne as possible. Life is so simple, really; everyone wants to make it so complicated. Simple as fun, and how much a soul can fit in his life before the old murdering jackanapes is upon one. Well, my dear," she said, turning to Roselind, "you were quite the sensation of the Assembly last evening, weren't you? Every time I turned about, there was some other young fellow declaring how much he adored you."

Roselind flushed, much to the duchess's amusement.

"There, now, child! Don't go crimson on me. You must learn, now you are in society, to take these fatal passions as lightly as possible. As lightly, in fact, as they are bestowed! You shall find, I make no doubt, that you have half a dozen young hellions on your heels at every moment. Pay 'em no heed, if you like them very well, and a great deal if you don't. By the by, who was that famous young gentleman—Black or White, or was it Grey?"

"Grey," replied Lady Agatha, suppressing a smile. "It was Mr. Grey, I believe."

"Ah, yes—his name is as impregnable as his manner. I liked him exceedingly. There are so few really amusing young men about nowadays, quite dreadfully tiresome, it is. But your Mr. Grey, or what's-his-name, *there* is a manner for you! Likes to pull people's tails, I think. And very handsome indeed, don't you agree?"

The duchess seemed to have addressed her last question to Roselind, who only smiled demurely and replied, "Very handsome, as you say, your Grace."

The duchess chuckled and gave her a sharp look, her keen green eyes taking in everything.

"And no more than that? If *I* was a young girl, I should be half mad for 'im, I assure you! Lord, they seldom make them like that anymore—handsome as a new guinea, and fine-mannered as you please."

"I am amazed to hear you call him so, your Grace," said Roselind. "I thought just the opposite. *I* found Mr. Grey impertinent in the extreme, and utterly abusive in his remarks."

The chuckle sounded again. "Did you indeed?" Georgina looked with great interest at her young friend. "I imagine you are a great deal more solemn than *I* am, then, for the idea of giving Reginald Darnley a set-down in the middle of the London Highway tickles me immensely, I assure you. *Ma foi!* The very idea of it makes me laugh!"

"I wonder you find it so amusing, since he is such a great intimate of yours," said Lady Agatha, smiling.

"Oh, really, Agatha! You think it is quite as amusing as I do, do you not? Don't contradict me—I see it in your eyes, though you have got that wonderful opaque look in 'em. Roselind, dear, your aunt is a wonder. She should have been the greatest hostess in London, as I've often told her, with that look, but she'll have nothing to do with it! Prefers sitting over tea with poets and scholars all day long. But, Agatha, my dearest, don't attempt to fool me. I know you dislike Darnley as much as I am fond of him. Still, one can't help liking his being piffled about now and again. Oh, he is as witty and charming as any man alive, but he *does* take himself immensely seriously, don't you agree?"

"I will not argue with you there, Georgina."

"Ah! And why do you loathe him so much, if I may ask?"

Lady Agatha smiled. She was aware that Roselind, too, was watching her very hard.

"I never said I loathed him, Georgina," she said carefully. "I only refuse to love him, as everyone else does."

"Still, you must admit," said Georgina Devonshire, "that what he did for the young Montague was quite wonderful. Lord, he could easily have ruined his own reputation, you must agree."

"I had no idea there was anything to lose," said Lady Agatha. "It seems to me Reginald Darnley had very little reputation before he risked it to help his friend." She smiled faintly. "If, indeed, there *was* any risk."

"Well, well . . . you are too deep for me." The duchess laughed. She adjusted a wrinkle in her glove, and rose to leave a few moments later. Lady Agatha and Roselind followed her out into the hallway, where Buxton was waiting with her parasol and pelisse.

"I nearly forgot!" cried their guest, twirling about just as Buxton had managed to arrange her pelisse in a suitable position for slipping it over her blue sleeve. "I did mean to tell you, when we were on the subject of Darnley—my dear, it is the most amusing thing! Whom do you suppose I saw, just on my way up the hill? None other than the gentleman himself. And whom do you suppose he was with? Louisa Chumley and her poor little Clarissa! He was following along behind the mama, looking obedient as a puppy, while Dame Chumley lectured his ear off, and Clarissa looked the perfect little waif. Poor little thing—and so pretty, too—I hate to think of her being bamboozled into a match of that kind! But to think! Darnley, who's scorned every match in the kingdom, succumbing to the charms of Louisa Chumley!"

The thought set her off into a gale of laughter, which was still audible when the front door had closed behind her and the hoof-steps of her handsome white pair began to sound on the cobble-stones outside.

5

"**B**y Jove, Grey is a fine fellow!" Bertie declared. He was languishing in a large chair which was not, however, quite large enough for his long limbs, splayed as they were, with one hessianed leg thrown indecorously over an arm.

"I thought he was very agreeable," remarked Lady Agatha absently from her desk. She had made a futile effort to return to her work as soon as Georgina Devonshire had left, and had been immediately interrupted, first by her husband, who, having come in from the stables, was off again to his club, and then by Bertie, fresh from a most enjoyable turn about the Crescent with his new friend.

"You have no idea!" continued Lord Iseleigh. "Such a dandy hand as he has got with the reins! I shouldn't have trusted my little barouche to anyone, you know, save him. And knows everything about Fox, and Fox's policies. I am ever so eager to know," he continued, staring out the window, "what he was up to in India. Uncle says he cannot have been traveling only for pleasure. It's a damned beastly climate, and no one goes there for pleasure—not for five years, at any rate."

"I do wish you would not use that word, dear," said Lady Agatha from her papers. "Why? Perhaps there are some people who enjoy hot weather and stifling jungle."

"Aye, for a month or two, perhaps. But five years? Anyway, I hope it was not that. I hope it was some adventure, like smuggling jade or pirating."

"Goodness! That does not sound very nice."

"Oh, but it would be, Aggie," Bertie replied with great earnestness. "I shouldn't mind doing something like that myself."

Lady Agatha looked up, smiling. "For a young man who has been talking so much about reforming agriculture and feeding the poor, you suddenly have some very peculiar ideas!"

Just then Roselind put her head in the door. She had gone upstairs as soon as Georgina Devonshire had left them.

"Is there some errand I can do for you, Aggie?" she inquired. "I think I shall just go out for a little walk. I should like to get a ribbon or two, and go to the library."

Lady Agatha looked up to see her niece looking very pale. It was plain the poor child had been suffering some torment, and little as Agatha liked it, she was quite well aware of what the source of her anguish must be. "I should like to wring Georgina Devonshire's neck sometimes," she said to herself. But a happier thought struck her, or at least a more productive one.

"Why, there is something, as a matter of fact, dear. Perhaps Bertie will be good enough to drive you in his wonderful barouche, about which we have all heard so much, but never seen."

Bertie seemed to accede to this suggestion, jumping up from the chair.

"I have got an old friend at Bath," continued Lady Agatha, "that is, not really an old friend … I mean to say, I've known her a number of years, but she is very young. Not above two or three and twenty now, I should think. A charming young lady, and most unfortunate. Her name is Miss Quimby. Maude Quimby. She wrote to me not very long ago, and though she never complained once, nor hinted that she might be very poorly off, I sensed that she was most unhappy. Her father, you know, was at one time very rich. Exceedingly so, in fact. But then he lost all his fortune in a foolish scheme of investments, and died soon afterward, leaving a daughter and a son quite penniless. Miss Quimby is herself come to Bath to take the waters, I gather, for she has suffered from a lung ailment these many years. I feel dreadfully sorry for her, and meant to go at once to visit her on getting back, only I should so much like to get these invitations off before the day is quite over. But if you would be so kind, my dear, and only take her a shawl I have which I never use—a very pretty cashmere, only the shade is all wrong for me—and give her my particular regards, and assure her that I shall come round very soon, I should be ever so grateful."

Roselind complied at once, and went to fetch her bonnet and pelisse while her aunt went off in search of the address.

Bertie was not half so enthusiastic about the mission. The idea of visiting invalids, no matter how pathetic and deserving, did not please him half so much as a turn about the park, which would, he was convinced, show off the splendors of his chariot to much greater effect than a slow rumble through city streets. Roselind, hearing some of these sentiments voiced, and reading the rest in the petulant droop of her brother's mouth, assumed a sister's prerogative in reminding him of his duty.

"Oh, I know it's horrid," he replied, handing Roselind up into his barouche, a very pretty contrivance all done in sky blue, with the golden arms of the earldom painted modestly in very small figures on the doors, "but I never said I liked visiting invalids. I only said they should be properly fed and clothed, with decent places to live."

"I am sure," said Roselind, "that Miss Quimby will be quite as grateful for a visit—more so, in fact—for it requires your real attention and concern."

The fresh air began to do its work on Roselind almost instantly. She had been feeling shockingly low, much lower than she was used to, and yet, no matter how she tried, she had not been able to raise her own spirits. But the prospect of a drive, and of a tour of the city with her own dear brother, brought a greater degree of relief than she could have expected. A young person of naturally happy temperament, a young lady with Roselind's health and joy in living, cannot remain long despondent, no matter how severe the blow life has dealt her. As little a thing as the feeling of a gentle breeze ruffling her skin and the tendrils of dark hair around the rims of a bonnet will raise those spirits. The company of a brother, and one dearly loved, will do the rest. The barouche had not gone very far, therefore, it had not traversed all the length of Pulteney Street and Laura Place and begun its descent into the old part of Bath, before Roselind was talking merrily, and listening with great interest to her brother's anecdotes of school life. The spectacle of so many fine ladies and gentlemen in the street, the view of shops and coffeehouses, did much to animate her.

Only one circumstance was not as welcome as it might have been. Whatever subject Bertie touched on, whatever figure walking in the street caught his eye, everything seemed to remind him of his new friend, Grey. It was forever "Grey recounted to me this," and "Grey assures me that," until Roselind would have been glad to hear the gentleman was vanished from the face of the earth. Each mention of his name called up the image of that laughing, impudent face, and revived in her the memory of his words. It did not occur to her to question why the fellow should irritate her so much. She knew, or thought she knew, what displeased her in him. He had no shred of seriousness, nothing to make her believe he was capable of sincerity. Everything was a joke, and a poor one at that.

A comparison between that light way of going on and the very different manner of Reginald Darnley could not help but follow. The thought brought Roselind full circle, until she was forced to look again, with, oh, how many blushes, at her own naiveté. What mortification she had felt on hearing the Duchess of Devonshire's laughing announcement! With an effort she forced herself to shake off this mood and attend to what was going forward around her.

As soon as the barouche entered the center of town, the young people's ears were greeted with the sounds of city life. The quiet luxury of Pulteney Street, with its peaceful sunshine, its magnolias, and its promenading nurses with their charges gave way to the hubbub of a bustling Union Street. Cries of hawkers competed with the rattle and rumble of carriage wheels over cobblestones. The elegantly clad ladies and gentlemen who had descended on the resort in the last week mingled indiscriminately with roughshod hawkers and ragged flower girls. A throng of gawkers had turned out to watch the spectacle, increasing the air of chaos in the narrow streets and making them all but impassible. The Earl of Iseleigh's barouche was soon forced to draw up at the juncture of Union Passage and Cheap Street, that infamous crossroads where the London Highway and the Great Southern

Road intersected with local traffic. The junction lay just beside the entrance to the Pump Room, giving the earl and his sister an excellent prospect of the crowd going in and out of that notable establishment.

"By Jupiter!" cried Bertie after they had been sitting in the same position for fifteen minutes hoping for an opening in the traffic. "There is Grey!" He pointed to the tall figure of a gentleman just emerging from the great doorway at their right the one giving in to the Pump Room.

Roselind looked up with a frown. She had no desire to meet that gentleman again, least of all now, and feared, from what her brother was saying, that it might be inevitable.

"Let us get his attention, Rosie!" the earl was exclaiming. "Perhaps Grey can be persuaded to come along with us."

But Mr. Grey, to Roselind's relief, did not notice them. He emerged from the Pump Room, looked neither to right nor to left, but with his head bent very obviously in thought, crossed the street just before them without looking up. Bertie cried out, but to no effect. In a moment he had disappeared into the crowd.

"Devilish strange," murmured Albert Arden. "I thought sure when he left me, he said he was going home. He has rooms in the Circus and they are in just the opposite direction."

"Perhaps," Roselind could not resist suggesting, "perhaps he had need of some of the waters to cure his ill manners."

Bertie gave her a peculiar look. "Why do you say such things, Rosie? There is nothing ill-bred about Mr. Grey."

"Is there not? I was certain there was. His behavior last evening did not impress me as quite gallant."

"Oh, he was acting peculiar then, wasn't he? I could not make it out. He seemed bent on teasing everyone. But I think it is only modesty."

"Modesty!" exclaimed Roselind. "He does not seem very modest to *me*," she added to herself.

The traffic just then dispersed enough to let them pass. Lord Iseleigh concentrated all his attention now on steering his team through the winding streets, until they had left the most populous part of the town and begun to ascend a long incline into another district. Miss Quimby lived on Elizabeth Street, just at the other end of Bath from the Banforths. It was not long before Roselind was looking about her at a very different scene from any she had ever witnessed. A maze of streets, reeking of squalor and poverty, led off a central square. In the middle of the square a band of raggedy children were beating a stick at the head of a tiny puppy. The sight made Roselind cry out in horror and grasp her brother's arm.

"Oh!" she cried. "What are they doing to the poor thing? We must make them stop at once."

But Bertie, who had himself taken on a rather yellow color on seeing the game, made her turn away and ignore it.

"I suppose their fathers are about somewhere, Rosie. They would not think much of our interfering, I don't imagine."

And so they passed on. The horrors of poverty were everywhere about them. Old buildings, which it seemed a wonder had not fallen down from neglect and fragility, crowded together along the filthy streets. A scrawny mother lolled in one doorway with a baby at her breast. Poor wretches, their eyes grown over with scabs and dulled by starvation, gazed wonderingly at the handsome carriage as it passed by. Before the barouche had gone very far into the district, a herd of ragamuffins had collected about the wheels, exclaiming at the wonderful conveyance and the still more marvelous young people inside it. The servant riding on the back had little success in persuading the children to go away, and at last the carriage pulled into Elizabeth Street looking exactly like a caravan of gypsies led by a prince and princess.

"I wonder," said Bertie after a little of this, "that Aggie allowed us into this part of town. It is well enough for me, you know, but I don't like the idea of your coming, Rosie. She should have warned me, I think."

Roselind did not reply. She was consumed with the sights about her, and fighting off a growing sensation of faintness. Never before had she witnessed such unhappiness, such misery. In the eyes of the ton, she might have been mistreated by a father who relegated her to a dull life in the country, neglecting to bring her out, and visiting his own home only once or twice a year, and then accompanied by all his friends. But in the eyes around her, the dull eyes clotted with disease and suffering, she saw something approaching worship. She must, indeed, have seemed like a character from a story to these poor wretches. "Never again," she swore to herself, "never again shall I feel any self-pity. To think that only this morning I was desolated to think I had not more than fifty thousand pounds to give my brother! I wonder if any of these poor souls have ever heard of such a sum!"

The barouche drew up before a large stone building a little less disheveled than its neighbors, and Bertie gave up his reins to the servant, who implored his master not to be too long. The entranceway was dark as they went in. Roselind, taking in her breath sharply as a woman reached out a scabby, scrawny hand to touch her frock, immediately repented. She gave the woman a kind smile, and reached into her purse for a coin. Nearly falling over herself with gratitude, the woman scurried off.

Four flights of rickety pitch-black stairs were climbed before the earl and his sister reached a landing on which burned a faint light. No sign of humanity was there anywhere. A single door showed light in the cracks below and above it. Tentatively Bertie put up his hand to knock.

"Come in," said a woman's voice. The sound nearly made Roselind jump. She had not known what to expect. Indeed, she had been bracing herself for anything but this. The voice was low and musical, with a beautiful accent. Lord Iseleigh pushed open the door. What they saw then made Roselind freeze in astonishment and wonder.

6

The room Roselind Arden looked into was small, and though furnished modestly, so neat and clean and flooded with sunshine that it seemed like splendor after the squalid street outside. Everywhere was the graceful touch of a woman. A beautiful old highboy, no doubt preserved from better times, stood in one corner. A vase of flowers on a little incidental table, a chair or two, and a chest made up the balance of the furnishings. In the center of the room was a sofa, and lying on it, the most beautiful woman Roselind had ever seen.

Maude Quimby was quite tall. Even lying down, the length of her limbs under the alpaca rug was evidence of this. A long, slender, graceful arm rested at her side, and another had been just in the process of reaching toward her hair when she had been surprised. But it was her face, a face which could only be described as ethereal, which lent her, and all her surroundings, that air of perfect harmony. The bones were exquisite, with strength and delicacy merged in the aquiline nose, the beautiful proud brow, the high, fine, arched eyebrows. A cloud of pale ashen hair framed her features, with a wave escaping at her neck from the slender ribbon which held it in place. Her enormous expressive brown eyes were open in astonishment and the beautifully shaped mouth formed into an expression of amazement. Even the dark circles beneath her eyes and the hollows under the high, prominent cheekbones added to her loveliness. They seemed to lend her an otherworldliness, an aura which transcended health and vigor.

Roselind stood quite still, feeling her brother's amazement also.

Miss Quimby was the first to speak. "Why, you must have come to the wrong place! Whom do you wish to see?"

"Miss . . . Miss Quimby?" Roselind murmured. "I am Roselind Arden, Lady Agatha Banforth's niece. She asked us to come and give you something."

The gentle eyes looked reproving. "You had better not have come," Maude Quimby said. "It is a very disagreeable neighborhood, is it not?" There was laughter in her voice. The realization startled Roselind more than anything.

"I wonder she would send you all alone, Lady Roselind," she continued in a very amiable way, "I have heard a great deal about you. Oh, a great deal, indeed! Lady Agatha is always talking of you—or at least she was, when last I saw her. And you must be Lord Iseleigh, are you not?" The great eyes turned on Bertie. He nodded dumbly and attempted a bow.

"Well, come along in, since you are here! Really, you should not have come at all, but it is a very agreeable surprise. Invalids are dreadfully low company, you know—always eager to get anyone to listen to them who will bear it. Heaven, I hope there are enough chairs! Bring up that one, will you? I am sorry not to be of any help, but you see, my legs won't function properly—horrible nuisance, most tiresome, indeed! I really think I have not any tea to give you. Will you forgive me? My nurse, Mrs. Dean, comes in three times a week, and when I am expecting a visitor she puts out the tea things for me, but of course I did not know you would be coming." Miss Quimby gazed at her guests, who had by now arranged themselves in chairs beside her couch, with a proprietary air.

"What a delightful surprise! But I am talking a great deal, aren't I? You must forgive me—I have so seldom anyone to chat with that I am afraid I shall talk your ears off. Lucius tells me I am in the habit of talking too much, but then, he is my brother, and brothers are very fond of teasing their sisters, don't you think? Do you tease your sister very sadly, Lord Iseleigh?"

Bertie stared at his hostess in wonder, unsure how to respond. Miss Quimby, however, seemed very well content to keep up the conversation on her own.

"Oh, I am sure you do not! Your sister does not look half so abused as she might! I am sure *you* are a much more sympathetic person than my brother."

"Why?" Bertie demanded gruffly, finding his voice. "Why does he abuse you?" The thought seemed to shock him deeply.

"Oh, well!" Miss Quimby laughed. "You know how it is! I am very fond of my flowers and my little gossips with Mrs. Dean. These women are wonderful, you know. Quite wonderful! They go about to a great many houses, nursing, some of them very great houses, too—and they hear all manner of things. Mrs. Dean goes to Lady Hardcastle in Milsome Street—a most horrible, overbearing kind of woman, I think—who tells her everything about what is going on in society. Mrs. Dean keeps me informed and amused regularly, on Mondays, Wednesdays, and Saturdays.

I warrant I know as much of what goes on in the great world as anyone!"

"Do you really?" inquired Roselind, more for something to say than anything, for she had still not recovered her shock from finding so much cheerfulness in such a strange quarter.

"Oh, yes indeed! I know, for instance," said Miss Quimby, turning her great brown eyes on the young lady, "that you made a great success at your first ball. It *was* your first ball, was it not? Mrs. Dean told me this morning, when she came, that there were a great many mamas looking ever so disgruntled afterward. I think Lady Braknell must have been one of them. I was most curious, you know, and very happy, too, for I knew it was to be your season, and of course your aunt is a very, very dear friend of mine. She has always been so kind to me! Fancy her sending you along like this! I suppose she was too busy to come herself?"

Roselind nodded. "She bid us tell you she would have come, and will, at the first possible moment. Only, this afternoon she was eager to get off the invitations—"

"Ah!" exclaimed Miss Quimby. "I imagine the invitations were to your come-out, were they not? When is it to be?"

"In three weeks' time," replied Roselind, feeling increasingly enchanted by this woman. Or girl, rather. It was difficult to make out. Lady Agatha had said she was not above two or three and twenty, but it was difficult to think of this lady as being any particular age. Her beauty seemed to regard time as her manner disdained her misfortune. Here was a tragic figure indeed, and yet, to hear her talk, one would have thought she had never had anything but happiness in life.

"Oh, indeed. It will be a very grand affair, I make no doubt. I should love to have been able to come, you know—don't think me impertinent—it is only that I have known your aunt for a great while. I feel as though I know *you* quite as well from hearing of you!"

"Perhaps," interposed Bertie in a tentative voice, "perhaps you could come?"

Roselind looked at her brother in astonishment. He had been ever so subdued since coming into the room, she had thought at first from unease, and then from boredom. But the expression on his handsome young face was full of admiration, full of a sincerity and earnestness greater than anything Roselind had ever seen there before. She was very glad. It made her prouder than ever to think that her brother was kind enough, and grown-up enough, to see the good in Miss Quimby.

"Perhaps," Bertie went on, "you would let us send a carriage for you. There would be servants, of course, to help you . . ." He stared uncomfortably at her legs, unsure whether to go on.

"That is very, very good of you," said Miss Quimby with every sign of serious gratitude. "Really, it is quite beyond everything to suggest it. But impossible. Quite impossible."

"I don't see—" commenced Bertie once again in rather a stubborn tone of voice.

"Ah, but you see, it would never do. No, no. Once, perhaps, I might have come. Five years ago, seven years ago—but then I would have been too young. But now ... no, really, it is very kind of you to think of it. But I have nothing to wear, and in any case, it would look very foolish."

Bertie started to say something but thought better of it. A little silence filled the room. Miss Quimby was smiling very kindly at the young earl, who was looking down at his hands with a grave expression. Roselind tried to think of something to say.

"Well," she began, casting about in her mind for some subject which would not embarrass their hostess, "my aunt says you are living here with your brother. He takes care of you, I suppose. How lucky you have a brother to do so!"

Miss Quimby gazed absently into the air. "Oh, yes. Lucius is very good to me. It is horrible, I think, to spend one's life looking after an invalid. Not but what I'm not much better—oh, I am, to be sure! The waters have had a great effect already! I go twice a week, and every time feel a little stronger. I have no doubt that I shall be quite well again soon."

"Really?" said Roselind eagerly. "Why, that is wonderfull And where is your brother now?"

"Oh, he is at work. He is a clerk, you know, in a solicitor's office in the City."

Roselind calculated that whatever Mr. Quimby's wages, he could not, from the looks of this place, have very much money. She had already ascertained that the apartment was not above three rooms. One doorway seemed to give into a bedroom, and another into a sort of kitchen or pantry. There were no signs of a maid anywhere, or any other domestic helper. Roselind wondered how Miss Quimby managed to live, with her brother away all day long, and only a nurse who came in three times a week.

"Yes," Miss Quimby was saying, almost to herself, "Lucius is very good to me. I have often to remind myself of that. He has a great deal to make up for."

Roselind looked up curiously. Bertie, too, seemed to have heard that strange remark. It did not at all fit in with the picture either of them had had of an adoring brother sacrificing everything for his sister.

"Oh!" said Roselind suddenly, remembering, "I nearly forgot! My aunt sent you a present. It is a shawl, I believe."

Miss Quimby exclaimed at her friend's kindness. The parcel, which was wrapped up in brown paper and string, was proffered, and the knot proving too tight for either lady's fingers, a scissors searched for.

"They are in the drawer of that bureau," said Miss Quimby, pointing to the tallboy. Roselind went over to look for them. As she reached the bureau on which were various incidental ornaments and porcelain figures, she noticed a small portrait of a man, framed in a beautiful little enamel case. She could not help looking at it curiously. The gentleman was very handsome indeed, with dark wavy hair and a proud, amiable countenance. Something in the features seemed very familiar to Roselind, but she could not remember when she had seen those features before. "It is her brother, no doubt," she told herself, and looked away again. She was curious to know what Mr. Lucius Quimby had to make up for, which the life he was leading now did not accomplish.

The shawl, a pretty cerise cashmere, was duly exclaimed at.

"What a lovely thing!" declared Miss Quimby, wrapping it around her shoulders. "Lady Agatha is the dearest creature in the world. And now . . . now you must both go. I do not like the idea of your staying away so long. I am sure there are a great many things you should be doing instead."

Bertie seemed reluctant to obey these instructions, saying there was nothing in the world they had rather be doing, but was at last persuaded, provided he could come back again often, that the visit had taken up enough of his day. Regards were delivered to Lady Agatha, and shortly thereafter, brother and sister were once more driving through the streets of Bath.

The sights and sounds of misery no longer affected Roselind as they had before. Something had occurred in that room, with its cheerful, modest little appointments and its beautiful, courageous occupant, something which had changed Roselind's whole view of things. Never before had she witnessed such gaiety in the face of misfortune, nor seen such a welcoming look in a pair of eyes. She had felt, for all her initial embarrassment, instantly at ease with Miss Quimby. So much good humor and gentleness! She glanced sideways at her brother. Lord Iseleigh was immersed in his own thoughts. He, too, seemed to have undergone a transformation.

"Never," said Roselind warmly, "have I seen anything like her!"

"Nor I," replied Bertie very softly. "I never knew there was so much goodness in the world!"

Lady Agatha Banforth was dismayed to hear the young people's account of Miss Quimby's neighborhood.

"I should never have sent you, had I known what kind of place it was! Oh, dear, I am most sorry I did."

"No, no!" cried Bertie. "It was not nearly so bad as it sounds. And Miss Quimby ... Miss Quimby is an angel."

Lady Agatha smiled. "She is, rather, is she not? What a brave soul! And so cheerfully disposed to see the humor and merriment in every situation. I can only wonder at her courage. At one time, you know, she seemed destined to make a very great match. Poor child! Life seems to have conspired against her."

"I should like to do something for her," said Bertie.

"Oh, indeed! We shall get her to come to dinner in a day or

two, and send her a good joint of mutton. I have no doubt that will give her a great deal of pleasure."

"No," said Bertie with a peculiar look, "I mean something else. Oh, you may have your joints and shawls, but I have another idea."

Both his aunt and his sister looked at the young earl with curiosity, but he had turned away to stare out of the window.

7

Roselind had been so much moved by her visit to Miss Quimby that her fears in another area were, for the moment, laid to rest. She had seen courage in its most beautiful form, and was determined to emulate her new friend's cheerfulness in the face of tragedy. That Maude Quimby was a friend, she did not for a moment doubt. The young woman's parting expressions had been full of hope that she would see Lord Iseleigh and his sister again. Even while she had been urging them to go, a trace of regret had been in her wonderful eyes.

"I shall go to her as often," she thought, "as I am able. Nothing shall keep me away. It will give me a goal, to have another person to help, in what ever little ways I can." The prospect of a busy season full of balls and theater, outdoor fetes and breakfasts, dimmed before the idea of seeing more of that marvelous woman, and of drinking in as much as she could of the other's attitudes. She went to her room with that intention firmly planted in her bosom, and passed the rest of the afternoon in contemplating Miss Quimby's goodness.

But resolutions, no matter how earnest, are sometimes

dispersed before the tide of events. Dinner was planned for an early hour in Pulteney Street, so as to make time to reach the theater, where the family was going to attend Mr. Sheridan's new play, *The Rivals*. Roselind came down the staircase shortly before five, to see Buxton holding a strange cloak and hat. She found, a second later, on going into the drawing room, where the family was gathered to await their summons to table, that Mr. Grey was immersed in conversation with her aunt and uncle. For once, Bertie did not seem to be hanging on every word that issued from his friend's mouth. With a rapt but rather absent expression on his face, he sat gazing out the window into the flower garden. The gentlemen rose as Roselind came in.

"Ah, my dear Rosie," said General Banforth, "you see we have an unexpected pleasure this evening. I was able to persuade Grey here to join our little party for dinner, and the theater afterward."

"How very delightful," murmured Roselind as sincerely as she could while Mr. Grey bent over her hand.

"I am afraid," said that gentleman when he was upright once more, gazing into her eyes with a slight frown in his brilliant blue ones, "that you find very little to rejoice in at the news."

"Oh! Oh the contrary, I am sure," mumbled Roselind. A little flustered, she found her chair with some difficulty, for however much she tried, she could not help feeling an agitation whenever she looked into that face.

"Mr. Grey was just telling us about his sojourn in India," said Lady Agatha. "It is a most diverting narration! I had thought there were only lions and tigers and other kinds of frightful monsters in the country, but I find I am quite wrong. It seems it is a most civilized place."

"Its civilization dates back so long," said Mr. Grey, smiling, "it would be a wonder if it were not. But I am sure such talk will weary Lady Roselind."

Roselind could not help reading a criticism into this remark, as indeed she read one into every one of Mr. Grey's comments. The look he leveled at her as he said it could only be interpreted as contempt.

"Why?" she demanded now, bridling slightly. "I hope you do not assume that simply because I am young and female, I have no interest in history and geography!"

With a surprised look Mr. Grey replied that such an assumption had never been his. He added with a faint smile, "But since it is history and geography that fascinate you, ma'am, I am afraid my little bit of wisdom will bore you to extinction. I have no expertise in these subjects—as, no doubt, you must have—for all I know is a smattering of human nature, legend, and the ofttimes exotic habits of some of the peoples I have encountered in my travels. There is nothing like scholarship in it."

Roselind pressed her lips together to keep from replying. It was quite plain now: Mr. Grey despised her. Well, and it was no very great loss if he did! What was his opinion to her? She looked determinedly at her hands, and after the little awkward pause that inevitably followed upon the last exchange, listened only halfheartedly to the rest of the conversation.

Mr. Grey was now leaning well back in his chair, his long legs stretched out before him in what Roselind considered a most impudent familiarity, speaking fluently upon the subject of India. Lady Agatha seemed nearly as much fascinated as the general, who continually interrupted the narration to put some question or other, and at last remarking, as they rose to go in to dinner, that "It is a great pleasure—a great pleasure indeed—to hear a man of sense speaking on the subject. There are so many young fools, you know, my dear," he added to his wife, "who come back from a month abroad, thinking they know everything. But Grey knows what he is talking about and understands it very well indeed!"

Dinner passed without any comfort for Roselind. She dreaded meeting Mr. Grey's eyes, and focused on the stream of passing dishes. Her aunt was delighted with him—that was plain—and General Banforth, usually a man of such good sense, could not agree heartily enough with everything that passed those lips. Roselind longed for a little relief from all this adulation from her brother, but Bertie was toying with his napkin at the other side of the table during the whole meal, only looking up once to inquire if Mr. Grey was acquainted with a Miss Quimby.

"No," said that gentleman, smiling in his impudent way, "I do not believe I am. But then, you know, I have no acquaintance at Bath—I come here almost a stranger."

"Come now," put in General Banforth in his hearty way. "I cannot believe a fellow of your breeding and knowledge has not *some* friends here!"

"But it is quite true!" protested the other. "I have neither family nor friends, but am quite alone in the world."

Such a confession would normally have drawn sympathy from Roselind, for she was by nature a warmhearted creature, given to liking anything homeless and lonely. But Mr. Grey's remark had been made as if it was a challenge to the world, for all the world as if he were proud of it!

"And where do you mean to make your home, now you are returned?" asked Lady Agatha. "You must have some idea, some preference for one part of the country over another."

Mr. Grey's reply characterized, in Roselind's mind, his whole attitude. With a laughing, mocking look and a wave of his slender, bronzed hand he said laughingly, "But I assure you, I do not! I have no plan at all, and no intentions whatever, but to pass my time as pleasantly as possible. I have a great deal to learn about England; I think the best way to accomplish it will be through diversion. One always meets a great deal of people in that way, and learns more, perhaps, than through any serious endeavor."

"Why," exclaimed General Banforth, laughing, "that is a very well way of looking on the matter for a young man! I can think of nothing better!"

But Roselind was not so delighted with the idea as her uncle seemed to be. Mr. Grey, in her view, seemed to combine all the worst aspects of frivolity. Not only did he practice idleness, he even boasted of it! So much did Mr. Grey remind Roselind of her father that she was forced to look again, to be sure the dead man had not come to life again. Diversion as a rule and a life plan had been Lord Iseleigh's guiding principle. It had made him lazy, selfish, and vain, and in the end had ruined his family.

"How different," thought Roselind, "is Mr. Darnley! *He* does not lie about all day long, I warrant! His life is full of useful work, and when he helps a friend, as he did Roderick Montague, he never even boasts of that!" The difference between the two gentlemen was very plain, but it did not comfort Roselind much. Instead, she was forced to remember her recent humiliation, and in the effort to justify her view of Darnley, found herself again searching out all sorts of excuses for his conduct.

The family rose from the dinner table and in a while they were traveling toward the theater. Mr. Grey, seated opposite the young earl, regarded his friend with amusement. Bertie had hardly opened his mouth all the evening, and even now was gazing out the window with a rapturous expression.

"So, young Albert," said the older gentleman in a teasing fashion, "what flaxen-haired beauty has captured your imagination? Do not protest! I make it out a . . . Let me think." Mr. Grey put his hand to his eyes in a mockery of concentration. "Ah, I have got it! A Miss Quimby, is it? With eyes like stars and lips like rose petals, I believe."

"How did you know?" demanded Bertie, looking up in astonishment.

"It was not very hard to make out. I had but to be in the same room with you for two minutes together to see what had taken place since twelve o'clock, when you were as natural and happy as a young skylark, and now, when you are as low and curmudgeonly as only a fellow in love can be."

"What," thought Roselind, sitting silently in her corner of the carriage, "can Mr. Grey know about such things? It would be useless to tell him that Bertie is not consumed by the image of starlike eyes and rose-petal lips, but a noble courage wholly unknown to such people as Mr. Grey! *He* would never understand what it is to sacrifice selflessly, nor to admire a woman, without any trace of demeaning passion!"

But Bertie did not look offended at the suggestion. On the contrary, he smiled at his friend in a dreamy sort of way, which made Lady Agatha stare at him in astonishment, and General Banforth, who had no idea who Miss Quimby was, laugh outright.

The Rivals commenced on an unlucky note. Roselind found herself seated next to Mr. Grey in the box before she could contrive to get away with some excuse. He was not content until he had made a great many foolish commentaries upon theater in general and comedy in particular. Roselind tried to ignore most of it, but was forced to respond to his most direct questions. This she endeavored to do as coolly as possible, without encouraging any further conversation. She hoped to make him see she did not care a fig for his observations, nor his opinion, and quite soon she saw she had been successful, for Mr. Grey gave her one piercing look and settled back in silence for the rest of the act.

In due course the opera glass was handed round, and Roselind, when it came her turn, put it to her eye. The spectacle on the stage was very amusing, but not enough to capture her attention. Her eye had been wandering round the theater all the time, resting chiefly on a dark corner of a box, directly opposite, which contained Lady Chumley, her daughter, and a sheepish-looking Sir Walter. Miss Chumley had been turning now and again to speak to someone in the shadow. Roselind could only guess who it was. She turned the glass in that direction, and hardly suppressed a little gasp when she saw it was Mr. Darnley. No matter that she had expected to see him; no matter that she had already—or so she thought—steeled herself to the notion that they were already affianced. It came as a shock to see the evidence of it so blatantly before her. It would have been one thing had they been together at the opening assembly, or together in the street, or had they once sat in the same theater box. But to have done all three—it was impossible to believe they were not promised! How else would they dare be seen together so much?

For the remainder of the act Roselind needed all her attention to keep from glancing away from the stage. She longed to know for certain if her suspicions were correct. If they were, she would make do. Once her last traces of hope were proved futile, she would steel herself to another way of going, but until then she must still cherish some residue of optimism. The curtain dropped at last. Roselind stood up, as if to stretch her legs, and positioned herself deliberately in the light next to the rail, where she could be glimpsed by the whole theater. Without any reason to hope it might occur, she longed to see Mr. Darnley walk in at the door to the box, come with an apology and some explanation of his absence. She stood in exactly that same spot for ten minutes, and then glanced around. Mr. Darnley had left his box. The sight made her tremble inside with happiness. In a moment his broad figure would appear at the door. Roselind gazed expectantly at it, unconsciously replacing a tendril of hair which had crept out from her coiffure. She accepted a glass of punch proffered by Mr. Grey with hardly any realization of what she was doing. He would come any second now...

The bell signaling the end of the interlude sounded. Roselind sank into her chair with a hollow feeling in her stomach. She saw that Mr. Darnley had returned to his place, and was conversing with a group of people who had followed him in. He never even glanced in her direction.

Mr. Grey had been saying something. Dumbly she turned to him.

"I said, 'What are you staring at?'"

Roselind crimsoned. "Staring? I? I did not know I was staring! I was only wondering what will happen in the second act!"

"I believe the rivals discover each other. It is too soon to come to grips, but in the last act, of course, there will be a duel."

"Why? Have you seen the play before?" inquired Roselind, surprised.

"No. But they are all alike, don't you agree? Certain elements meet and blend, in different proportions, but to the same effect. The romantic hero and heroine, the blackguard, and the comedic lovers—it is always the same. First each unveils his motive and his objective, which, having been revealed, seem to be stifled, and at last are fulfilled. It is a neat pattern, and would work very well in real life, only it is never the case."

"No," said Roselind, "it never does work out like that, does it?"

For a moment she forgot to dislike Mr. Grey. He seemed almost sympathetic in that moment, smiling down at her. But in an instant he was odious again.

"Very rarely. Now, let me see. If theatrical formulas were to be applied here, I wonder what we should have."

Roselind smiled unsuspectingly up at him.

"Who are the characters, first?"

"Oh! The characters!" Mr. Grey laughed. "It seems to me *they* are obvious. We needn't mention them. To begin, we should have your brother, Lord Albert, and his *amour*—Miss Quimby, I think?"

"But they are not lovers at all! Miss Quimby is an unfortunate young woman, very ill—Bertie only feels, as I do, a great affinity for her!"

Mr. Grey raised one blond eyebrow. "Indeed? A tragic heroine? How interesting. But let us say, only for the sake of argument, that they are in love. It is always that way, you know. It would be thought dreadfully dull to have a mere 'affinity' where grand passion ought, by rights, to be. So, let us *say* they share an undying love."

"Really! You are beyond everything! We only just met her today."

Mr. Grey smiled at her as a grandfather might smile at a backward child. "Yes, yes, but in fiction, one look is enough, you know. One look reveals body and soul, past, future, and everything in between. In short, one glance is all there should be! So, we have Bertie and your Miss Quimby arrayed on the stage. They shall be all right. Bertie, being an earl and very rich, will no doubt carry Miss Quimby away on his white steed in short order. He will start by making her well, through some miracle of devotion, and end by making her rich, and a countess to boot. Where does your Miss Quimby live?"

"In Elizabeth Street."

"Ah, yes—Elizabeth Street. A Miss Quimby in Elizabeth Street. Not very good names, to be sure, but they will do. By rights, they should be—let me see—I think Blanche, yes, Blanche . . . Blanche Hargrove would be ever so much better, don't you agree? But the curtain is going up. We shall have to save the rest of our predictions for later."

Roselind hardly noticed what took place in the second act. Her mind was far too much occupied with a thought, which, though incredible and utterly impossible, nevertheless could not be shaken off. It was quite ridiculous to think that Bertie was in love. No, no, completely preposterous! But what if he *should* fall in love? Even if the object of his affections were not Miss Quimby, but someone altogether different, even should she (in that far-off time when he would be old enough to feel such sentiments) be a lady of family and means, what would he have to offer her? The thought of Bertie as a man had entered Roselind's consciousness, up till now, only as a single entity. The thought of his meaning eventually to marry and to have children, to form a family in fact, filled her with astonishment and fear. But of course he would marry in the due course of things! And then, what would her fifty thousand pounds avail him? A modest income, by his present standards, a house and perhaps two carriages. But would his wife be content with that? Should not an earl offer his loved one more? And would not he want to leave lands and income to his children? Roselind had not many notions about money. She had never had to, to be frank, but she was aware that fifty thousand pounds, while a fortune by other standards, was as nothing for an earl. In distress she gazed across at Reginald Darnley, still seated in the shadow of his box. He was, she realized increasingly, her only hope.

Mr. Grey did not continue his predictions, as he had promised. The curtain rose and fell three more times, but he seemed absorbed in thought. At the final curtain he rose and offered Roselind his arm.

"You will accept my carriage to convey you home, I hope, Grey?" asked General Banforth as they went out into the night air.

"No, no … I thank you, sir, but I believe I shall walk."

"It is a great way to the Circus, man, you had better come in the carriage."

Mr. Grey declined the offer once again, with every show of gratitude. Turning to Lady Roselind as he took his leave, he murmured, "Mark what I said about the young lovers."

Roselind laughed, as though she did not put any weight in his words.

"Oh, indeed, I shall! But tell me, Mr. Grey—what part do you play in all of this?"

"I?" demanded he with a surprised look. "Why, I do not know that I play any part at all!"

8

"**P**oor angel!" exclaimed Mrs. Hogarth, regarding her brother's niece with a degree of pity hardly welcomed by that young lady.

Roselind had been sitting with her aunt and uncle in the morning room after breakfast when Mrs. Hogarth had rushed in, bursting with news, and barely stopping to excuse this early appearance and the wild-looking arrangement of her hair, crying, "My dears, I am so sorry for you!" It had been some minutes before either of the ladies, or General Banforth, who was trying to read his morning paper in tranquillity, had understood her meaning.

Such a wild rush of words, pinned together without the least semblance of coherence, had escaped her lips that General Banforth had stared blankly at her, and at last cried, "Clara! I demand to know what you are speaking of! Has the continent of Europe fallen into the ocean, or is it merely a question of your dressmaker delivering a crimson gown in place of a violet?" He could not help adding, with a smile, "Though really, you know, my dear, you had better give up both of them and order a nice quiet gray silk."

His sister stared at him in confusion. "Why, whatever are you talking of, brother? I am sure you have such a peculiar way of going on, *I* cannot make head nor tail of it!"

"My dear," said the general, getting up from his chair with a resigned look, "you have expressed my sentiment exactly. I suppose I am the one causing all the confusion. As that is the case, and as only ladies, it seems, are privy to your news, I shall just retreat to my study and leave you all in peace."

"A most exceeding difficult man," murmured Mrs. Hogarth, watching her brother out the door. "I wonder you can abide him as well as you do, my dear."

Lady Agatha murmured, with a faint smile, that she just managed.

"But what is all this about, Clara? You quite shocked me, rushing in in that wild way. Is there anything amiss?"

With an air of great importance and increasing sympathy Mrs. Hogarth glanced from one to the other of the ladies. She sometimes took as much delight in withholding information as in giving it.

"I have just come from my friend Louisa Chumley," she said significantly. "Or at the least, she was once my friend. I shall never again dignify her with the title! A very bossy, overbearing kind of woman, to be sure, and ranks herself quite freely with her betters!" Mrs. Hogarth sniffed. "Nothing but a baronet's lady, and fancies herself as consequential as a duchess!"

Mrs. Hogarth would have gone on in this same vein for a great while longer, for she was very expert in the dignities and honors owing each particular level of the aristocracy, a group for which untold admiration and jealousy mingled in her bosom, had she not been urged to continue.

"However, that is not much to the point, save, of course, it only makes her conduct more arrogant! Fancy, my dears, what she has just told me—and with such an air of importance, it quite made me sick to look at her! In short, she has just let me know (which she was very eager to do, you know!) that she expects Reginald Darnley to be her son-in-law before the autumn! Those were her very words." Mrs. Hogarth seemed torn between the triumph afforded by being the bearer of such news and the desire to look more pityingly than ever at Roselind. That young lady had moved to the window and was gazing out very hard at a lilac tree in full bloom, its blossoms trembling very prettily in a gentle wind.

The commiserating look was wasted, therefore, in that quarter, but Mrs. Hogarth lost no time in directing it at her sister-in-law, who only smiled back in a calm fashion.

"How interesting!" said Lady Agatha. "But I wonder why you considered *us* worthy of hearing it so soon?"

Mrs. Hogarth's chin dropped in amazement.

"For, you know," Lady Agatha went on, giving her companion no time to interrupt, "we hardly know Mr. Darnley at all. To be sure, he was on intimate terms with my brother, but as to my knowing him—why, I have barely spoken three words to him this last age. Still, it is very interesting news."

Mrs. Hogarth had decided, wisely or not, to ignore this speech. She moved to Lady Roselind's side, a thin hand raised to comfort her with soft pats and whatever other ministrations she could think of.

"Yes, yes, of course you would not admit it, my dear," she cooed, and then, in a softer voice added, "but do not think *I* do not remember what it is to be in love! Do not think I never saw you staring after him at the Assembly, or last evening in the theater!

Oh, no, I am not so old as that! It has not been quite *that* long since I suffered all those same little tremors and flutters which I can read quite plainly in your face this moment!"

Roselind cast the older woman one anguished glance. Shame, mortification, and the pain of being discovered all fought in her bosom. How was it possible that she had been found out? She had only spoken to the gentleman for the briefest moment, her only communication to her uncle's sister had been that she was going to drive with him yesterday! And then, of course, he had not come. Could Mrs. Hogarth know so much? To be sure, she had been looking after him all the previous evening at the theater, but how had Mrs. Hogarth seen her? She remembered distantly that Mrs. Hogarth had come in at one of the intermissions, but how could that have afforded her such a view of her own heart? What she had to be thankful for now was that it had been interpreted as love. No one should ever discover what her real motive had been, a motive which Roselind herself could only blush at in retrospect. How foolish, how innocent she had been! To have assumed a great man like Reginald Darnley would have given her the time of day! Only because he had approached her and spoken a few kind words! Her only consolation now, her only hope, was to preserve her dignity, not only for her own sake, but for her family's. She could not bear to be discredited in those eyes!

Roselind, in all the passion of the moment, assumed that Mrs. Hogarth had indeed made out her heart. She never suspected that the older woman's words had not been spoken from real knowledge and observation. She would have been amazed to learn that the truth of the matter was that Mrs. Hogarth had made a felicitous guess. She had used an old trick, a trick which had had much success in the days when her own daughters had been of a marriageable age and obstinately refused to like the gentlemen their mother thought they should. It was, precisely, to suggest their sentiments persistently, in such a way that by degrees the girls (who were, though fine-looking, healthy girls, not quite equal to their mama in subtlety) had come gradually to feel as they were meant. Mrs. Hogarth had predicted a long struggle for herself, for she badly wanted Lady Roselind to take the field against the odious Louisa Chumley. But now she saw, with a look of immense relief, that she had nothing to combat. Roselind's eyes were full of her feelings, feelings impossible to ignore or misinterpret.

"There, there, child!" she murmured, patting Roselind's shoulder with her scrawny hand. "I never bowed to Louisa Chumley in all my life, nor shall I, while I have breath left in my body. We shall find a way out of this perplexity, make no doubt."

It seemed to Roselind impossible that they should do so. Her only wish was to collect her emotions and endeavor to behave as if nothing had occurred to disrupt them. She barely listened to the balance of Mrs. Hogarth's remarks, and found with some astonishment on looking back into the room again that her company had been solicited for a walk.

"I have a great desire to get out into the fresh air, my dear," Mrs. Hogarth was saying to her aunt. "I suppose you could not spare me Roselind for the morning?"

Lady Agatha looked back and forth between the two. Roselind, pale and trembling, was wearing a forced smile on her lips.

"Oh," said Lady Agatha, "I am sure I can spare her, if she is up to it. How do you feel, my dear?"

Roselind did not like to let anyone think she was beyond her usual spirits, and readily complied. Bonnets and gloves were fetched, and in a few moments the strangely attired woman, with her orange locks tied up haphazardly in an incredible-looking bonnet of ostrich feathers and Spanish lace, and the small, pretty, demure young lady, in her high-necked muslin frock and parasol, were causing smiles and speculation on the street outside.

"I think we should just dash over to the Crescent for a spell," said Mrs. Hogarth innocently. "There is always something doing there, and then, it is such fine weather, too—just right for a walk."

Roselind agreed readily enough. She was too much taken up with scolding herself for her stupidity, and itemizing every misconception she had had about the world, and gentlemen, and her own powers, to notice where they went, or how. They walked along, Mrs. Hogarth chattering away in a gay kind of fashion, pointing out a wonderful gown here, and a magnificent bit of lace there, and seeming not to notice the distracted, cursory replies of her companion. In this way they attained Laura Place, and turned into the maze of residential streets leading off it, one of which led in the direction of the Royal Crescent.

Having paid no attention to the direction in which they had come, Roselind looked up in a moment to see, with some surprise, that they had come into Milsome Street, a grand avenue bordered on both sides by modern houses of luxurious proportions and design. She murmured absently that she had always thought Milsome Street led off another way from the one they wanted, but received Mrs. Hogarth's assurance that, "No, no, my dear—it is much the quickest way," without argument. Another moment had brought them to the juncture of a carriage lane leading between two mansions. Here they were forced to stop, to allow for the passage of a sleek black lacquered phaeton, driven by a groom, which was just rounding the bend. Mrs. Hogarth, much to her companion's surprise, began suddenly to complain of the heat.

"To be sure it is a very hot day," she wailed, fanning herself distractedly with her gloved hand and clutching at Roselind's arm. "I do not think I am equal to another step, my dear. Lud, I wish we had come in a carriage!"

"Why, ma'am, I wonder you feel it so," said Roselind in astonishment. "Not a moment ago you were praising the weather."

"Yes, yes," came the impatient retort, "but you have not my old legs, my dear. Were you half my age, you should know what misery the heat can cause! It is beyond everything, I am sure! Really, I must just lean up against this post for a moment. Give me your arm again, child. Oh, oh! I think I am surely going to faint!"

In distress Roselind sought through her reticule for a box of smelling salts, which Mrs. Hogarth promptly waved away. The phaeton by this time had left the alley and was just drawing up before the next mansion, a very splendid edifice of vast size.

Mrs. Hogarth gestured in the direction of a stone bench just in front of the mansion. "My dear," she said, "I wish you would support me to that seat."

Roselind obeyed, wondering all the while what could have brought on this strange transformation in her friend. They reached the bench just in time to hear a familiar baritone voice remark, "I shall be back in time for dinner, Parkins."

Roselind glanced up, her cheeks lit with color. The impressive figure of Reginald Darnley, his broad shoulders draped in a handsome brown riding coat, stood frozen at the top of the marble steps. Before she could look away again, her eyes had met his startled ones.

Mortification beyond anything Roselind had ever experienced

overcame her. Where could she look, how could she behave, to avoid the humiliation of the moment? Her first instinct, when she was capable of speech, was to turn angrily on her companion, but Mrs. Hogarth was crying, as innocent as a babe, "Why! If it is not you, Darnley! What a piece of luck! I was just telling Lady Roselind that I did not think I was equal to another step! We were just on our way to the Crescent, you know, when the heat—why, I thought sure I should collapse! I suppose *you* are not going in that direction, are you?" Mrs. Hogarth eyed the phaeton, with its pair of glorious blacks, with the hunger of a child gazing at a plate of dainties.

"How fortunate in that case," said Mr. Darnley, coming down the steps, "that you should find yourself within easy reach of a friend."

Roselind saw that his countenance had regained its usual composure. But despite the civility of his words and the smile he was directing at them, she could not help detecting a trace of sarcasm in his tone. "And no wonder!" she thought. "What must he think of us? Planting ourselves on his doorstep like a pair of flirts!"

"I was myself going to the Crescent," Darnley was saying, extending one elegantly swathed arm to the older woman. "Allow me to escort you there."

Mrs. Hogarth beamed in a sickeningly coquettish fashion. "Oh! It is too good of you, I am sure! We could not impose on your goodness so much!"

This was a strange way of accepting the invitation she had just solicited, but it gave Roselind the opportunity to exclaim, "Indeed, we could not, sir! It is much too kind of you, but Mrs. Hogarth and I are very able to walk."

"Tut, child!" cried that lady with an irritated look. "*You* may be equal to it, with your young legs, but I am sure I am not! No, no, we had better accept Mr. Darnley's hospitality."

So saying, the older woman jumped up from her seat, for all the world as if she had been three and twenty instead of three and fifty, and leaning on Mr. Darnley's arm in a very poor imitation of languor, hobbled to the phaeton. Roselind had little choice but to follow. Too mortified and angry to care anymore, she allowed herself to be handed up beside Mrs. Hogarth, avoiding determinedly the mocking eyes of the gentleman.

The journey to the Royal Crescent could not have been a matter of much more than five minutes, but to Roselind it seemed an eternity. She listened with increasing humiliation and pain to the senseless babbling of her companion, who seemed incapable of uttering one intelligent or creditable word. Prattling away as foolishly and as constantly as a magpie, she seemed barely to have begun to make all those little effusive compliments to Mr. Darnley's dress, his taste, his house, and his carriage, which she felt it incumbent on her to do, before the phaeton began to climb the little stretch of rising ground which preceded a first glimpse of the Crescent. Each comment, each phrase, inspired Roselind with fresh shame in her companion. An occasional stolen glimpse of the imperturbable face beside her told her nothing. She could only guess what was in his mind! What must he think of them, and of her? How would he now despise her for choosing the company of such a woman!

Darnley had not opened his lips during the whole ride, except to answer, wherever he was forced to, some one of Mrs. Hogarth's vulgar inquiries. This he managed to do without in any way betraying his feelings, but with a cool civility which only increased Roselind's distress. How kind he was to them! How much more she should have liked it had he been overtly cutting; at least in that way she should not have felt so much inferior to him in breeding and good sense! The faintly mocking expression in his eyes had disappeared. What was there now was only an unreadable expression, as he stared directly before him at the road.

At last the gentle hill gave way to a first panoramic view of the Royal Crescent, with its magnificent semicircle of buildings, its formal gardens and lawns, its avenues and ornamental waterworks. The sight was cool and refreshing in any case, with behind it the long vista of the River Avon and a ridge of chalky cliffs. The sight promised Roselind an end to this torment. At the first possible moment she was determined to get down, and never again to look into those dark eyes. The idea gave her a little ease, even as she was listening to the last of Mrs. Hogarth's prattling.

But that lady had very different ideas. Oblivious of her friend's suffering, she cried out, "Why! There is my good friend Louisa Chumley! Do pull up beside them if you will, my dear Darnley!"

"My dear Darnley" looked almost startled at this. Both he and Roselind glanced up at the same time, to see a little group of three, standing some hundred yards away. The ladies, one stout and proud-looking in purple linen, the other demure and gentle in pale blue, were looking about them as if searching for someone. Sir Walter Chumley was talking affably to the air in general, it seemed, for no one appeared to pay him any mind. Roselind could hardly believe her ears when she heard the command repeated. She could only look at her hands, and then at Mr. Darnley, and seeing nothing in *his* eyes, turn crimson with embarrassment.

The phaeton drew up alongside the party, and Mrs. Hogarth, giving no one any time to speak, and ignoring the expression of apoplectic rage in her good friend's face, cried, "Louisa, my dear! You see how elegantly we have contrived to come! Such a good fortune it was, for I was near dead with the heat, when who do you suppose came to our rescue? Yes, yes, it was this dear man, dear Darnley! He would hear of nothing but that we must climb up with him and ride to the Crescent. Though"—with a meaningful glance at Roselind—"I do not think it was *my* comfort that concerned him! No, no—what could he care about an old woman like me?" Mrs. Hogarth laughed delightedly at her own turn of phrase, for once not minding the label of age.

Mr. Darnley's expression was still impossible to decipher. Glancing from him to the dumbfounded countenance of Miss Chumley, who seemed all innocent consternation, Roselind could only suppress a gasp and try to keep her head. What more could Mrs. Hogarth be plotting? Was she not content with the damage she had already done her young friend? The answer was soon to burst upon the unbelieving Roselind.

"Do hand me down, Sir Walter," Mrs. Hogarth was saying, putting out her hand in an imperious manner. "I will just get down and walk a little with my dear friend, for we have not conversed in an age, and I dislike above all things interfering with the workings of young hearts"—this with another sly glance at the two still remaining in the phaeton. "Do you now just go along, my love," she said to Roselind, "and pay me no heed. Mr. Darnley certainly does not want *my* company! You had better have a delightful drive around the gardens and forget all about me!"

Lady Chumley's throat was puffed up, rather like a frog's. She no doubt would have liked to say something, but the words stuck in her throat. Unbelievingly she glanced at Mr. Darnley for support, but he was smiling civilly and said, "I should of course feel myself honored to have Lady Roselind's company for a tour of the park."

But what else could he say? Mrs. Hogarth had choreographed the little scene to perfection. Even Sheridan might have been proud of so quick a revolution of the chief characters, such concise and distinct hints from the new master of ceremonies to the old, so abrupt and yet so smooth a revision of themes. Barely two minutes had passed since they had driven into the Crescent, and already there was a new love scene in progress, a fresh heroine, and a discarded plot. It was a pity that no one but Mrs. Hogarth (and perhaps Sir Walter, who had never seen his wife spoken to in this kind of way before) derived any satisfaction from the proceedings. Roselind was mortified, Lady Chumley outraged, and Miss Chumley looked perplexed and vaguely hurt. Mr. Darnley's eyebrows had mounted to a position signifying wonder and perhaps amusement at what had gone on, but Roselind never noticed it, for she was too busy staring at her gloves and trying to collect her thoughts.

Absently she noticed that the horses had started up again, and supposed them to be moving toward the avenue which ran about the central park. But it was some moments before she had composed herself enough to look up, and longer still before she could open her lips to murmur, "How can I ever beg your forgiveness, sir? Mrs. Hogarth ... I cannot believe she understands her own conduct. She is but a child in some ways. Only, I beg of you . . . but how *could* you forgive us? We have maddened your friends, and perhaps ruined your own happiness—"

Roselind was surprised by a sort of snort beside her.

"Do not speak of *my* happiness, I beg you, my lady."

Roselind glanced up in wonder. Mr. Darnley was staring directly ahead of him, a smile in his dark eyes.

"It was wonderful to see Lady Chumley given a set-down, I assure you. Though, in truth, your relative does lack something in decorum."

"Indeed, sir, if there is any way—"

"No, no, never mind," he cut her off. "There is nothing to apologize for. Indeed, it is *I* should be grateful to you! That woman has had me in thrall these last three days, as much as if I had been a puppy and she my domineering mistress. And all because she claims to have come to my aid the other day in the highway when an absentminded farmer pushed his cart under my wheels. I thought I should never be free of her, I assure you!"

Roselind's jaw dropped. The expression on her face betrayed only part of her amazement.

"Then you are not ... I mean to say, Miss Chumley is not promised to you?" she stammered.

"Good God, no!" Mr. Darnley put back his head and laughed as if it had been the best joke in the world. "Little Clarissa Chumley? Lord! She is in love with that young officer—Wedgeworth, or Wedgewood, I can never recollect which. Her mama abhors the notion, for he has not a farthing, and all the world knows she has been trying to make her daughter look elsewhere. Well, but she had better set her sights somewhere else. Miss Chumley is quite well-looking, but has got no wit, and even if she had, I should not be able to stomach her mama. By Jove, what a dragon she is!"

Words could hardly describe Roselind's emotions on hearing this. To think that a moment before she had been wishing she could jump beneath the carriage wheels! And now such a flood of joy—a sensation that, she could not help thinking, even while she experienced it, was not wholly laudable—rushed over her that she was once again at a loss for words. It was true that Darnley's sentiments as regarded Lady Chumley and her daughter were not exactly chivalrous, but in the rush of pleasure, Roselind never noticed it. All she could think of was her darling Bertie and what she might yet be able to do for him. It was true this was only a beginning—but what a more propitious one than it had seemed at first! All her self-reproaches of the morning were forgotten as she listened to Darnley's next words.

"To be sure," he was saying, leveling at her that glance which had become famous in the boudoirs of England's greatest belles, "I had wanted an opportunity to speak to you in any case. I had meant to do so last evening at the theater, and started to come to speak to you in fact, but was cut off by that . . . woman. The reason I never came for you, for, you know"—again the glance fell on her flushing cheeks—"I never meant to break my word, was that, just as I was coming out the door to fetch you, who should drive up but Madam Chumley with all her entourage. I tried to get away—in fact, every moment thought I should—but every moment brought a fresh delay. In the end, I found I was delayed beyond all pardon, and feared sending a servant. I wanted, you know, to beg your pardon in person." Mr. Darnley's voice had begun on a direct note, but had grown gradually quieter, until now he was speaking quite softly, with a sort of honeyed tone. So much sincerity was in his look, and so much desire to be forgiven in his words, that Roselind could only blush to think she had been tempted to think ill of him for not sending news.

"Oh!" she said very lightly. And then, in a most mendacious spirit: "I never thought twice of it! I assumed you had been kept away on business of some kind."

"Did you indeed?" Mr. Darnley's black eyes seemed to be looking into her soul. "I should have known you would be some kind of an angel! When I first glimpsed you at the opening assembly, I could hardly contain my astonishment that that . . . little elf I had seen in Devonshire was grown into such a beauty! I see now there is wit and understanding also mingled in that ingenuous look."

That so much could have been read into her eyes (seen, after all, for a very short time, and under the least satisfactory conditons) did not surprise Roselind much. She was certainly flattered, and a little amazed at this open praise, but not unduly so. That Mr. Darnley was a gentleman of great taste and understanding struck her instantly. The admiration in his eyes only underlined his words and made her flush with a different sensation from any she had had before. Here, indeed, was breeding and sense in a gentleman! Never had she thrilled to the sight of any pair of eyes as she did to his. For the first time it struck her that her machinations on behalf of her brother were not wholly self-sacrificing.

With eyes half-veiled, and a demure look, she murmured, "You flatter me too much, sir. I only did what any woman would have."

"No, that is untrue. Only an angel would have interpreted my rudeness in such a way, your ladyship," said Mr. Darnley with the same intent gaze.

The horses had by this time slowed to a walk. The glorious day, with its dappled sunlight and soft shade, the gentle breeze, and even the singing of the birds seemed to echo Roselind's emotions. What had for so long been a muddy stream seemed miraculously to have cleared into a rush of sparkling water over pebbles; what had once been like an impassible tangle of complexity, with a goal only remotely visible in the background, now lay like a smooth route ahead of her. Even in her most optimistic moments, when Roselind had thought she could win Reginald Darnley's affections, she had envisioned a future with a man she would respect, but never love. The sacrifice had seemed worthy, if it could assure her brother's happiness. Indeed, having nothing to compare it with, it had appeared very promising. Roselind had never known those little tremors and flights of fancy so familiar to young ladies in love; having been for twenty years exposed to hardly any gentlemen except the vicar and her father's occasional guests, having seen very little of society and nothing of the great world, she had founded her plans on pure pragmatism. Never, certainly, had she expected to feel anything like this! In wonder did she gaze at the gentleman beside her, his eyes still playing over her like an expert fiddler's fingertips. There was obvious admiration in his glance, which made her almost blush and look down again, but none of that attitude, so common in very young men looking at their beloveds, which resembles nothing so much as a slightly sick sheep. No, Darnley was beyond the awkwardness of love. He was as practiced in the art of wooing pretty women as he was in the business of running his complex affairs. And there is nothing, as any female will attest, quite so conducive to lovesickness as a sophisticated suitor.

Some moments passed before another word was spoken. Too much was in the air between the lady and the gentleman, too many inarticulate, unspoken phrases, for there to be any need of verbalization. Roselind's heart was in her eyes, which had a very becoming effect, and made her naturally pretty face, her immense gray eyes, and animated look glow from within. Reginald Darnley, too, seemed nearly overcome. That witty gentleman, renowned for the ease with which he could dispense maxims under the most awkward circumstances, for once appeared beyond the ability to make light of his feelings. He sat looking down at the little figure beside him, as if he could not get enough of the sight. The horses were pretty well left to their own devices, wandering for a little in a halfhearted manner, and at last coming to a halt beside a little patch of very edible-looking grass, of which they made short work. Neither their master nor their master's companion seemed to care, and the tiger, riding up in the back, who had listened in amazement to his employer's remarks, sat staring dumbfoundedly into the air and wondering if the fine dasher he had served for so long was about to succumb to the ardors of love like so many lesser men.

At last, and with a little reluctance, Darnley took up the reins again and commenced in a homeward direction. It is not, unfortunately, our business to detail the conversation which occupied those two for the next minutes. Let it suffice to say that, though little was said of a direct and comprehensible nature, much was understood by each. Pleasant remarks were made about the landscape and the day, but nothing to thrill anyone save the listener. Roselind was a little astonished, it is true, at one juncture, to find her companion staring very intently at a small, nervous-looking fellow with hunched shoulders who had darted across their path and seemed to be gesturing at them from the cover of a clump of rhododendrons. Remarking on the sight, she received a curt retort, accompanied by an angry frown, but in a moment Mr. Darnley remembered himself, and with a renewed energy he turned his attention back to her. His ministrations were so pleasant, so altogether soothing to her nerves and no less to her vanity, that she was soon distracted from every other concern but the very delightful one of gazing into his admiring dark eyes. It was decided between them to leave Mrs. Hogarth to the mercy of her friends. *She* had made her bed so thoroughly, that a long rest therein seemed the best remedy for her interfering nature. However, Roselind was determined that the punishment should be short-lived.

"After all," she told herself with a smile, "had it not been for her, we should never have discovered each other's sentiments! To be sure, she was dreadfully misguided to act as she did, and yet I would not wish she had done anything else!"

And with this charitable sentiment, born out of gratitude, and nurtured by the gentle weather and the devotion in the gaze of the gentleman beside her, Roselind gave herself up to the warm sensation which seemed increasingly to envelope her.

9

"I don't like it, Desmund," said Lady Agatha Banforth a few days later. "I don't like it one whit."

Lady Agatha was walking up and down her dressing room in a distracted manner very unlike her usually calm self. General Banforth, reclining in an armchair near the fireplace, watched her with a slight frown. The late-evening *tête-à-têtes* which had been a pleasant custom since they had been married, had been marred, in the last days, by just this sort of nervous distraction on the part of his wife. The general leaned back a little, sighed, and prepared to listen. There was not much more he could do, aside from offering up a little piece of patient wisdom now and then, to help her.

"Roselind is a changed creature since we came to Bath," Lady Agatha went on. "I cannot make her out! It seems so strange to me—there was a time when I thought I knew those two children as well as if they had been my own."

"Very difficult, to be sure, my dear," murmured General Banforth. Then, with a smile, he added, "Though, in truth, it would be a difficult business if they *were*. I mean, you know, Rosie is little more than a dozen years younger than you."

Lady Agatha gave him an impatient look. She was not in the mood for jests this evening.

"Do be serious, Desmund! I hardly know which way to turn, and you can only make ridiculous jokes. It is not very helpful, you know," she said with a reproving look.

General Banforth's expression spoke eloquently of his wish to be forgiven. He subsided with a little all-suffering sigh.

"Go ahead, my love. I am all ears. Exactly what has got you in this state tonight?" Implied in the phrase was the idea that for many consecutive evenings Lady Agatha had had cause to feel distress.

"Only the same thing," said his wife, "that has had me worried for the past six months! Only my worst predictions have come true! Indeed, I sometimes think I may have brought it about merely by the power of suggestion." Lady Agatha frowned, thinking to herself, and continued after a moment, "What an *homme fatale* that man is! I wonder, is there such an expression?"

"If there is not, there should be. Darnley, I suppose you mean?"

Lady Agatha nodded. "Did you see how he was making eyes at Georgina this evening? I don't suppose either of them noticed the singing! And all the while, Roselind sitting there with rapture in her eyes! I have never known her before to be impressed by people simply because they were stylish or were considered 'consequential figures,' as your sister likes to say. But Rosie has spoken of nothing else for nearly a week! It is always 'Mr. Darnley says this' and 'Darnley says that,' until I think I shall surely scream! She talks of nothing but his carriages, his friends, and his manners—as if they were something to be admired!"

Lady Agatha subsided with something nearly approaching anger in her gentle face.

"Well, you know," her husband pointed out, "she has not had much exposure to his sort of grand style of life before. It is only natural that a young girl who has lived such a sheltered life should be a little swept off her feet by all that splendor."

Lady Agatha nodded, sinking into a chair.

"I suppose you are right. But still, I should never have expected *her* to be fooled by him! She is no simpleton, even if she is innocent."

"Are you sure she is fooled, then?" inquired General Banforth. "You said yourself you suspected her of encouraging him, you know... to help her brother."

"And that is how it began, no doubt. To help Bertie. But I can tell something is different. She has normally a very candid view of things, but it seems to have evaporated in these last days. Now she has—what is the line?—'eyes of a fool, a slave in love.' Well, nothing quite so awful, but nearly so. What frightens me is that she has lost all her sense of humor, as if she had forgotten her sense. No. I think something quite different has happened than perhaps even she planned. I think she has fallen in love with him!"

The general was smiling in his good-natured way. "That is not very uncommon in young girls, I think—to fall in love. No doubt it will pass over soon enough, and some other young macaroni will be the object of her affections."

"But she won't let it happen," said Lady Agatha. "If once she has got him, she won't for a minute think of giving him up. Not when she knows how much he could do for her."

"In that case, my dear, perhaps we should be grateful for this new development. Better to have her wed happily, after all, than sacrifice herself to save young Albert."

Lady Agatha stared off into space.

"If I thought she *could* be happy with him, my dear, I should do nothing but encourage the match! Little as I like him, if I thought he could make *her* life happy, I should swallow my feelings."

"But you think he can't? Or won't?"

Lady Agatha did not reply. She was thinking deeply.

Her husband was forced to prod her a little. "What exactly have you got against the fellow, Aggie? You certainly seem to loathe him!"

Agatha Banforth let out an almost involuntary shudder.

"Do *you* like him?" she demanded. General Banforth had often very good sense about these things. She made up her mind to trust his judgment as much as she could.

"I haven't given it much thought." He shrugged. "On principle, no, I suppose not. He is far too arrogant, and never looks quite human, you know. Those neckcloths are always arranged a little too perfectly to be believed, and his manners are—how shall I say it? Unflappable. He is always perfectly civil, perhaps too much so, without ever being quite believable. I never know how to take him, and suspect that just as he is complimenting me on my splendid maneuvers against Bonaparte, he secretly harbors the suspicion that he should have done it better himself. Vaguely contemptuous, I should say."

Lady Agatha nodded.

"There is no crack in his fortress," she murmured. "And yet ... and yet ..."

General Banforth looked up, curious.

"It is very odd. I think he *does* care about something. He looks as if nothing could move him—always the faint drawl and the bored lift of an eyebrow, quite the fashion now, you know, to look as if nothing mattered whatsoever. But beneath it all, I believe he does care dreadfully about something ..."

Lady Agatha did not finish. She was remembering something her brother, in one of their infrequent bouts of friendliness, had told her once. "Darnley is impregnable." He had laughed in his own devil-may-care fashion. "I will never understand what makes him tick. I believe that is one of the things which fascinates me—and Prinney, too, perhaps. *But I do know one thing,*" he had said with a surprising intensity, "I am quite sure that Darnley would have nothing to do with me if I weren't an aristocrat. No, not even that—if I weren't the rank of earl, at least."

And it was quite true. Lady Agatha had never known the famous nonpareil to speak to anyone beneath the rank of baronet. Not, at least, with any trace of the kindliness he lavished on their superiors in the peerage. The exception, of course, was Brummel. But even Brummel received none of the flattering attentions sometimes paid to even improverished members of the aristocracy. Some last residue of resentment, she supposed, at having been born a merchant's son.

"Do you know anything about Darnley's father?" she asked suddenly.

General Banforth looked faintly surprised.

"Why, nothing aside from the legend," he said. "An immensely clever man. Rose from the lower classes by sheer strength of character and hard work. Began, I believe, as a clerk in the East India Company, when it was a fledgling firm, and shortly took it over. He died, as you know, with the greatest fortune in England."

"Which his son has only added to, despite all his lavish style of living."

General Banforth regarded her with astonishment.

"Don't tell me, my love, you are entertaining reservations on the basis of his birth? Even *I* don't like the idea of Rosie's marrying beneath her, but Darnley can hardly be considered *that*."

Lady Agatha drew herself up. "I should never object," she said, "to Roselind's marrying a gentleman, whether he were titled or not, provided she loved him, and he her. But I don't call Darnley a gentleman. No amount of money could make him *that*."

"You are grown quite old-fashioned, my dear." Her husband laughed. "Imagine talking of gentlemen! The thing now, I believe, is to be a dandy, or a Corinthian, or at the least, some kind of macaroni. Gentlemen are quite out of fashion."

"I'm afraid I'm very much out of my depth." Lady Agatha sighed.

General Banforth said he did not believe there were any depths in which his wife did not feel at home, at which she smiled and shook her head.

"This one, my dear, is quite beyond me."

"I've no doubt you'll find a way to work it out, my dear," said General Banforth, kissing the top of her head. "You always do."

Her husband's faith, while welcome, did not do much to reassure Lady Agatha. She sat late into the evening cogitating certain things, things she had heard, as well as merely things she *sensed*. There were areas, she felt, where a woman's intuition was worth all the masculine logic in the world. And this, she was quite sure, was one of them. But Agatha Banforth was not the only one who lay awake that night. She was rather astonished to hear her husband's first remark the next morning. She had come downstairs for an early solitary breakfast, as was her habit, and was just sitting over a second cup of coffee and fingering a brioche, when she heard: "After all, Aggie, there was that business of the Montague scandal."

Agatha looked up in surprise, a smile breaking in her hazel eyes. General Banforth looked vaguely shamefaced.

"I *have* been thinking over what you said, my love, and though I admit I never liked the man, I cannot think of anything dishonorable about him. On the contrary," he said, lowering himself somewhat painfully into a chair, for his gout had reappeared the moment he set foot on civilized land again, "there is nothing *but* honorableness in his past. Stood up for his young friend against every reasonable objection, and even went so far as to defend him publicly. Devil of a business it was, too. In *my* day it would have been thought highly unsuitable for a mere merchant's son to stand up for the honor of a duke's heir, but times do change, I suppose."

His wife was frowning at him, or rather, past him.

"That has always puzzled me," she murmured, half to herself.

"What? My archaic prejudices?" demanded the general, nodding to the footman who came forward to remove his plate to the sideboard, where an elaborate array of dishes was spread out.

"Darnley's behavior to his friend. Roderick Montague, you know, was much in society when I made my come-out. One of the favorite young men of the season, in fact. I even,"—Lady Agatha glanced slyly at her husband—"entertained a grand passion for him once. It lasted quite a fortnight, I think. I never knew him intimately, but we became quite friendly, and he flattered me once or twice by making me think he might be going to offer for my hand—"

General Banforth interrupted gruffly, "Better not say any more, Aggie. Make a fellow green with jealousy, to tell him you might have made a brilliant match, and been a duchess, instead of ending up with an old soldier like myself."

"Nonsense!" was the only reply Lady Agatha would grant that piece of tomfoolery. "You know I never saw another gentleman I really loved. Roderick was, in any case, so exceedingly *frank*—so open and sincere, rather like a trusting puppy. There is a kind of subtlety in older men which, say what you like, cannot be out-done by young men, however dashing."

"Ah! You married me for my subtlety, I see," said General Ban-forth, smiling. "I had hoped it was for my noble brow and dash-ing manner."

Lady Agatha ignored him. "It was exactly that frankness," she went on, "that makes me wonder. I never knew a man as honest and forthright as Roderick Montague! I have never been able to believe that he did all the things he was accused of. Adored his father—rather idolized him, in fact. Why would a son like that, a son, furthermore as cosseted as he was, resort to such methods? If he wished to gamble, why did not he do it openly? And if he had a debt, why not apply to his father for the sum? Hamilton was as indulgent with his son as any man alive, and was certainly never short in the pocket."

"But a fierce old codger, I believe," said the general rather in-elegantly. "I do not wonder Roderick was afraid to own up, once he had gone beyond his father's authority."

"But to sign away a deed of land to his father's estates?" de-manded Lady Agatha, pushing her cup away. "I cannot believe it! No, I *will* not believe it!"

The general smiled at her stubborn expression.

"Come, my love. All these young fellows are alike. They gad about, running up immense debts, and then are astonished when their creditors try to collect 'em. No wonder Montague could not keep up with what he owed. It is accounted shockingly unfashionable to live within one's means. In the circles he frequented, I do not wonder he ran up fifty thousand pounds in a year or two of gaming."

"That is just the point," said Lady Agatha intently. "He never ran in those circles! He lived rather quietly, as far as I could tell, and though accounted fashionable enough, was never one of your beaux! I do not believe," she finished in a softer voice, "that he was even acquainted with Reginald Darnley."

General Banforth would have objected to this statement, on the basis of its contradicting all the known facts, but he was prevented from doing so by the entrance of his niece.

Roselind seemed to float into the room, and sank into a chair as if she were sitting on a cloud instead of satin upholstery. She greeted her aunt and uncle with a rhapsodic look and embarked immediately on the consumption of a large quantity of sweetbreads and breakfast buns. Having polished off the entire plateful, she stretched, smiled, and looked at her companions, who were both regarding her balefully.

"Where is Bertie?" she inquired. "I looked in to see him on my way down, but he had gone out."

"Ah! I suppose he is gone off with his friend Grey again," said the general. "He mentioned something of the kind last evening. Those two are practically inseparable."

Lady Agatha smiled. "And I, for one, am very pleased by it, too," she said. "Mr. Grey is in every way amiable and gentlemanlike."

Roselind did not, as it happened, agree with her aunt on this point, but she contented herself by saying, "Well, I suppose it is better he should have a friend like that than none at all. It keeps Bertie merry and occupied at the least."

"Since he has been deserted by the one friend whose company he really cherishes," remarked Lady Agatha with a faintly accusatory look.

Roselind looked down and flushed a little. It was true she had not glimpsed her brother much in the last days. She had been too occupied with Reginald Darnley and his glittering circle. Lord Iseleigh had been left, for the most part, to fend for himself while she went off on endless walks and drives and pleasure expeditions. She reminded herself, however, that what she was about was infinitely more important to the earl's continuing happiness than a few hours of companionship.

"And where are you off to today, my love?" inquired Lady Agatha, glancing at the elegant new riding costume, with its feather trim, which had been made up in a sudden fit of fashion-consciousness. Roselind had been made suddenly aware of her lack in that area by the subtle but nevertheless pointed compliments of Darnley's female friends on her "sweet natural quality" and "sublime disregard for everything artificial," which was meant to mean, as she had slowly gathered, that her clothes were plain to the point of homeliness. Roselind's hair, too, had undergone a striking change. What had once been a gentle cloud of glossy dark waves tied simply back by a single ribbon was now a meticulous arrangement of ornamented curls. The effect, thought Lady Agatha Banforth, was not half so pleasing as the former. Roselind's manner, too, had undergone a change. Her formerly happy, unconscious good humor, her direct way of meeting people's eyes, and her ingenuous smiles had given way to a forced kind of laughter and unnatural sophistication. Whether she was conscious of all this now, thought her aunt, she could not help feeling that her darling niece was very soon to suffer from it. The idea made Lady Agatha frown and bite her lip to keep from betraying her emotions.

"We are all to go to the Avon and see a launching of pleasure boats," said Roselind.

"I suppose Georgina Devonshire will be there?" inquired General Banforth. He did not usually interfere, but did not like the idea much of all this gallivanting about without some respectable older woman.

"Oh, yes—she is always with us, you know. I am grown very fond of her grace. She is always very kind to me," replied Lady Roselind. She did not add that there had been moments when, but for the kindness of the duchess, she would have felt quite stupid and dull.

"Well, then," remarked the general affably, "I can see no harm in the scheme. I suppose I am old-fashioned, but I do not like to think of you dashing about without a chaperon of some kind." He laughed good-humoredly, as if to excuse this betrayal of his old-fashioned instincts but his niece only smiled at him in a way that Lady Agatha thought fleetingly betrayed her gratitude.

10

The launching of the pleasure boats, an event much anticipated by the cluster of tonnish men and women who had gathered at Bath to avoid the *ennui* of Brighton in a summer when Prinney was ill with the gout, a condition which always brought out his most temperamental and difficult nature, was to be held at one o'clock. A goodly crowd had already gathered on the shore by the time Roselind, conveyed with another of Mr. Darnley's fashionable friends, arrived in that gentleman's black phaeton. Immediately there arose cries of welcome, which Mr. Darnley received with the conscious smiles of a popular hero. "Here is Darnley at last!" cried one lady, a woman of between forty-five and fifty, but corseted so tightly, and wearing such a mask of powder that she managed to look as young as her daughter. "Now we shall certainly be entertained! It has been shockingly dull this past hour."

A murmur of agreement rose in a knot of young dandies, whose collar points were so high as nearly to obscure their mincing expressions.

A crowd of townspeople, who had turned out as much to view the spectacle of the fashionable audience as to see a bottle broken over the hull of a riverboat, craned their necks to get a better view of the man who was causing so much commotion.

Darnley, smiling all the while, maneuvered his vehicle past the common herd and into a favorable position for observing the proceedings. Half a dozen other chariots were lined up along the banks for a similar purpose.

"I wonder they permit such a flock of wretches to gather here," said Miss Henrietta Burlingame, who sat next to Roselind in the phaeton. Miss Burlingame was a tall, haughty-looking beauty who had been accounted the belle of the winter season in town. She addressed her remark to the driver of the phaeton, with a proprietary smile, while simultaneously grimacing at the common folk.

"I suppose they have as much right to be here as we do," remarked Lady Roselind. "After all, it is their city."

"Still," sniffed Miss Burlingame, "I think it is shockingly unclean! They should not be allowed to mix with their betters."

Roselind kept silent. She had at first admired Miss Burlingame for her wit and astonishing beauty, but was increasingly pained to hear her constantly deriding those about her. Nor did her habit of leaning up against Mr. Darnley's arm whenever opportunity permitted, and of directing her every remark, accompanied by a brilliant smile, to him, please Roselind much. Mr. Darnley, however, seemed never to notice. He replied to her incessant questions with every air of civility, but with none of the intimacy for which Miss Burlingame seemed to hope.

Mr. Darnley was looking about him as if hoping to catch sight of someone. At that moment a gay female voice called out, "There you are, Darnley! And I see you have got my lovely little friend with you!"

Georgina Devonshire, driving an elegant landau emblazoned with the ducal arms, pulled up alongside of them.

"Hello, my dear!" she greeted Roselind, and nodded to Miss Burlingame. "I shall stay but just an instant. I must rush home and see that everything is ready for this evening. I know people who leave everything to their housekeepers and butlers, but I do not dare, I assure you! No, no, there is always something ready to go wrong at the least urging!" She laughed her delightful laugh, and then turned to the young lady.

"What a pretty driving costume that is, my dear! Did Madame Renault do it up for you? Oh, she is a wonder, is she not? I do not know how I should make do without her! Really, Darnley, you do always contrive to have the most wonderful-looking creatures with you! But I do not see your great friend Lady Chumley anywhere about. Do not tell me you have had a falling-out!" This last was accompanied by a sly grin, which Darnley ignored.

"My dear Roselind," she prattled on, "I depend upon you and your dear aunt to come this evening. How is my good friend?"

Roselind replied that her aunt and uncle were both in the best of health, and imagined that they did indeed plan attending her grace's soiree.

"Ah, *bon!*" exclaimed the duchess, glancing around. "I have not seen dear Lady Agatha this past age, not since last week at least. But then they are a very quiet kind of people, are they not? Given to staying at home always. Ah, love! Is not it a wonderful thing? What a marvel, after twelve years of marriage, to prefer the company of one's spouse to any other!"

The lowering of a large, brilliantly painted vessel into the water at that moment distracted the group for a little. Her grace, keeping up an almost constant patter of bright conversation, interspersed with remarks on nearly every subject, from the fashion in parasols to the question of whether a riverboat should have a rounded or a flat bottom, remained beside them for half an hour. Miss Burlingame, looking petulant, hardly said a word, and seemed increasingly abused by the little amount of attention paid to her by the illustrious lady in the cerise driving costume. As always, Mr. Darnley kept his impenetrable expression, somewhere between a smile and a sneer, remarking occasionally, in his familiar drawl, on some one of the proceedings. Since the fateful day in the Royal Crescent, Roselind had not known his manner to change. Sometimes he would give her one of those long, penetrating looks, which made her by turns flattered and uneasy. It was impossible to make him out, to know what was in his mind, or what he demanded of her. If only he would let her see what was in his heart! It was impossible not to know that he admired her; why else keep her constantly about, parading her before his friends? And even those looks, which seemed to pierce right through her, were, though infrequent, ample proof of his attraction. She felt increasingly flattered and bewildered. Her admiration of *him*, her respect for his conduct, never waned. On the contrary, she was more than ever under his sway. The envious looks of his female acquaintance, too, could not help but make her a little dizzy. She only wished that he would tell her which way to go, for as it was, she was forced to guess what he required of her in the way of manner and appearance, taking her cue from those little critical looks from his friends, and their frequent backhanded compliments. She felt more and more foolish, and would have been glad, at some moments, to be able to give up the whole charade.

For it was a charade. Roselind felt increasingly that she was playing a part in a comedy the end of which she could not divine. And yet she was compelled to dress for the part, to speak lines which came to her as if from recollection, but which she could not feel were her own. She seemed a stranger to herself, and yet, uncertain where it was all leading, she could not shake off the compulsion to stay upon the stage and to respond to what the other characters said to her. Mr. Darnley seemed to be playing a game with her sometimes. Without warning he would look deep into her eyes as if she were a well of cool water, and he a man dying of thirst, and then as suddenly, he would look away and no trace would remain of his emotions. She could not divine what was in his heart, and yet she felt certain he must love her, that the longed-for proposal was not far-off.

"I must be off, my dear friends!" the duchess exclaimed, cutting into Roselind's thoughts. She leaned over from her seat in the little landau to say, "Roselind, my dear, do persuade that delightful fellow, your brother's friend, you know—Mr. Grey, is it?—to come to me this evening. I suppose you see him rather often?"

"He is sometimes at home with my brother, ma'am," said Roselind. But her grace was immersed in turning her little chariot about. She looked up, smiling brightly, and then exclaimed, "Why! But there he is. I shall just speak to him myself."

Roselind looked in astonishment to see the duchess drive over to the crowd of common folk and draw up beside the familiar figure of Mr. Grey, who seemed much surprised at being recognized. She watched them converse with a combination of irritation and fascination. Her grace was smiling and gesturing at their own little group. Mr. Grey said something, evidently something amusing, for the duchess laughed delightedly. They were both looking at Roselind.

Mr. Darnley, too, had been watching the scene with some little interest. Now he frowned and said, "Who is that man Georgina is talking to?" The sharpness of his tone took Roselind by surprise.

"Why," she said, "it is a Mr. Grey, an acquaintance of my brother's."

"And do you know him well?"

"Not particularly. I believe, in fact, that no one knows him very well. That is to say," she continued, on seeing Darnley's inquiring look, "I do not believe he has any acquaintance at Bath. He is just returned from India, I think, where he has been these last four or five years. A very peculiar gentleman, for he has no home in England, and seems vague on any idea of where to settle." She could not resist asking, "Why? Have you met him, sir?" Roselind was curious to see what Mr. Darnley would reply, after the tale she had heard of their encounter on the London road.

Reginald Darnley looked coldly at the other gentleman and only said, "No, no, why should I know him? I only had the misfortune of seeing him once, when he was very rude."

"Lud!" cried Miss Burlingame, who had been looking about her with every sign of impatience this last half-hour, hoping for some opening to further impress the fact of her presence on her escort. "They are about to put the last boat in the water! I have a great desire to walk down and look, my dear Darnley." Miss Burlingame raised her lovely eyes in a petulant look to that gentleman, who, obviously seeing no alternative, offered to hand her down and escort her to the river's edge.

"I think it will be very muddy," said Roselind doubtfully, eyeing the shoreline, which was a mess of trod-down grass and muddy bootmarks.

"Pooh! I do not care about a little dirt!" replied Miss Burlingame scornfully. "*You* may stay here, if you like, and be bored to extinction, but Darnley and I are going down to get a better look."

So saying, she jumped down, and proceeded to lean against Mr. Darnley's arm in a very familiar fashion. Seeing no alternative, except to remain conspicuously alone in the phaeton, Roselind followed suit. Walking on the other side of Mr. Darnley, she disdained taking the same familiar attitude as the other young lady, sometimes falling behind the pair when there was not room for three. In this way they made their way through the crowd, receiving a great many interested glances from those they passed, and, Roselind was a little chagrined to notice, a few pitying looks directed at herself.

Miss Burlingame had no eyes for anyone but Reginald Darnley. Her every remark was directed at him, and always with the same proprietary attitude. It was "My dear Darnley, is not that a wonderful vessel? I should like to have one just like it! Fancy drifting along down the stream, with a dozen servants to fan you! I suppose you have done that kind of thing very often, have you not? When you were in India?" Roselind was amused to see Mr. Darnley look coldly at the speaker after hearing this remark.

"I never was in India in all my life, Miss Burlingame."

"Oh, were you not?" Miss Burlingame gave a toss to her head. "I thought sure you had been. I was positive you had been working there, when you had been a merchant!"

"I believe you have mistaken me for my father," said Darnley in chilly accents. He seemed to move a little farther away from his fond companion as he did so, but she, not noticing, only grasped him the more tightly, and continued prattling away.

After a little of this, Roselind could bear no more. She saw that they were beginning to sink up to their ankles in mud, and refused to subject herself to another minute of it. Murmuring that she would stay behind and watch from where she was, and receiving no objection from Miss Burlingame, and only a doubtful look from Mr. Darnley, she moved up the bank a little ways. Here was a cluster of people gathered whom she knew to be Darnley's friends. They had often spoken to her in the past week when she had been in his company. But now they returned her smiles with nods and cold looks, and continued talking among themselves.

Roselind grew gradually more miserable. Her feet were wet, and beginning to grow cold. These people, whom she had first considered agreeable and elegant, were showing themselves as uncivil and even rude. She heard them whispering among themselves, and could not help overhearing her own name mentioned once or twice. She saw a curious glance directed at her, accompanied by a little titter, and saw them staring down at the spectacle Miss Burlingame was by now creating with Mr. Darnley.

"Why won't he come back?" she demanded of herself. "He must see how unhappy I am, and how foolish I appear! Why will he not make her stop, and come back?"

But another minute passed, and then another. Miss Burlingame had approached one of the workmen who had been laboring to get a vessel into the water, and was asking animated questions. A few dark clouds, which had begun to gather in the west, moved across the sun. The formerly sparkling waters of the river grew dark and surly, and a gust of wind swept past, nearly taking off Roselind's bonnet. She held her skirts down with one hand, clapping the other onto the top of her bonnet, feeling all the while more foolish. A clap of thunder sounded. All at once the crowd, sending up cries of distress, began to swarm about, some moving in the direction of their carriages, and some going toward a large shed which had been put up to protect a vessel.

Much dismayed, Roselind looked about her. She expected any minute to see Mr. Darnley run up the hill to get her. By now she had completely lost sight of him in the throng of running figures. She bit her lip and determined to stay where she was until he should do so. But all at once the rain began to come down in sheets. Blinded at first by the natural moisture, and then by the tears which had sprung suddenly into her eyes, she commenced running, without knowing in the least where she was going. Running figures swarmed past her, but no one seemed to notice her existence. Her feet moved from instinct, she felt the slippery mud creep into her slippers, and then suddenly, tripping on some invisible obstacle on the ground, she fell heavily to her knees. Unable to move, too miserable even to struggle back to her feet, she stayed where she was, the tears streaming down her cheeks. The pressure of strong fingers round her arm jarred her from the unhappy reverie she was falling into, and pulled her to her feet.

"Come in here, your ladyship," said a familiar masculine voice just next to her ear.

She looked up in amazement to see the bronzed face of Mr. Grey looking down at her, a smile in his blue eyes.

It was some moments before Roselind was capable of speech. She had been conducted rather forcefully into a small shed, where a dozen other people had also taken refuge. Her bonnet was sopping wet, and looked, she suspected, as ridiculous as the rest of her. With a good deal of embarrassment she made what repairs she could to her appearance, and then looked up again. Mr. Grey was not smiling now. A steely look had come into his eyes, and the muscles of his jaw were working in anger.

"It was well I was close at hand," he remarked tersely. "I suppose otherwise you would have stayed exactly where you were and been drowned, or else struck down by lightning."

His tone immediately irritated Roselind. It seemed to take for granted not only her stupidity but also his own invaluable presence. "What does he think?" she asked herself hotly. "That I have no other friends? I suppose he considers himself the only person with any gentlemanlike instincts!"

She looked him directly in the eye and replied archly, "Mr. Darnley should have come to fetch me at any moment. He was only down at the riverbank with Miss Burlingame—"

"Aye," Mr. Grey cut her off, "I saw them very well. But I doubt they were thinking much of *you*."

Roselind could stand no more of this.

"You may know very little about gentlemen," she said warmly, "but I assure you, Mr. Darnley does! He only conducted Miss Burlingame at her own request, and, I believe, to his own annoyance."

The last phrase had slipped unwittingly out of her mouth, and now she bit her lip and stared defiantly at her rescuer.

"Be that as it may," replied Mr. Grey, "they did not wait about to see that you were safe. I saw them drive off just now together, as if the devil were on their heels."

"I do not believe you!"

"But I assure you it is true." Mr. Grey smiled down at her, his

anger having given way to something like amusement at her vex-
ation, which, in truth, combined with the state of her clothes and
hair, and a little droplet of water that was running down her nose,
made her look quite marvelously ridiculous.

Roselind would have liked to stamp her foot in a childlike
show of rage, but she just managed to contain herself. She contented herself by saying, in a cold voice, "Well, then, I am sure
there was some reason. They would never have left me alone had
there not been. Perhaps Miss Burlingame was taken ill . . . or . . ."

She trailed off without much conviction.

"Or perhaps they thought you had suddenly grown wings and
wished to fly home instead of being driven," said Mr. Grey. "Indeed, there are a great many possibilities. I am sure one or another of them will account for their rudeness."

Roselind stared dismally at the ground. The first shock of what
she had heard had begun to wear off. She felt now only cold and
miserable, and exceedingly ill-used.

"And what are we to do now?" she murmured with a remark-
able lack of willfulness.

"I think we had better stay here until the worst is past. After
that, I shall take you home myself—that is, if you can bear my
company. I am aware it distresses you immensely."

Roselind did not reply. She felt a little ashamed at having been
so blunt to the gentleman who had rescued her, but she was not
about to admit it. After all, he had been far from civil himself. A
long silence ensued, during which Roselind endeavored to repair her appearance a little, and Mr. Grey walked distractedly
about the shed, gazing out to see how the storm was progressing.
It showed no signs of letting up. In fact, the thunder had only

grown louder, and nearer at hand, and lightning streaked across the sky at more and more frequent intervals.

"I am glad to see, at least, that you are not frightened of thunder," said Mr. Grey, returning to her side.

"Oh, no. We have always a great many storms in Devonshire," she replied.

"There are a great many young ladies who, though they have no fear of natural disasters, pretend to have, so as to impress their fragility on their male acquaintance."

Roselind regarded him indignantly. "Well, I assure you I am not one of them!"

"No," replied Mr. Grey, smiling, "I see that very well. I do not believe cowardice is one of your leading characteristics."

Roselind did not reply.

"Well, I suppose we had better try to have a little civilized conversation, as we are doomed to be in each other's company this hour at least," said Mr. Grey after a little. "What do you propose talking of?"

"I have no idea, I assure you."

"Well, then, I suppose it is up to me to choose the topic. How do you find Bath?"

"Very well, thank you."

"You are amused by it? You find the diversions of town better than those of the country?"

"They have both something to recommend them."

"Ah! Indeed. A very philosophical turn of mind. And you are not bored by the diversions here? Do they not weary you, so many balls and breakfasts, so much going to the theater, viewing of operas, and paying calls on your friends?"

"I have not had time to be weary of them yet."

"Indeed!" Mr. Grey looked surprised. "I believe it is common, among young ladies, to grow very weary of things before they have been exposed to them a week. They plead to come to town, saying how dull it is at home, and then, after their mamas and papas have gone to all the trouble of preparing the way, of taking a house in a desirable neighborhood, and fitting it up, of sending servants, luggage, and necessaries ahead of them, and finally of conveying the precious darling herself with all her trunks and bonnets, feathers and lace—newly made up for the purpose— and seeing her schedule busily filled with every sort of interesting diversion, the dear girl announces she is fed up and wishes to go home."

Roselind looked at him coldly. "You do not know very much about us, I see, Mr. Grey, and even less about me! If you did, you should know that we are most of us much more grateful creatures than that, and do not desire more than to make ourselves agreeable and useful to our families. To hear you go on, I imagine you have had the misfortune to be acquainted with only a few females of the worst kind. I pity you for it, and wonder you do not hate us all!"

Mr. Grey looked suddenly regretful, and replied thoughtfully, "It is true I have not had much contact with the fair sex. I never had a sister, you know, and I have been out of England so long— but, I am glad to hear you defend your sex so warmly. It does much to change my own prejudices, I assure you."

"I doubt that." Roselind stared moodily into the air. "I doubt anything *I* could say would change your mind at all!"

"You underestimate your powers, my lady," said Mr. Grey with what Roselind considered a very impudent and scornful smile.

"I think we had better give up this experiment," she said after a moment's silence. "It is leading nowhere that I wish to go."

Mr. Grey acceded readily enough, and for a little while neither spoke. But suddenly Roselind looked about her in surprise.

"Why, where is my brother?" she asked.

Mr. Grey seemed startled by the question.

"I do not know, I assure you. Why, what made you think I should?"

"I was convinced he had come out with you this morning. That is what he told my uncle."

"Did he indeed?" inquired Mr. Grey with an amused look. "But I have not seen him this day or two at least. Lord Iseleigh is a changed creature of late. I should ask a certain Miss Quimby what has taken place to make him so, if I were you."

Roselind stared at him with an unbelieving look.

11

Lord Iseleigh sat in the little chair next to Miss Quimby's couch with a wretched look upon his face.

"If only there was some way . . ." he said, and then stopped. He did not really wish his companion to know what was in his mind.

Maude Quimby was watching him intently. Although she had been keeping up a very happy rattle of conversation for the past hour, a sober expression was in her beautiful luminous eyes which belied the lightness in her tone.

After a moment she said, "I know what you are thinking, my lord, and I wish you would forget all about it."

Bertie looked up sharply.

"You mustn't call me that. How often have I told you?"

"Bertie, then. I should rather call you Albert. Bertie is the name for a child, and you are not a child."

It was quite true. A miraculous transformation had taken place in the face, the eyes, the whole expression of the young man. A week before, he had been a slightly awkward youth, uncertain where to put his hands, or what to say. And now, although there was still a vestige of that awkwardness, still some traces of his former self-consciousness, the chief of it had changed. Now, where there had been sometimes solemnity but more often irrepressible merriment in his eyes, there was the hunger of a starving man. He was torn mercilesssly between delight and misery, looking at that exquisite face before him. At one moment he felt like singing, and the next like weeping, but always he was mesmerized. It was impossible to take his eyes away from her, and when he was forced to, in order to go home and eat and sleep, and pretend that nothing had occurred to change him, it was as though he was in prison. Only when he could get away again, to race back to this darling creature, this miracle of gentleness and gaiety, with her manner as if nothing in the world could be better than the way she lived, did he feel really alive.

"No," he said, looking at her solemnly, "you are quite right. I am not a child anymore—but you're the only one seems to realize it! They all treat me, the others, as if nothing had changed, when really, everything has changed! Everything is different!"

"But," said Maude Quimby, smiling, "that is how we arranged it, didn't we? So that no one should suspect. It's much better that way, you know."

"Is it?" asked Bertie, getting up and walking to the window with a distracted air. "Is it really better? I am sure it is not. It will only be perfect when everyone knows how much I adore you, how much I should like—"

But here Miss Quimby cut him off.

"Hush," she said. "Better not to say such things!"

"But if I feel them?" Bertie whirled about in anguish.

Maude Quimby smiled. "Then you must feel them alone. It will not make *that* any better, to tell anyone."

"No, in a way you are right," said Bertie, coming back and

sitting down again. "Really, it has been wonderful, these last days, with only *us* knowing! But . . . but I am afraid I couldn't bear it for very long, you know. No. Sooner or later, I shall *have* to tell someone. Besides . . ." he began, but then stopped.

"Besides," said Miss Quimby, "you have your Mr. Grey. You could tell him, and no one in your family will be any the wiser for it. I like your Mr. Grey enormously, from all you have told me. Perhaps sometime you will bring him to visit?"

"Oh, yes, Grey's a fine fellow," said Lord Iseleigh stoutly. "He would understand, you know. In fact, I think he already does. Not that I've said anything, mind you, but I've just mentioned you once or twice, and told him what an amazing creature you are. He wants to come to see you, too, I think. In fact, he told me so himself."

"And will he approve of me, d'you think?" Miss Quimby smiled mischievously.

Bertie laughed in delight. "Approve of you!" he cried. "Why, I shall murder him if he doesn't! Ah, Peter'll approve of you, all right. How could he not?"

But Miss Quimby looked a little startled and said, "Why, is his name Peter, too?"

"Yes, yes, that's his first name. Peter Grey. Why d'you ask?"

Miss Quimby looked vague. "Nothing, really. It is only that I once knew someone with a friend called Peter. But it was not Peter Grey."

There was a short silence, while Bertie watched her with a fascinated look, a look which was often on his face when he was in this room. He could hardly believe there was really a woman like this in the whole world, and still less that she could find anything to love in him.

"What are you thinking about?" he asked after a moment.

"Oh, only about my old friend," said Miss Quimby, looking up.

"It was a very long time ago, however—very long. Five years it has been since I've seen him."

Suddenly Bertie began to grow a little red.

"Not some old suitor, I hope! I warn you, I shall be green with jealousy. Perhaps ... perhaps I'd even kill him!"

Miss Quimby laughed. "You're very fond of the idea of doing murder this morning, aren't you? But," she continued more seriously, "it would be impossible. You see, he's already dead."

There was so much sadness in her eyes as she said this, that Bertie wanted to cry out. He never wanted to see any pain of any kind in that sweet face. But he didn't dare ask what it was. There was something rather remote and aloof in Maude Quimby, despite all her gaiety, that awed him a little. He contented himself, instead, by saying, "Well, let's think when we can persuade you to come and dine at Pulteney Street. Aunt Aggie, you know, is very determined you shall come."

"Dear Agatha," murmured Maude, half to herself. "When I think how much I owe her. First of all for inducing you to come and call on me that day!" she finished, laughing.

Bertie looked rather shamefaced.

"Yes, I was a bit reluctant about that. I envisaged sitting for hours with some withered-up old invalid! I certainly never expected to see anything like you!"

Miss Quimby laughed.

"And how is your sister? Such a pretty girl!"

"Oh. Rosie's all right, I suppose. I hardly ever see her anymore. She is always away gallivanting with that Darnley fellow."

Suddenly Maude looked intent, and although the merriment never left her voice, she continued looking very keenly at the young earl as she spoke.

"I suppose she is often in his company?"

"Oh, yes, a great deal. An awful starch-breeches he is, too, you know. Great pal of my father's."

"Was he?" Miss Quimby looked interested. "I never knew that. Of course, there is a great deal I do not hear, even from Mrs. Dean. She tells me nearly everything, but perhaps not quite all of it. So," she continued right along, but with the same keen look, "I suppose they are getting quite intimate—your sister and Mr. Darnley, that is."

"Lord, I hope not!" Bertie laughed. "I do not think I could bear to have him as a brother-in-law. What an odious life we should have to live then, always buttering him up and pretending to like his friends!"

"But you think they may get married?"

Bertie looked quite serious, contemplating the matter. He had never considered it in just that light before, but then, he had never much contemplated the idea of Rosie's marrying at all. Still, he supposed she would, eventually, and as he was determined to marry himself as soon as he could, it did not distress him overly.

"Yes, I suppose so," he said finally, but without much enthusiasm. "I suppose that may be what will happen in the end. But I do hope not! Unless Roselind finds something in him that I have never seen, I should think he would make her dreadfully unhappy."

Miss Quimby neither laughed at this nor made any objection. Instead, she lay gazing into space with a very worried look. At last she murmured, "Yes, he might very well make her miserable. He has made a great many other people miserable."

—   —

Lord Iseleigh was lying in wait for his sister. He had been

impatiently pacing up and down the little study in Pulteney Street which gave off the front hall, hoping to detain her as she came in. The butler had said she had gone out some hours before with Mr. Reginald Darnley, but now it was nearly two o'clock, and a downpour was well in progress, and she had not yet returned. After a great while, and just when Bertie was about to give up his wait and repair to his own apartments, he heard the front door open, and two voices conversing with the butler. Bertie was amazed to hear the voice of his friend Grey mingling with that of his sister. At any other time he would have rushed out into the hall to speak to him, but the speech he had prepared and rehearsed was too carefully laid in his mind, and of too fragile a nature to allow for any untoward interruptions. He determined to remain as he was.

As it happened, Roseline stayed only a moment in the doorway. She passed the study a second later, and turned about in surprise on hearing her name called out.

Bertie noticed with some amazement that his sister was looking rather the worse for wear. Her bonnet was sodden, as was her skirt, and a good deal of mud appeared to be clinging to her hem and the heels of her shoes.

"Good God, Rosie!" he exclaimed in astonishment. "What have you been doing? You look exactly like a wet rabbit!"

Lady Roselind Arden was not in the peak of good humor. She returned her brother's greeting with a grimace, and begged to be excused while she changed her clothes.

"I have passed the most dreadful day," she moaned, "and all I want now is a bath and my bed."

Intrigued as Bertie might have been at any other time as to the source of all this sorrow and discomfort—for even he could see quite plainly that Rosie was hobbling about like an old woman—there were other, more pressing matters in his mind. With some little difficulty he persuaded his sister to postpone her longed-for comforts till he should communicate to her an item of the utmost urgency. Roselind, with very little of those sisterly shows of concern which might have been becoming in one who had been mentioning to herself very frequently of late that she was ready and willing to sacrifice her whole life for the comfort of this dear young man, complied unwillingly, and dragged herself into the room. Refraining from sinking her weary bones into a pretty satin-covered chair, she remained painfully on her feet, with her only support a campaign desk to lean up against. In a few moments she was regretting that she did not have some sturdier support, for her brother was pacing distractedly up and down the room and revealing a most unsettling piece of news. On the young man's face was a most unfamiliar look, an expression half of anguish and half of crazed excitement, which, had Roselind not been so immersed herself in other matters of late, she might have noticed increasingly to have adorned that handsome young visage.

"Do try to be a little calm, and tell me what you mean," she demanded at last, when Bertie had been blurting out a number of disjointed phrases, which all seemed to revolve around a wonderful "she" and still more marvelous "we." "Whom are you talking about? Who is this lady who needs assistance?"

Bertie stopped dead in his tracks and gazed doubtfully at his sister.

"Why, have you no idea, Rosie? It is Miss Quimby, of course."

Suddenly a light began to break in Roselind's mind. Phrases began to revolve in her head, phrases she had heard through the half-mist of her distraction in these last days, from Bertie himself, and, lastly, the mocking voice of Mr. Grey echoed in her thoughts. "I should ask a certain Miss Quimby, if I were you," he had said only half an hour ago. And the other evening, at the theater, it had been, "They are the romantic pair, of course. Bertie will rescue her on his white charger and bear her off to the happy-ever-after of his castle."

How she had doubted him then! How she had defended her own blindness by saying he was only a child, too young to fall in love! Even now, looking at him standing stock-still before her, with that pleading look in his gray eyes, she could not really believe it. No, no, it must be some mistake. Endeavoring to take a great hold on herself, she inquired calmly, "And Miss Quimby needs assistance? But you know, dear, we are all very eager to give it to her! Agatha has sent her a great many presents, and she is invited to dine with us whenever she likes—"

"No, no," Bertie cut her off impatiently. "You don't see at all, do you?" He looked reproachful. "I thought *you* at least would understand, Rosie!"

He turned about and walked to a window, where he stood gazing out at the storm raging over Pulteney Street with a moody expression. "It's not like that, you see," he said very softly. "I am in love with her... I want her to marry me!"

For a few minutes Roselind was incapable of saying anything. Several times she opened her mouth to speak, but each time seemed to change her mind. A number of questions came immediately to her lips, questions she would have liked answered, but on second thought realized that her brother was the last one in the world to be capable of satisfying them. At last she said, "Miss Quimby is an angel, darling—I should be the first one to say so. But . . . but is not she a great deal older than you? And besides, even if she were to accept you, you know, it would be several years before you would be of age."

"One year," said Bertie, who had not had this matter very far from his own mind lately. "And Miss Quimby is barely twenty-two. There is a difference of only two years. *She* does not seem to mind! I wonder you should!"

"Still, two years, if it is the lady who is the elder of the two—it is a great difference in experience. And then, there are a great many other restraints to take into consideration ..."

Bertie whirled about, an angry expression in his eyes.

"You mean, she is so far beneath us in society? You do mean that, don't you?"

Roselind said gently, "No, no, dear, it isn't only that—" But she was not allowed to finish.

"You forget that she was once quite an acceptable member of society! Very much so, in fact. Were it not for an unlucky stroke of fate, she should be this moment paying calls on us as an honored guest, I make no doubt! She might even have married higher than me, I think . . ." But here Bertie's face grew red, and he subsided.

Roselind hardly knew which way to turn. Only an hour before, she thought she had reached the very bottom of the abyss of misery. Mr. Darnley, on whom all her hopes had rested, had proved himself an unworthy object of her admiration. He had discredited himself, and her, by his action, which, she felt increasingly, could hardly be explained by any amount of generous thought. She had been made a thorough fool of, and in front of a great many people. Had it not been for the intervention of Mr. Grey (who, no matter how she disliked him for herself, she was now forced to admit had acted in a very chivalrous manner), she might still be standing quite alone on that horrible wet bank. She had not had time to digest all of this, but one thought had been clearly in her mind. Perhaps that was not the way to put it. It raged through her rather, with all the fury of outraged pride and indignation: she would never be able to look Reginald Darnley directly in the eye again.

And now, added to her own humiliation, was this further distress. And how much more profound it was than her own petty mortification! That, she now realized, she could bear, if painfully. If the mist had been cleared from her eyes regarding the true character of Mr. Darnley, if she no longer held him in the esteem she had once, it now looked more than ever as though she needed him. If Bertie were to marry—and marry, once more, so far beneath him (in a matter of fortune, in any case)—he would more than ever need her help. The idea that Miss Quimby, unaware of the turn the Iseleigh fortunes had taken, had had this view precisely in mind, had at first crossed her mind. But on second thought, she blushed to think so ill of that poor creature. That gentle, cheerful spirit, who laughed in the face of her own misfortune, was quite incapable of encouraging a young man for the sake of being lifted out of misery. The thought made her blush; she had inwardly accused Maude Quimby of a scheme she had herself entertained, and with far more cunning, if with much less need.

"I know what you are thinking," said Bertie suddenly, eyeing her in a fierce way. "You suspect Miss Quimby of snaring me for my fortune."

The color rose in Roselind's cheeks. If he only knew how close he had come to the truth!

"No, no!" she protested hurriedly. "I never thought anything of the kind!"

"You see," Bertie went on, barely listening to her, "you are quite mistaken! It is she who has been trying to persuade me out of it in the first place! She forbade me to tell anyone, although I wished to beyond everything, and urged me to wait until I had finished at Oxford before making any public engagement. I only agreed because I saw how much it meant to her, and I should never, in any way, wish to make her unhappy—even if it tormented me!"

Roselind looked at him in wonder.

"She made you promise all of that?"

He nodded. "I only ... I am only breaking my promise to tell *you*, well, because first I wanted you to know, and second, because although she would never permit it, I am determined to do something for her now. You have no idea how much she must suffer! Her legs are always painful, though she says nothing of it, and she has no one to help her—not even the simple comfort of a servant! She has only that nurse, Mrs. Dean, who comes to her three mornings a week. But for the rest—how she manages to live, I hardly know!"

"She has a brother, however," said Roselind. "Cannot he help her?"

For a moment the determined look that had been in her brother's face gave way to doubt. "Yes, there is the brother. I hardly know what to make of *him.*"

"Have you not met him?"

"Never. I only passed him once, in the corridor. A very sickly, nervous kind of fellow, with stooped shoulders and the look of a hunted animal. But Maude . . . Miss Quimby never speaks of him, unless I ask her. She seems ashamed of him, in a strange kind of way."

"And yet," said Roselind, "he seems to have done so much for her . . ." She remembered, suddenly, something Miss Quimby had said that day, when she had first laid eyes on her. Something to do with having a great deal to make up for. It had struck her then as very odd, and came back now with a sudden austere ring.

"Do you remember," said Roselind now, "what she said on the day we first visited her? About her brother having a great deal to make up for?"

Bertie looked at her curiously. "You remember, too? I have never been able to make it out. Only . . . only, something she said today . . . Well, it is probably nothing."

Lady Agatha put her head in the door just then, saying she had heard voices. The conversation was, for the moment, brought to an end.

12

Roselind went to her own bedroom as soon as she could escape. So much had transpired in the last several hours that she felt as if her mind and heart could not cope with all the sensations which tore at her. The inquiring looks, moreover, of her dear aunt did little to allay her suffering. In one morning she had experienced elation (which now seemed, on looking back, as unfounded and ridiculous), she had been embarrassed and then humiliated in front of a great mass of people, had suffered the mortification of being subjected to Mr. Grey's cool cynicism, and now she was forced to confront a new and even greater difficulty.

In the quiet of her own apartments she sank down into a little window seat which afforded a view of the street, but her mind was elsewhere. Rain continued to pummel at the window casements, and only a furtive figure or two, hovering in the shelter of a doorway, populated the scene. Roselind's own troubled attitude seemed to match the natural mischief going on outside. For months she had endeavored to fight a difficult battle, and to do so alone, without the help or comfort of any friend's advice (for Lady Agatha, who was her dearest confidante, had been ostracized of necessity, as her niece believed the lady could never approve her plans, and would do all in her power to foil them). And now she felt doubly alone, when her troubles, as it seemed, were just begun.

For a great while she remained as she was, turning over and over her predicament. Bertie's news had been startling indeed; it had done much to unravel what little calm she had left. And yet, on looking back over the past week, she was forced to admit that it was not altogether astonishing. He had been very unlike himself, had she only noticed! But she had been consumed with Reginald Darnley and all his friends, which she had supposed was all being done for her brother's good. In retrospect, it did not seem quite true. Lady Roselind was forced to bite her lip, and blush a little, and condemn herself of vanity and self-flattery. What had begun as sacrifice had soon developed into something else, something which had nothing to do with Bertie or even Bertie's legacy, but with no one besides herself and her own desire to be admired, and petted, and to be shown about as the Earl of Iseleigh's daughter, who had been closeted in the country for so many years, but who was in truth very pretty, and very charming, and worth noticing.

Roselind lectured herself for a good while, with all the passion of a just mind which had caught itself out in an act of selfishness. The passion was not diminished by the fact that she had been humiliated in her attempts. Roselind was incensed at her own folly, but she would not have been human had not some part of fierce resentment mixed with all her righteous feelings.

"He should not have left me there," she said to herself. "It was not the act of a gentleman, much less of a noble mind." But then she was forced to add, "And yet it was I encouraged it, in a way, by being always available for his every wish, and hanging on his words, as if he were some kind of oracle and I an adoring child! I should have been more cool and let him see that I was not merely his for the asking!"

It was true that Roselind had been a little less exacting than she might have been, than, for instance, any knowledgeable lady of society would have been. She had flattered him, perhaps, too much, and hung on his every word, and let him know, through looks, and smiles, and gently lowered eyelids, that she was ready to be wooed. No properly conscious lady would have done so much. Such a lady would have done more, perhaps, in plotting and scheming, would have encouraged him a little, and then let him out again, rather like a skilled fisherman with a playful trout, but she would never have let him know that any thought at all was put into her machinations. Roselind was exactly the opposite. Her encouragement had been given out of artlessness, because she really admired Darnley and really wished him to know it. Her nature was to be forthright with herself and others, never to pretend she liked anyone when she did not, except to be civil, and never to feign coolness when she did not entertain it. It was her way to be completely openhearted, which everyone knows is not the best way to get a man, and which, in this present case, made everything more difficult.

The Lord only knows how she would have contrived if she had not admired Mr. Darnley to begin with. She had had a plan born out of a fertile imagination which had no rub with reality. Her plan had been all goodness, and never been dishonorable in her own mind. It had been simply to wed, as many had done before her, for a purpose other than love. And yet she had had very good reason to do so, for the future of her darling brother depended on it, and she had never intended to marry without the firm intention of being a devoted, and kind, and admirable little wife. Love had never played a part in her scheming, but then, she had never loved anyone besides her family. Love, in any case, she had assumed, would grow out of a further acquaintance with her husband, and if it was not to be one of those great passions so often alluded to in novels and poetry (and which, it must be admitted, Roselind had sometimes dreamt about with a little flurry of anticipation), then so it must be. Her elation at discovering Mr. Darnley to be so much more dashing than she had anticipated—the kind of gentleman who easily inspires the tender sentiments—had been that much greater for not having been expected. She had really believed she could love him, had just, in fact, on the very moment when he had disappointed her, been beginning to think she really did love him. She had been very glad, too, because she had always doubted a little her motives, and whether she was being fair to him.

But now everything had changed. In one stroke Reginald Darnley had managed to destroy all the first stirrings of love. The fact was that it did so much to distress Lady Roselind Arden that for a great while she thought she could never look at his face again. He had behaved abominably, whatever the cause. Even had he been called away by some emergency, he should never have left a young lady alone as he had done, even had the weather been fine. This much Roselind knew, and although she was a young lady much given to looking for the good in everyone, and to inventing excuses for those she liked, she could find nothing to condone his behavior in this present case.

And so she was left with a first conclusion: Mr. Darnley, for all that he was credited with doing in the past, for all his generosity in larger cases, was not a real gentleman. She knew she could never love him, even if, by degrees, she could find it within her courage to look him in the eye again without blushing for shame. In any other circumstance, she would surely not have tried even to do that. She would have made a point of avoiding him, have hidden from his looks, and perhaps stayed away from any public entertainment for a week or two. But things had arranged themselves in such a way that Roselind could not afford to be so modest, and shy, and human. Bertie wanted to marry, and to marry, moreover, a lady who deserved him but could do nothing to help him. On the contrary, Miss Quimby would be a great weight on him, not only on his fortune, but even on his strength. And yet there was so much to love in her!

It was, Roselind concluded with a great deal of warmth, impossible to deny him that basic right of humanity: to love whom he chose, and to bestow on his beloved what he could. There was, it seemed, no way around it. She would have to rally her forces and do what in the past she had been spared: she should have to swallow her pride and learn to deceive.

After a great while—for Roselind's reflections lasted above an hour—she rose up from her seat and rang the bell for her maid. Not long afterward she stood in front of her glass before going down to dinner. The reflection which came back to her was very strange, though beautiful. Her upright, slender little figure was draped in a splendid gown of ivory silk with a slip of bronzed gauze. Around the delicate neck, with its proud straightness, was fastened a necklace of diamonds and pearls, which had not been worn since the late Countess Iseleigh had been alive. It glittered, for all its brilliance, no more brightly than the pair of great gray eyes which seemed to challenge the very air. The fragile complexion was heightened in color and the stubborn little chin held proudly aloft as Lady Roselind Arden descended the staircase to dinner.

⸺ ⸺

The Duchess of Devonshire kept a mansion near Bath, about twenty minutes from the center of that city, on a verdant sweeping stretch of the River Avon. It was a very grand place, with acres of carefully tended lawns, ornamental waterworks, and miles of formal flower gardens laid out in a dizzying array of color and scent on the riverbanks. Her grace kept no real park at Bath, for these she had at other residences, in Scotland, and Devon, and Yorkshire. The house at Bath was merely a little country retreat, where she came very seldom, and never for long. It was exactly suited to small entertainments of an intimate character.

The duchess was much given to entertainments on the whole. A week never passed in her life when she did not hold at least three dinners and one or two soirees. She never gave a ball— what need had she to do so? There were never fewer than fifty at the smallest gatherings, and there was always dancing as well as cards, conversation, and exquisite suppers. In her little country place she was very fond of having intimate evenings, which consisted of one or two hundred guests, and which were enlivened by some human beings she would never allow into her house in town. It was true that the Duchess of Devonshire was very popular. She was gay, and handsome, shrewd as any lawyer, and above all, she was consequential. Ministers and generals loved her as much as everyone else, and often depended on her judgment in matters of state and war. In short, Georgina Devonshire could command the attendance of anyone she liked at her "little soirees." But what she liked, and whom she chose to invite, was often a matter of astonishment to some of her admirers. Perhaps because she had everything she ever needed, and had attained the apex of fashionable elegance, she delighted in nothing so much as cultivating people whom no one else took any special notice of. It was a kind of arrogance, in a way, and had she not been who she was, she might have been frowned on for it.

The latest of Georgina's series of peculiar friends was Mr. Grey. Now, it was admitted by everyone, and especially that reputable group of English citizens, the mamas, that Mr. Grey was very handsome. Whether he was anything else, it was hard to say, for he had no acquaintance, and there was no determining what his position in life was. Mamas are very dependent on knowing such things, before they approve a young gentleman. They like to know if he is a Grey from Cornwall (where a family of very prominent Greys have made their domicile) or of Lancashire, or no Grey worth noticing at all. They are very likely to admire a handsome Mr. Grey, and even more a rich one. But no matter how handsome or rich such a Mr. Grey may be, there is no countenancing him if he has not some good position in life. How else is one to be sure of his character, to be certain he will not abduct a tender Belinda under the guise of love and honor, or, more probably, whether he is posing as a man of solid income, when he is no such thing? Such things are the business of mamas, but not of duchesses. Duchesses may choose to like whom they will, and if the object of their interest appears to have no friends, and if his income is but five hundred a year, or even if he is in trade, it is of no consequence. Once he is approved by such a *grande dame*, he has gained a kind of stature even if he had none before, and mamas are more ready to approve of him on these grounds alone.

Now, Mr. Grey had been seen about frequently of late, although no one had conversed with him very much—not, at least, enough to dispel the suspicions necessarily accompanying mystery. That he was very well-looking was acknowledged by everyone, though more wholeheartedly by the younger ladies than the older, who depended on some more viable form of exchange than an aquiline nose to decide their regard. He had gained a good deal by being seen about with the young Lord Iseleigh, and though there was some talk in certain circles that he had formed this intimacy merely to be in close contact with the earl's sister (whom, it was thought, he might be cultivating for her fortune), it was soon clear to the majority that such was not the case. For Lady Roselind was very clearly setting her cap at Reginald Darnley. Mr. Grey could never be expected to remain in the contest when that nonpareil was his competitor. But still, some said, it was very telling the way Mr. Grey was always watching the two of them, with a kind of loathing in his eyes. Such loathing could only be accounted for by the fact that he despised Reginald Darnley, or feared him, and that he wanted more than ever an opportunity to get the upper hand. It was all very unlikely, however, and until the word was spread about that Mr. Grey had been seen talking intimately to Lady Roselind that very afternoon, in a closed hut in the middle of a thunder shower, such notions were brushed off with contempt.

Georgina Devonshire had heard none of this gossip. She had not the fortune to be intimate with those few ladies whose business it was to spread rumors, nor did she make a habit of sitting by the hour in other people's drawing rooms speculating on the marriage mart. She had spoken to Mr. Grey once or twice, but had not paid much attention to where his glances were directed.

She liked him chiefly because of what she had heard about him—that he had stood up to Reginald Darnley in the middle of the London Highway, demanding that he make recompense to a farmer whose cart he had turned over. The very idea made Georgina laugh. And when she had spoken to Mr. Grey herself, she had found him astonishingly attractive. He was quick, and well-spoken, and did not hesitate to say what he thought. He seemed, moreover, unimpressed by the complexities of society, which had everyone else in thrall. He did not seem to understand that if you are a plain Mr. Grey, without consequence or family, you should do everything within your power to cultivate the regard of personages such as her grace. The result was that Georgina found him refreshing, and quite delightful to talk to. Because of this, she had made a point of inviting him tonight, and when she was finished with her duties of greeting her guests and seeing that they were all comfortably bestowed, she sought him out.

Mr. Grey was quickly found. He was standing in one of the small drawing rooms overlooking the gardens, leaning up against a mantel and watching the proceedings with evident amusement. In one corner of the room two young ladies were battling for the attention of a young swain who seemed torn between the prettiness of one and the singing of the other. The pretty one was standing beside the piano while her friend played, and making bashful eyes at the young man. The rest of the room was occupied by little groups of men and women, and in the center was a gathering of dowagers immersed in gossip. It was this conversation which Mr. Grey seemed to be watching with the most interest.

"Why are you all alone?" began Georgina in her forthright

way, which was never offensive. Mr. Grey smiled and bowed, and said he never noticed if he was alone or not.

"But where is young Iseleigh?" inquired the duchess.

Mr. Grey nodded in the direction of a French window.

"He has gone outside to moon. It is very hard being in love in a room full of people, I suppose." He smiled.

The duchess exclaimed at this, and demanded to be told whom Bertie was in love with. The answer, that it was a certain invalided young lady by the name of Quimby, aroused her interest. "Lord," she said, "I believe I know that young lady. Was not her father a merchant? I think he lost all his money some years ago! And she is at Bath—that is very interesting. Have you met her?"

Mr. Grey replied that he had not so far been fortunate enough, but that he expected every minute to be invited along to Elizabeth Street.

"That is a hard fate! She was once very rich! And now, you say, she is sick, and living in such a poor district?"

"But Bertie will save her," said Mr. Grey, smiling. "I have no fear for *her*—he is a most devoted do-gooder, and will not rest until she is well, and rich."

Georgina Devonshire looked at her companion as he said this. He seemed to attempt lightness, but there was real fondness in his smile and in the way he spoke.

"I suppose you never were in love," she chided him, "or you should not mock the passion of another."

Mr. Grey seemed to stiffen slightly.

"Believe me," he replied, "I would never make light of a genuine love. Where there is real feeling, I have nothing but tender admiration, both for the emotion and the man who feels it."

Georgina Devonshire followed Mr. Grey's glance, which had

strayed away from her while he had spoken, and was fastened on the spectacle of Reginald Darnley, who had just walked in from out-of-doors with Roselind Arden on his arm. Mr. Grey's expression was chilly, and his voice equally frigid. The duchess could hardly suppress a smile. A light had begun to dawn in her.

"And there is a man, I suppose," she said slyly, "who feels nothing like that particular kind of love of which you think so highly?"

Mr. Grey seemed a little surprised.

"Oh, do not look so startled," said the duchess. "I may be old, but I am not so blind, nor so ancient, that I do not see *some* things!" She saw that her companion had colored a little, and went on, "I thought it was no more than outraged justice that made you attack my old friend in that way which I have heard so much about, but I see there was more driving you than that!"

Now Mr. Grey was really flustered. He had at last got the duchess's meaning, and did not seem to know how to respond. However, he was not a man to hem and haw very long, and said at last, with an attempt at his usual lightness, "I am sorry to disappoint you, ma'am, but you have got it wrong. I never saw Mr. Darnley before that day in the highway—in fact, even then I did not know who he was until a very large and bossy woman did me the honor of enlightening me."

"Yet you do not like him," said the duchess.

"No," said Mr. Grey shortly, "I do not. I cannot find it in me to love anyone who goes about disregarding the feelings of others."

"Only farmers?" inquired Georgine Devonshire with a mischievous look. "Or does your contempt spring more out of pity for some other creature—some young, female creature, perhaps?"

Mr. Grey turned coldly away and watched the couple at the

other end of the room, who seemed joined by some unspoken intimacy, with a great loathing in his eyes.

"I once did pity her," he murmured, "but now I have changed my mind. Where there is no pride, but only avarice, I cannot respect very long."

The duchess had not caught all of Mr. Grey's words, for they had really been spoken almost to himself, and in a very soft voice, but she saw the look in his eye and heard the word "pride."

"Oh, Darnley certainly is proud." She laughed. "But then, he is so rich and so much sought after, I suppose one cannot blame him!"

She was called away just then to attend to some one of her guests, and did not see the animosity with which Mr. Grey continued to stare at Darnley and Roselind, nor see the little contemptuous shrug he gave soon afterward, before he turned away and left the room.

Roselind had anticipated her evening's work with much more dread than she soon found had been necessary. She had not known what to expect from Mr. Darnley, but certainly she had not thought it would be he who would rush up to her, as soon as she had come into the Devonshire mansion, with eager apologies on his lips, and many expressions of contrition. That he had looked for her long and hard before driving away was professed, and that it had been nearly a half-hour before he had been persuaded that she must have been rescued by some other friend. "I realized Georgina must have taken you home with her," he said, smiling, and Roselind, thinking that Mr. Grey had told her, only minutes after the downpour started, that Darnley had been seen leaving the pleasure grounds, did not contradict him. She knew that he hadbeen as much aware of the duchess's early departure as she had been herself. Surely it was a false testimony, but the eagerness in Darnley's look and the sincerity with which he spoke almost persuaded her otherwise. Indeed, only twenty-four hours earlier she might have swallowed it all. Something had transpired within her, however, to make her see this evening a kind of falseness in his tone and manner. He evidently expected her to accept his apology without a murmur, and this, above everything, made her wish to withhold it. There was an arrogance in his assumption which angered her beyond anything she had ever known. How she would have liked to turn coldly away and never speak to him again! But as it was, she smiled (though without the warmth which had been lately in her look) and said, "Oh, it was nothing."

"Then Georgina did bring you back to Pulteney Street?" he demanded with something of relief in his look. "I was sure she would, you know."

Roselind did not reply, and so the matter was ended. Mr. Darnley, however, devoted himself to her from then on with a kind of diligence which had never been in his treatment of her before. He stayed by her side, addressing every remark to her and hardly once straying off to speak to some other of his friends. Very recently such a change would have delighted her, but this evening Roselind had no strength to appreciate it. She felt as if something in her had died, and with a cold, empty feeling she allowed herself to be guided in and out of rooms, to converse with people she had no interest in, and to pretend to delight in everything. She would have been glad to sink into a chair and remain unmolested for the evening, but a reserve of strength and determination kept a smile on her face and animation in her look. "I will think only of Bertie," she told herself, "and of Miss Quimby, who is a much more deserving creature than I."

Each time she glanced up at the dark face beside her, she saw there something new to dislike. Mr. Darnley's treatment of his friends, she noticed now for the first time, was divided between an almost fawning eagerness with some and a cold reserve with others. It was a little while longer before she was able to discern just what made the distinction. Where he was confronted with someone of a superior rank, Darnley played the solicitous puppet, nearly approaching obsequiousness in his looks and smiles. Such was the case even with a rude old dowager, a countess whom Roselind knew to be quite penniless. Anyone who was not consequential received a curt nod and an uninterested glance. What had seemed at first to Roselind as gallantry looked now like exaggerated courtesies, and what had puzzled her at first as an unreadable countenance began to betray signs of contempt.

At first she could hardly believe it. She wondered that she had ever thought him the finest gentleman in the world! But with her eyes now cleared of the cobwebs, she was able to see much that had passed unnoticed before. All the fine ladies and gentlemen who had once impressed her looked artificial and snobbish now. Those who had once had the power to make her cringe in distress when they had implied her gowns were homely and the dressing of her hair so plain as to be almost ugly (all the while complimenting her on her "wonderful simplicity of appearance"), or that her manner was not what it ought to be, while saying she was "so sweet and quiet—a pretty little mouse," were as incapable of shaming her now as they were of raising her spirits by their approving looks. Word had not yet had time to spread that she had been abandoned at the boat launching in a thundershower by the very gentleman who was now hovering over her in a way quite unlike himself. Her grace's guests saw only what was before them, and from the look of it, Reginald Darnley had at last been snared.

Roselind received their overt gestures of congratulation without any pleasure. When Mrs. Hogarth, who had been going about telling all her friends that she had arranged the match all by herself, sidled up to the couple to lurk in the shadow of their glory, Roselind had not even the heart to smile to herself.

"Well, my dear," said the older woman when she had the opportunity to draw Roselind aside for a moment, "you see that I had your best interests in mind, after all! I know you did not understand what I was about that day in the Crescent—perhaps you even disliked me for it!—but see *now* how satisfactorily everything is worked out!"

Roselind could hardly believe her ears, and would at any other time perhaps have replied with some sally, but tonight all she could do was murmur, "Why, what has happened, ma'am?"

"Pshaw! Do not tell me you are so innocent, child! Why, all the world is saying you are to be Lady Roselind Darnley soon! But I see you do not like to speak of it just yet. Perhaps it is just as well. Very modest and becoming of you, too, my dear—but still, you may speak to *me*, you know! I am your good old friend!"

Roselind had not much strength to listen to any more of this. She quickly drew herself away and mingled for a while with the crowd of guests who had gathered to listen to a young lady playing at the pianoforte. Mr. Darnley was still at her side—indeed, he had hardly moved more than three feet away from her the whole evening. She was hardly aware of anything he said, or what she was seeing. The music came to her as if through some silk screen, barely audible, and just recognizable to some distant part of her mind. There was only one face in the whole crowd which stood out, which seemed clearly in focus. Mr. Grey was part of the audience as well. He stood, as usual, a little away from the main part of the crowd, leaning up against a decorative column and watching everything. She had seen him several times this evening, and had really longed to go up to him. She wished to apologize for her rudeness this afternoon, for she was aware that she had been brusque and ungrateful. It had been, indeed, a very great service, and she had repaid his kindness with abominable incivility. Twice she had been about to approach him, but each time she had seen him cast her a look of thinly disguised contempt. She felt that really she could not blame him, and yet she longed for his forgiveness. It was extraordinary, to be sure, but it was true nevertheless: some great transformation had taken place inside her bosom, to make her wish for his regard. It was not only that he had been the first to understand Bertie's state of mind—a thing which Roselind had always prided herself on being able to do better than anyone else; that, indeed, must have played a part in it. But there were subtler reasons, reasons which Roselind would perhaps have been the last to make out. Be that as it may, in almost exactly inverse proportion to her increasing disgust with Mr. Darnley she began to like Mr. Grey better. Perhaps it was his aloofness from everyone else—*he* would never fawn over an old dowager only because she was a countess! Despite all his frivolity, Mr. Grey seemed, at heart, more sound and solid than anyone else in the room. There was a quality to his look, when he was not aware he was being watched, which struck her, almost, as sadness! Could she be mistaken, or did not he seem deeply grieved by something? But no, she must be wrong. She had never known anyone who seemed to care less about what troubled others most. Neither friends, nor family, nor wealth seemed to move him. His stated belief, what she had heard him say very often, was that life was for the living in that moment, and that it was foolish to worry about the future. How, then, to reconcile that expression of ineffable sadness with his usual devil-may-care attitudes?

Roselind had been watching Mr. Grey longer than she realized, and so immersed in her speculations had she been that she hardly noticed when the music ended and the guests, after a little polite clapping of hands, began to move toward the supper room. For a moment she stood rooted to the spot, and then absently began to wander in with the others. Mr. Darnley was out of sight, but she made no move to find him. She found herself beside the great supper table, laid out in a marvelous array of cold dishes, carved-ice statues of swans, and an exact replica of the mansion in spun sugar and glaze. A voice beside her made her start.

"It is a very grand spectacle, is it not?" said Mr. Grey.

Roselind, who had hardly noticed the lavish display of dishes, did not at first see what he was talking about.

"Why, yes," she said after a moment. "It is very pretty." She longed to open the subject of the afternoon, but held back on seeing the coolness in her companion's eyes.

"You shall very soon keep such a table as this, I suppose," he continued. "I make no doubt that will please you."

Roselind looked at him in confusion. Had it not been for the look of contempt in his face, she would not have been able to understand him. "What must he think of me?" she wondered, coloring, for it soon dawned on her that Mr. Grey thought she was pursuing Mr. Darnley for his wealth. That his idea was exactly right did not comfort her much.

"Will you," continued Mr. Grey, "have a replica made of Darnley Park, or Darnley Manor, or whatever he calls his chief house, and ornament it with candied fruit, like this? Or perhaps you have some other idea—"

Roselind could bear this no longer. She cut him off, nearly crying out, "I beg of you, stop! You must take me for a very wretch! I was hoping to ask your forgiveness for the vile way in which I thanked you this afternoon for saving me. But I see I have done too much harm to ever make it up. You despise me utterly."

Mr. Grey looked at her thoughtfully for a moment, and for a moment his sardonic manner left him. He seemed to regard her with a passionate tenderness, which brought a blush more quickly to Roselind's cheek than anything she had ever felt. Her heart seemed to leap quite out of her bosom. But in an instant Mr. Grey regained his chilly composure and said, "You have no need to thank me, or to apologize. I was only as uncivil to you as you were to me. I am a little sorry to see that you have not learned your lesson, however. Do you always so easily forgive gentlemen who have used you ill?"

Now Roselind's agitation came from shame. She could hardly lift her eyes to his as she replied, "You do not understand me, sir! Indeed, if you did, you could never think of me as you do! If I were free to tell you what drives me . . . But there, I am not! My own happiness would make me explain, but there are others whose happiness is dearer to me than my own."

And with this Roselind turned away and fled from the room. Tears were burning in her eyes as she made her escape, and when she at last reached a quiet corner empty of any humanity, she sank down onto a sofa, hidden from passersby by a row of flowering bushes, and wept until she thought her heart would break. The thoughts which passed through that mind, torn by conflicting emotions, need not be noted here. Suffice it to say that even Roselind did not know exactly what made her cry, or what, in that censoring blue gaze, had made such an impact that for many minutes it would not leave her mind's eye.

At last her grief was vented, and by degrees she grew calmer. After a little rest, a little spell of composing herself, she drew herself up with a proud lift of the shoulders, and although her heart was very heavy still, she left her sanctuary for the hard fight she knew was ahead of her.

13

Bertie went early the next morning to Elizabeth Street to inform his beloved that he had broken his promise of secrecy. In fact, although he was a little ashamed to confess this, he felt so strongly that Miss Quimby would forgive him, when she learned that Rosie, at least, seemed to approve the match, that he meant to tell her right out. It was true that his sister had said nothing absolutely sanctioning his marriage, but then, neither had she rebelled against it, except to remind him that he had not attained his majority yet and to caution him against haste. But Lord Iseleigh knew Roselind very well. He knew that she could not hold out long against real love, and especially where his happiness was at stake. He knew, too, that Roselind admired Maude Quimby almost as much as he did himself, if that were possible, and in the euphoria of happiness and the first passion of a passionate heart, he practically flew up the five flights of rickety dark stairs which were by now dearer to him than any castle could have been.

Miss Quimby received him very happily, as she always did, although there seemed something not quite right about her today. She was very vague, and hardly listened to his confession, or even to his account of Roselind's reaction to it. She was completely lost in thought, and after Bertie had finished, feeling rather let down at her attitude, she burst out, "Tell me—is your sister engaged to Reginald Darnley yet?"

Bertie did not know, and in truth cared little at the moment. He was too astounded to say much, but replied, blinking his eyes, that Roselind had been with him all the evening before at the Duchess of Devonshire's soiree.

"Yes, yes," said Maude, "I know it. Mrs. Dean was here earlier." Bertie had ceased to be astonished at the wealth of information which Mrs. Dean had always at her command.

"Well, then," said he, "they were together. But that is nothing new, you know. They have been together ever since we came to Bath."

"But now the word is out that they are going to be married," replied Maude Quimby, looking at him intently.

"Good God! I suppose the word is always out before anyone knows a thing! I think, though, really, you know, that I should have been told, if it was quite a settled thing. I don't suppose Rosie has forgotten me that much."

Miss Quimby did not seem much convinced by this assertion, but she let the subject drop. After a moment, however, she said, "Have you never thought it odd that my brother is never here when you call?"

Bertie had, in fact, thought it very odd. He had wondered more than once about that mysterious fellow, whom he thought he had glimpsed once on the stairway, a small, frightened, ferrety type of creature, with shifting eyes. He had wondered, too, as had Roselind, what Quimby had done that had to be made up for. But he said none of this out loud, and only nodded.

"I suppose," said Maude, smiling at him, "that you think it very strange gratitude from a sister, to avoid mentioning the name of a brother who has sacrificed independence, and marriage, and perhaps even a fortune to look after her? To be, in fact, ashamed of him, and to resent him?"

Bertie could only blink, and stare.

"Well, you should be very just to think ill of me for entertaining that kind of thought about my brother Lucius. And yet you would not, perhaps, be quite just enough, for my brother once forfeited *my* happiness, and even a brilliant marriage. And even that I could have forgiven. But what I have never been able to conscience is something else—something Lucius did many years ago, which began a chain of evil, and eventually ended in the death of a man very dear to me, and who had done more for my brother than anyone else in the world, save perhaps our parents."

Miss Quimby paused for a moment, staring intently into the air. At his post beside her, Bertie sat forward in his chair, unsure what he should say. He could read very great distress in that dear face, and was torn between a desire to learn what caused it and an equally strong urge to see it cleared away. After a little, Maude went on.

"I mentioned once," she said, "that there had been a gentleman in my life before I knew you. I always meant to tell you about it, but not just yet; I wished first to be assured that your own affection for me was strong enough to endure the test which a previous affection for another man must always cause in the mutual feelings of a man and woman. Oh, don't look at me so! It was nothing of the kind you are imagining, but something altogether different. At any rate, I am convinced now that I must say it, for not to do so would be to risk wrecking your sister's life.

Mr. Darnley," continued Miss Quimby, looking very hard at her lover, "is an evil man. My brother, Lucius, was always weak, and that weakness led him into actions which he should not have undertaken. But where there is a weak mind and heart, there will always be folly. Though I cannot condone Lucius' conduct, I can understand it. Mr Darnley is something altogether different—a very devil, I think."

Again Miss Quimby paused, as if unsure how to proceed. When she spoke again, it was with the utmost care in what words she used, as if she had been picking her way carefully amid a field of sharp stones. During all the narration, Bertie leaned intently forward, hardly moving a muscle. What he heard was so astonishing that he could not at first believe it. It seemed as if he had opened an ordinary-looking door and found behind it a maze of dark winding alleyways peopled with ghosts and alive with the past.

"You know that my father was once very rich," began Miss Quimby. "In those days—seven years ago—we lived a very different life from the one you see now. My father kept a mansion in Grosvenor Square, we had liveried footmen and four carriages. My brother went to Harrow, and then to Oxford, in preparation for his life as a gentleman. Although my father was only a wealthy merchant, and his own family had been a humble but respectable kind of people, Papa's dearest wish was to see his own children grow up to be accepted members of the society which scorned him. If he could not gain admittance to the drawing rooms of the ton, he wanted us to do so. To that purpose, he struggled, and if in his great longing to see us rise above his own level he sometimes lost sight of the values and honorable feelings which a gentleman must have to deserve the name, it was all done for love and a real wish to see us happy. I went to the best schools, governesses and tutors were brought from the Continent to teach me drawing and music, French and Italian. My brother, as I have said, was sent to Harrow, and then to Oxford. My father, thinking only to help his son, gave him a huge allowance, bigger by five times than any of the other boys.' But Lucius was a sickly child, with a nervous disposition, and grew into a puny man with no sense of his own worth. When he was scorned and teased by his comrades, he took it very much to heart, although scorn and teasing in young boys is very common, I think. He soon learned the value of money, and in his eagerness to be accepted and loved by those who held him in contempt, he began to use his wealth to win them over. Of course, as anyone knows who has ever studied human nature, such a course will never succeed. Men are very glad to take anything given to them, without giving anything in return.

"At all events, Lucius began to play at cards. It was a common practice among his friends—or those he wished to call his friends—and he discovered very early that, being a poor player, and given to losing the huge stakes he put up, the others were eager to play with him. He took their attentions, at first, as gestures of friendship, and played more and more heavily, until at last he was paying all the tailors' bills, the club dues, and incidental expenses of half the population of Christ Church College. The men who were happy to take his money—sons of aristocrats and peers, often impoverished ones—still laughed at him behind his back. But this he never knew, or else, perhaps, never wished to know. He continued gaming until at last he was addicted to the pastime. It was a dangerous entertainment for anyone of his character, and could not but end in grief.

"There was another gentleman at Oxford at the same time as Lucius, a man altogether different in character, fortune, and blessings. He was a duke's eldest son, in line for one of the great titles in the kingdom, and one of the vastest fortunes. Besides this, he was a person so blessed by nature that others could not help but envy him. Tall, beautifully made, with a noble face and almost unbelievable charm, this gentleman was considered the most popular of all the men at the university. Besides all this, he was so open and naturally generous that one could not help but love him—and nearly everyone did. But where there is so much good fortune, there must also be envy, and even hatred. And yet this fellow inspired almost everyone with love—everyone, that is, except another scholar, a merchant's son, like Lucius, but more powerful in every way than Lucius ever dreamt of. Reginald Darnley was already one of the richest men in England, but he, too, suffered from the knowledge that his heritage was not lofty. In any case, he hated the other man with a consuming passion."

Maude Quimby broke off for a moment, staring across the room. With a gesture she asked to be brought the little portrait which sat always on her bureau. Bertie fetched it obediently, wondering all the while who the handsome gentleman represented in the miniature could be.

"You have heard, I suppose, of the Montague scandal?" said Miss Quimby at last, fingering the miniature.

Bertie nodded, with a puzzled look.

"Yes," he said, "I know the story. Montague paid off his gambling debts with a deed of land to a part of his father's estates, and then, disgraced, fled England."

Maude Quimby smiled with a cynical expression.

"Yes, that is what the world thinks," she said. "And it is also believed that Reginald Darnley defended his reputation, at the risk of his own, and even paid the debt from his own pocket to assuage the old duke's wrath. But what would you think if I told you that the debts were my brother's, and that Darnley had tricked Montague into the scheme out of pure hatred? What would you think if you knew that, as surely as if he had put a knife in Roderick's stomach, Darnley killed the man he calls his 'great friend'?"

Bertie could say nothing whatever to this. His eyes grew round in disbelief, and perhaps, in half an hour, he might have been able to organize a question, for this news, coming from such a quarter, disavowed everything he had ever heard about the case.

But Miss Quimby allowed him no time to question her. She went on immediately, "For that is the truth, I swear! It was Roderick Montague, the best-loved scholar at Oxford, who befriended poor Lucius, and tried to make him stop gambling. It was Roderick Montague, of all the men in England, who stood by him when my father made a series of rash investments and lost all his money. It was Roderick who did not scorn to come to us in London, when others would have been ashamed to visit the house owned by a nabob, and who, when we were no longer rich, but cast on the world as penniless orphans, undertook to see that my education was finished, that I was presented at Almack's in a decent gown, and that Lucius did not sink into a gutter of ignominy—for he was still addicted to gaming, although he had no money to lose." Miss Quimby sighed, and looked very hard at Bertie. "I will not tell you the whole story, for it is very long, and I have not much energy for this kind of horror, but I'll only tell you what you must know, to save your sister.

"Darnley hated Roderick Montague, as I have said, and for

many years he must have harbored a twisted resentment against him. In the years when they were all at Oxford, he did nothing, but must have been consumed with a kind of jealous rage. I do not know—it is only what I imagine, for something incredible must have been in his mind. When they all came down from university, after the death of my parents, I saw Lucius only at infrequent intervals. He had taken up a residence at Bath, and was living a very ignoble existence, hardly surviving, yet managing to play constantly at cards, all the while increasing his already sizable debts. I was by now established in London with a respectable lady, provided by a settlement in my mother's will, before she died, when she had been moved to make some precaution against what she must have suspected was an almost unavoidable fate. Roderick, too, was living in town. He came very often to see me, and though I never knew it until later, it was due to him that my life was made much easier than it might have been. I was still very young—only sixteen—and had no idea of the ways of the world. If I had, I might have seen that his affection for me was grown beyond that of a kind older friend. He had always been dear to me, as I think I was to him. When we were still living in our former life, he had been used to bring me toys and little gifts of an ingenious nature, and had never tired of playing with me, or helping to increase my little knowledge of history and geography, bringing me books, and helping me to study them. He was always a gay, openhearted fellow! So easily amused, so delighted with life, and yet with a kind of firm and immovable belief in right and justice—he could never have done the things which he has been accused of. I loved him, I think, as dearly as I had ever loved anyone. But I never knew how his own affections were changing.

"Roderick was still as much in demand as ever. Everywhere

he went, people were drawn to him, and he could easily have made a brilliant marriage. He was handsome, charming, and rich, and besides everything, he was to be the Duke of Hamilton very soon, for his father was dying. The old duke, in fact, wished for just such a brilliant match, for Roderick was his darling son, on whom he doted, although by all accounts he was a fierce man to everyone else, even to his younger son, which I know always grieved Roderick immensely, for he was very devoted to his brother.

"It was, therefore, most unfortunate that Roderick should have chosen me as the woman he loved. Had he chosen some other . . . Well, perhaps he might be alive today. And I was so young and innocent, I had no idea of what sacrifices he was prepared to make!"

Miss Quimby went on after a moment, "In any case, I loved Roderick, and when he asked me to be his wife, I readily, and very happily, said yes! I never thought what it might cost *him*, nor did I even question my own feelings above thinking that he was the dearest man in all the world. The engagement was made between us, but secretly, for Roderick wanted to wait until I was eighteen—and perhaps until his father had softened a little—to make it public. Lucius, in the meantime, had argued with him, for Roderick always was urging him to leave off gaming.

"One day Roderick was called away to Bath. He never told me why, but only that he would not be able to keep his usual appointment with me in the morning—he came every day to call, as it was the only time we could speak freely together, without causing suspicion in our friends. I never thought of it, for Roderick was often called away to see his father, or to conduct some business of the estate, which he was increasingly charged with as his father's health declined. In a week, I had heard no other news, but one morning I received a letter."

Miss Quimby did not speak for a while, recalling, it appeared, the pain of those days. With a sigh and a look of great exhaustion she began again.

"I am not certain exactly what took place in those days, but from what I can gather, both from Lucius and from Roderick's letters, it seems that Lucius had incurred a huge sum of debts—nearly twenty thousand pounds—in the interval since Roderick had last seen him. Reginald Darnley had offered to pay them and to give my brother, as well, a sum to live upon. A year passed, and Lucius was beginning to give over his former life. He had now some semblance of respectability, and was on the verge of a new feeling of self-respect. He had agreed to pay Darnley back very gradually, and was working to that end as a clerk. But one day Darnley appeared and demanded to be paid back all at once, and immediately. He must have threatened my brother, for Lucius still lives in dread of him. Lucius wrote to his old friend Roderick, whom he had used so ill already, and begged for help.

"Roderick had a large income, but was unable to procure so much ready cash at such short notice. Instead, he made an agreement with Darnley that the other should accept, as a guarantee of payment in the next quarter, a deed of land worth fifty thousand pounds—twice the sum of the debt. This must all have been done at great cost to Roderick's feelings of right, and I can only imagine that he was motivated to it in part out of a concern for myself. Darnley agreed to accept the deed merely as a guarantee, and all seemed well. But within a few days the word was out that Roderick Montague had incurred all those debts and had paid his fee with his father's lands! The old duke was one of the first to hear this—one can only imagine who had told him! The letter I received that morning was to tell me (without any mention of this) that Roderick was forced in honor to leave his own country, abdicating both inheritance and title. His father would not see him, and refused to recognize his son and heir. Reginald Darnley, who had laid his plans for years, who had been inciting my brother to gamble more and more, then went about declaring his 'great love for his dear friend Montague.' His own position rose instantly in the ton, when it was learned he had paid off the debts himself. No word was ever mentioned of my brother, and he—weak as he was—never came forward to tell the truth. The whole kingdom chose to believe the word of a man they had hitherto paid no attention to, over the honor of a man they had known and loved for years! That is the nature of our great country, Albert—it will believe anything to the discredit of a good man, so long as there is gossip and interest in the belief!"

Maude Quimby broke off, her immense brown eyes, usually so gentle in their gaze, brightened by moisture, and full of a wrath like that of an avenging angel. Bertie could only stare and long to comfort her. A silence followed which seemed to echo in the small apartment, with its streams of sunshine, its threadbare but tidy furnishings, and the air of order and tranquillity so out of context to this story.

At last Bertie managed to ask what had become of Roderick.

"He died some months ago," murmured Maude. "In India, where he had been these last five years. He used to write to me, saying he was well and happy, and urging me to marry. I never knew how much he concealed, in order to help me, until I received this letter, from the commandant of the army in Calcutta, a Colonel Morrison."

Miss Quimby asked for a little inlaid box, which had been lying next to the miniature, and, opening it, took out a folded missive, which she handed to Bertie. The letter was short and so businesslike that Bertie, who had heard the story with the concern of one who had been part of it, could not help but feel horrified. It spoke of the remains of a body, nearly unrecognizable from starvation and the ravages of malaria, which had been found in a hut in the midst of a tiny village some hundred miles from the capital. The man, who had been identified by the natives of the village as a Sahib Monten, was at last discovered to be English. Another Englishman had found him, one who claimed to be an old friend, but he had not stayed long enough to give any information to the commandant of the regiment. It had been through a native, one supposed to have nursed the dead man, that knowledge of an English friend had been acquired. Miss Quimby had been informed of the death as a matter of course, though, said the colonel, "I entertain little hope that you will know the fellow, or that his death will affect you very much. It is only out of duty that I write to you, as there is no knowledge of the man's family. I enclose a golden chain which was found on his person, in case this may be of any help in recognizing him. Some medal or trinket must have been torn off from it."

When Bertie had finished the letter and put it down with a look of disgust, Maude said, "The chain was all I had—aside from my own sentiments—to go upon; I had given Roderick a lock of my hair, which he kept in a tiny locket, with a miniature he had ordered made of me. I suppose the locket must have fallen off in the jungle."

Bertie regarded his companion with a combination of fury and horror.

"And you are sure it was Darnley?" he said.

Miss Quimby nodded.

"There is no doubt about it. For a long time I lived in misery, unsure what had made Roderick rush off, wondering if perhaps he might have had some doubts about marrying me, or if something else—something I had not known about—had happened. He protected me, you see, so completely, even in his death, that I never knew the truth. I never believed he had done what he was accused of, of course, but I had nothing else to hold onto. He only said, 'Believe that I have done no wrong, and that I love you.' It was not until a month ago that Lucius finally told me the whole truth."

"But why did your brother not go forward and proclaim it to the world?"

Miss Quimby smiled.

"There, you see," she said, "there is the difference between you and my brother. You—as could Roderick—can see only what is right, what should be done, and must, regardless of the harm it will do you. But Lucius is a weak man, he always has been. I do not despise him for it, I only pity him. But even allowing for his weakness, you cannot realize what danger he is in every moment. Reginald Darnley is a powerful man, more powerful, perhaps, than any other man in England. The prince himself is in his debt, and would be glad to do him any favor. He is accounted a great man by everyone, even those who should be able to see him for what he is—a person so deformed in his heart, so twisted by malice and ambition, that if he ever had a soul, it must be a thing horrible to look upon by now. He has no mercy, no softness, nor any human warmth. I am convinced he would kill Lucius at the least provocation. I am convinced, too, that Roselind is in as much danger, though not of the same kind, as Lucius. He cannot love—he does not know the meaning of the word. He must only want her for some other reason, something neither you nor I could ever understand."

14

In the eyes of the world, the Duchess of Devonshire's soiree had marked a triumph for Lady Roselind Arden. Mr. Darnley had shown himself so eagerly at her feet—more emphatically than he had ever been seen to do with even the brightest belles of Mr. Brummel's London—that the word had quickly gone around hinting at the likelihood of an interesting event, and hinting, moreover, that the event would no doubt take place before the encroachment of winter. The news spread as fast as wildfire, and by morning the very young lady who had been laughed at for being left all alone in the rain while her suitor dallied with another young woman by the river's edge was being proclaimed the soon-to-be Mrs. Darnley. The title, even in anticipation, was capable of great things. To be Mrs. Darnley, or a prospective Mrs. Darnley, was better than being a countess, and nearly as good as being a duchess. What it lacked in ring and reverberation, it made up for in echoes, for the wife of Reginald Darnley would be among the first ladies of England, consequential enough to do as she liked, and rich enough to do it beautifully.

By the following morning, which was Friday, the world had

raised its eyes to look upon this fortunate creature with tenderness and awe. Who would ever have thought that eager young girl, so artless in her enjoyment of the dance at the opening assembly, barely a fortnight before, her gown so simple, her hair dressed with very little more ornament than a well-born governess's, could have caught the greatest fish in the sea of the British marriage market? There was speculation, to be sure, as to what had brought about the match (for that it was to be a match was doubted by hardly anyone), but no satisfactory answer could be found.

Mrs. Dean had told Miss Quimby what she had heard from Lady Hardcastle, which was that "no doubt they were intimate when the late earl was alive—it must have been arranged then." But neither this nor any of the other possible answers offered by a dozen busy gossips in as many drawing rooms that day could satisfy the question well enough. Still, that Lady Roselind had caught him was certain, and whatever wiles she had used, whatever slender artifice had been in those mild gray eyes, it had done its work to perfection.

Lady Roselind, however, was not so pleased as she might have been, considering that a week before she had been longing for the familiar nods and mincing greetings which she found everywhere about her today. She had walked out alone quite soon after breakfast, refusing even the company of her maid, and saying she had an errand or two to do. The device had been inspired as much from a desire to get out into the fresh air and let the throbbing in her temples subside as from a wish to get away from the curious, worried glances of her aunt.

She had refused Lady Agatha's offer of company with a little rending shake of the head. How she wished she might confide now in that dear friend! How she longed for the freedom to confess all her foolishness, all the hopes which had been recently shattered, and to have the luxury, after such a long self-confinement, of absolute freedom with the lady she loved best in all the world! But it was not to be so, not yet; in a day or two, when she had collected her own thoughts enough to behave without any fear of betraying her real emotions, she would go to Lady Agatha, and then her purpose would not be the great heave of relief she longed for, but a self-contained little speech announcing her intentions. She would not even contemplate it now, nor all the artifice which would necessarily accompany such a speech. For, if Roselind was to be Reginald Darnley's wife, she was determined to do it as well as possible. Never would she breathe a word of her own doubts as to his character, not even to her aunt. Especially not to her aunt! She would be the best wife that anyone could be when there was no love, nor any real tenderness to help her. Even the respect she had formerly thought would always be in her thoughts had abandoned her. And so now all that was left was courage, which she held on to as tightly as if it had been a thin wire which alone prevented her from falling to her death. And yet the feeling that even that thin wire was available helped her. It gave her a new confidence in herself, and made her feel, for the first time in all her life, like a grown-up woman who was equal to anything.

As she walked along Pulteney Street, hardly glancing up from the ground, and only painfully aware of the interest she was attracting, she thought of a great many things. First and foremost in her thoughts was Bertie and his beloved. Maude Quimby! She tried to bring that delicate, strong face into focus, and to conjure up the image of that lady's bravery in the face of such great hardship. She clung to that image as others crept into her thoughts—the look of contempt that had been on Mr. Grey's face the night before, which injured her more than she could bear; her aunt, Lady Agatha, watching her always with that half-veiled look of distress and concern, torn between her desire to speak and her respect for her niece's silence; finally, there was the dark, unreadable countenance of Mr. Darnley as it had been when she had first seen him at the opening assembly. In that first impression, she had read into his countenance wonderful things, things which she had certainly wanted to find there. She had read a sincerity and love of decorum and honor, the modesty of a man who has done a great thing for a friend and wishes to go unlauded; she had even—and thinking of it now, she almost shuddered!—read into it an ability to love, which she now knew was more present in a stony wall than in his heart. It was very odd, but the more Darnley had seemed to soften to her, the less she had believed him. It was quite true, she thought now, turning into the little park which surrounded Laura Place, and which seemed, save a nurse with her charge, deserted of humanity, that just as Mr. Darnley had *seemed* to be in love with her, she saw only artifice. His lips, as he had gazed smiling down at her, had looked suddenly very thin, and almost cruel in their lines. There was a slight curving downward at the outside of that mouth, which, as it flashed into Roselind's mind, sent an inexplicable shudder through her.

She tried to calm herself, staring hard at the trees and grass, listening to the laughter of the child and the sound of wind in the leaves overhead. She entered a small alleyway formed by two rows of shrubberies, and told herself to be sensible. "After all, even if he does not love me, he must want me—how else could he behave as he does? And if that is the case, I have no fears as to my own conduct. I want him, too. It is a very fair exchange, provided I behave exactly as I ought, and never even allow myself to think anything but good of him. After all, there must be good: how else could he have done what he did for poor Roderick Montague, without it? No, I will only think of that. Whenever I am troubled or in doubt, that is what I shall hold on to."

And consumed by these thoughts, Roselind wandered up and down, and hardly noticing where she went, at last arrived at a little tranquillity. She had come out into an inner courtyard, hidden from view by the bushes, and at the center of which was a small marble fountain in the shape of an urn. At the side of this fountain was a bench, and seeing the edge of it, just obtruding into the path, she started toward it. But just as she rounded the corner, she saw that there was already someone occupying the seat, a gentleman, who seemed to be looking at something in his hand. Roselind began to turn away, thinking she would find another place to rest, when a familiar voice spoke behind her.

"Why, it is Lady Roselind," said Mr. Grey in a surprised voice.

Roselind started, and colored. She desired nothing less than another one of those recriminating looks. But civility made her respond as if she were happy to see him.

"And what brings you to this quiet corner of the wood?" inquired Mr. Grey, standing up and putting whatever it had been in his hand into a pocket. Roselind just wondered, in passing, why he was staring at a locket, for that was what the object looked like.

"I thought you would be off driving about with all the tonnish set of people," he finished, staring at her quizzically.

Roselind colored, and replied that one could not always be

driving about, expecting any minute to see that same contemptuous expression come into the gentleman's eyes.

But instead Mr. Grey looked at her in quite a different way. He seemed torn between sadness and sympathy, and gazed long and deep into her eyes, as if by doing so he could communicate some message. The look made Roselind color more than ever, and glance away. She had no notion why those keen blue eyes, which had such a wide range of expression, were capable of discomfiting her so. In any case, she no longer wished to run away, although no word would have described her feelings worse than "comfort." She was neither comfortable nor particularly happy to be here, but she was as incapable of leaving as if she had been rooted to the spot. She sank onto the bench for lack of any other idea of what to do. "I hope I am not disturbing you," she said feebly.

"Oh, no! Nothing could disturb me less than such an interruption. I was only ... only contemplating something."

"Were you indeed? And so was I."

There was a little silence.

"I hope your thoughts were not so sad as your expression," said Mr. Grey with a voice that was less teasing than earnest. "For if they were, I should not like to have been the subject of them." The idea seemed to irritate him, and he added cynically, "Which, of course, is a very egotistical idea. I suppose you were thinking of your wedding train, and your sadness sprang from irritation that there is a war on in France, and you cannot have it made up there."

Roselind made no protest. She was too sick and weary to be piqued by this sort of comment, which, in any case, was becoming very familiar to her now. She sat silently, staring ahead of her, and at last Mr. Grey seemed to repent.

"I am very sorry," he murmured in confusion, "I have no idea why I say such things to you."

"It is probably because you despise me, sir," said Roselind softly. "And I do not wonder much. You must see only one side of me, and anyone seeing only that one side, and blind to the others, must wonder at my conduct. You saw me treated abominably by a gentleman, and then act as if nothing of the kind had happened. You must think I have no pride, nor any sense of propriety. And yet, I am sure if you knew anything about it, you would not despise me! Have you a brother, sir? Oh, but I forget. You have no family. But perhaps you have some friend or relative who is very dear to you?"

Mr. Grey seemed very startled, and replied softly, "Yes ... I once had such a friend. He was dearer to me than life."

Now it was Roselind's turn to be startled. She looked up to see an expression unlike any other she had ever beheld in that face, one so full of sadness and sincerity that she was for a moment embarrassed to have witnessed it. It was as though she had interrupted a very private conversation, a love scene, perhaps, or a last meeting between friends before the death of one. But the expression passed as quickly as it had come.

"I once had such a friend," said Mr. Grey in a brighter tone. "You must believe me. Perhaps you think I am devoid of all feelings, but I assure you it is not the case. Only, sometimes it is better to pretend to have none. In the deception, one sometimes loses oneself, until at last it is possible not to be so aware of pain. But! You have no interest in these thoughts of mine, broodish thoughts, born out of too many months of living alone. You were speaking of your own brother, I think? Of young Bertie? How goes his Miss Quimby?"

Roselind was forced into another vein of thought, and had soon forgotten the impression which, for an instant, had made her wonder that two such different men could inhabit the same body.

"I think she is well. I have not"—Roselind flushed a little—"been to see her myself lately. But Bertie goes very often. Your predictions, after all, have come true—I am forced to confess that I was utterly blind!"

Mr. Grey smiled.

"Well, that is no great sin. It is sometimes easier to discern the truth from a distance than so close at hand."

"But I should have been aware of it," said Roselind warmly. "Indeed, I hardly understand how I was not! It is almost . . . almost inexcusable that I did not! For one who feels as I do about my brother!"

"It is easier than one would believe," said Mr. Grey, staring into the air, "to misjudge the people one loves best. One thinks one understands them, and then some evil is imputed to them, or they undertake a certain action, and we, who think we know them best, are the first to misinterpret them!"

Roselind looked up eagerly.

"Do you think it is so?"

"I have, unfortunately, a certain knowledge of it. I once did the same. I once thought I understood what made a man whom I dearly loved do what he did, and once was enough to scar me for life! I only hope that, in future, I have courage enough, and strength enough, to believe myself above anyone else."

This little speech did much to restore Roselind's peace of mind. She had been longing, in a sense, to trust the judgment of others lately. But now she saw, as one sometimes does see, all in a flash, that she must do what she knew to be right.

Mr. Grey suggested they walk, and together they began to make their way through the alley of shrubberies. They went along in silence for a little, and after a while Mr. Grey inquired if it was true that she might be going to marry Reginald Darnley.

"I could not answer that question," she said, flushing slightly, "until I have been asked."

Mr. Grey said quickly, "Then you have not been asked?"

"No."

"And yet it is a certainty."

"Nothing is a certainty, until it has happened."

"And you"—Mr. Grey seemed to hesitate—"you have no ... I mean to say, if it is asked, you will accept it?"

Roselind looked at him sharply.

"Do you suppose it is quite kind to question a lady in this fashion, sir? I think perhaps it is not quite gallant, for were I to say yes, and the gentleman never allows me to be so encouraging, it would look very ill, and were I to say no, and then to change my mind . . . well, that would not be any better, would it? So I think you had better not ask me. Only . . ." Something made Roselind add, "I shall perhaps be more likely to say yes than no."

"Yes," said Mr. Grey, "that is what I feared."

For a moment Roselind looked up and colored. But the expression she saw in Mr. Grey's eyes made her sudden fluster subside for there was nothing of personal interest in his look, but only a cool inquiry in his eyes.

"I do not see why you should fear it, Mr. Grey," she could not help saying. "It is not much of a cause for fear, to be married so well."

"I suppose that is your definition of 'well,' then? To marry a man who could buy and sell England at a whim?"

"Some people would say that was very well indeed. But I have no desire to buy England, only . . ." But here Roselind stopped.

"Only a hundred Parisian gowns a year?"

"I do not have any such idea," said Roselind angrily.

"But yet the idea of being able to does not displease you?"

Roselind could not answer immediately. She felt suddenly angry again, angry at the impudence of this gentleman, who took so many liberties with her, and angrier still that she could not explain what was really in her heart. She had no idea why she should wish so heartily for the good opinion of such a man as this!

"You seem to take the idea of money very lightly, Mr. Grey," she said coldly. "And yet it is not such a bad thing."

"No, no!" cried Mr. Grey. "Not such a bad thing at all. In and of itself, it is nothing, and sometimes very nice, too. It is only what it does to people, what it makes men do to have it! And in any case, money is not the essential ingredient of happiness. One needs, as I have learned, very little ready cash to be happy."

"Perhaps you are right," said Roselind. "At least in principle. But if money can change a man then so can the lack of it, and perhaps to an even greater extent."

Mr. Grey was silent. For a while they walked without a word, coming out of the alley and turning without thinking into Pulteney Street. Just as they approached the front door of General Banforth's house, Mr. Grey grasped Roselind's arm in a sudden gesture, which made her start.

"Do you really know anything about Reginald Darnley?" he asked quietly, but with so much intensity that Roselind could hardly reply.

"Why," she said at last, "I think I do. I know he is an honorable man."

"Do you?" The grasp relaxed. One fair eyebrow mounted to a position of cynical interest. "And what makes you think that?"

Startled, Roselind said, "Why, because he has done a great deal of good in his life. He tried to save Roderick Montague, for one thing. Perhaps you do not know the story—"

"Oh, I know it very well," said Mr. Grey sardonically.

"Then you must also know how well he is thought of," said Roselind.

"I know that, too. There is nothing but good to be heard of Reginald Darnley. I am grown very sick of it! I only"—and here his face took on a look of enormous distress—"I only ask you to think what *you* know of him, and to conceive what sort of actions a man who does not blink at the idea of abandoning a young lady who is in his care in the midst of a thunderstorm could be capable of under worse conditions."

"Do you," said Roselind hotly, "mean to say you know something to Mr. Darnley's discredit?"

It was a moment before Mr. Grey replied quietly, "Nothing absolutely. Nothing that can be proved."

"Then I beg of you not to speak to me like this again, sir! Remember I may be his wife one day, if … if my desires are fulfilled!"

And with this sharp outcry Roselind ran into the house, leaving behind her a man with an expression of torment in his eyes.

━ ━

Lord Iseleigh left Elizabeth Street with more anger than tenderness in his heart. He had been very much moved by the story he had heard from Miss Quimby, and for half an hour was incapable of any collected thoughts. He had gone on horseback to

Elizabeth Street, and now rode off in the direction of the North Field with hardly any idea of what he wanted to do. What he needed immediately was a great hard gallop and the feeling of wind on his hot brow. For half an hour he rode as hard as he had ever ridden, seeing nothing around him, hearing nothing but the repeated phrases of his fiancée. Albert Arden had never been called upon to decide so great a problem as the one which now lay before him, and with a furrow in his forehead which only hinted at the tangled emotions in his heart, he began to sort out the different issues.

Half an hour's ride will often bring relief to a young man, at least enough to ease the perplexities of the moment, to soothe them away with the pent-up energies which often complicate them. But the present case was too difficult to be eased by mere exercise, it involved the happiness of too many people, and seemed to warrant a more hardened mind than Bertie's. It had not been clear, at first, what he could do, and the question only increased in difficulty as he pondered it. He had sworn himself to secrecy as regarded the story of Roderick Montague; this Maude had exacted to protect her own brother's life, and even her lover's, who, as she knew very well by now, was not unlike any other young man of high ideals and principles with more love of righteousness than experience. And yet Bertie had also sworn to keep his sister from marrying the fiend Darnley. It had been to this purpose that Maude Quimby had revealed the story at all, and only to this end that she wished the intelligence put. "There is no point in trying to revenge Roderick's death," she had said. "What would it serve? Only to draw up horrible memories, and besides, I do not believe Roderick would have wished it for himself. He was always a peace-loving man, with a greater respect for gentleness than vindication. I believe he would wish us only to prevent any further unhappiness."

"But how can we let Darnley go free, living off the fruit of his evil?" Bertie had demanded.

"We have no other choice. Men like Reginald Darnley are too highly placed, too powerful, for the likes of us. Oh, you are an earl, and that gives you some strength; but who would believe us, against the word of Reginald Darnley, who will be defended by the regent himself?"

And at last even Bertie had been persuaded that to do anything against Darnley would be rash, although he could not shake off a hatred of that man which would have made him glad to commit murder.

And so for a great while Bertie racked his brain, trying to think of some way to warn his sister, without revealing the whole truth. He knew Roselind too well to think she would take an insult to her lover without anger. But insults, without evidence, were all Lord Iseleigh had. He longed for the counsel of some older, wiser man, someone who had seen more of the world. And yet he was tied hand and foot. He could not go to his uncle, nor to Lady Agatha. His next thought was Mr. Grey. Grey was a gentleman who had already roused an immense respect in the young earl. He felt for the older man both admiration and openness, a combination often difficult to find in a friendship. And so he turned his mount in the direction of the Circus, where Grey was putting up.

A servant told the earl that his master had gone out soon after breakfast and had not been seen since. And so to the Pump Room, the Crescent, and finally the chief commercial streets, Bertie went, hoping to catch a glimpse of his friend, for Grey was often to be found wandering about alone in these places.

Yet none of these, nor even the stables, rendered up his friend, and at last Bertie turned in the direction of home, hoping that no unlucky accident would bring him face to face with Reginald Darnley, whom, if Lord Iseleigh saw, he did not think he could look upon without giving away his intelligence. He was very glad, indeed, to catch sight of Grey walking away from General Banforth's house, on the opposite side of the street. Calling out, Bertie roused his friend out of a deep meditation, and was soon riding next to him.

"I have been looking everywhere for you!" exclaimed the earl. "I have been to the Circus, the Pump Room, and the stables, and have just come from riding up and down High Street."

"I have been walking in Laura Place all the morning," said Mr. Grey, "and have just come from conversing with your sister."

At any other time Bertie might have been glad to hear this. Roselind's peculiar antipathy for Mr. Grey had been causing her brother increasing irritation and distress in these last weeks, but there was too much in Bertie's head already to make way for happiness at what might have been a reconciliation.

"Have you indeed?" said he, and then added in an urgent voice, "Listen, Grey, I must speak to you! I never needed help so much in all my life, and you are the only one I can depend upon!"

Mr. Grey must have recognized a real urgency in these words, for although he himself had been much lost in thought, he now shook himself, and suggested they continue together as far as the stables, where Bertie could dismount.

"I hardly know what to say!" exclaimed Bertie at first, in a frustrated tone.

"It is about your Miss Quimby, I suppose?" said Mr. Grey, who was very used, by now, to hearing all the complexities of love from his young friend.

"Yes, yes—but not only her. That is, she has told me an incredible tale, which involves others, as well. It is really mostly to do with ... a friend of hers, who is dead. But it was told me because it involves Reginald Darnley also, and so may be considered to affect Rosie."

Mr. Grey had not expected this. He looked now at the young earl with a great keenness of interest and what seemed to be muffled excitement. And yet his words were very slow in coming, as though carefully chosen.

"And what is the tale, pray?"

"That I cannot tell you," replied Bertie with increasing frustration. "That is the very devil of it, for I have sworn not to say anything, and yet must warn Rosie, for I have reason to think this Darnley is the worst fiend in all the world."

"What makes you think so?"

"If I could tell you the tale, it would be as clear as day to you, but that I am unable to do. In essence, it is that Darnley is a heartless, depraved creature incapable of human feeling. He pretends to be what he is not, and cares nothing for anyone who gets in his way."

"That I could have told you myself," said Mr. Grey in tones of heavy sarcasm. "It is quite clear to me he is a very horror of a man."

"D'you think so? I wonder I never thought it myself! I only considered him a rather pompous, heavy fellow with a great gloating vanity, but it never dawned on me . . . Well should never have imputed to him what I know now, and you knowing it, I wonder I did not recognize it before. Still, think he was capable of murdering a man, as surely as if—"

But here Mr. Grey stopped him short, and turned to his young companion with barely concealed excitement. "You must tell me what you know, Iseleigh! It is more crucial than you can imagine. Only think what you are risking if Roselind marries him."

Bertie stared at his friend. He longed to unburden his mind and heart, and nearly began to do so. But he was not the only one who must decide the question, and so with a great feeling of regret he shook his head.

"I cannot, my dear Grey, it is beyond my power to do so. You see, Maude's brother may be in danger, and though from all I have heard I have no love for that paltry coward, I must think of her and of her natural affection for him. I should tell you, believe me, were it any other way."

"Perhaps," said Mr. Grey, "you could persuade her to tell me herself. I shall tell no one else, I swear it. You know you may rely on me."

"Of course I may! That is what I shall do! I will take you to her, and she will see what kind of man you are. She knows already how much trust I repose in you, and likes you, I think, nearly as well as I do."

Mr. Grey wished to go immediately, but Bertie could not consent to this. Maude Quimby was already exhausted from his visit and must be allowed to rest In the morning, she was to take the waters, and so the first possible opportunity of their going to her, which was the following afternoon, was agreed upon.

15

The intervening time was spent, at Pulteney Street, in a state of great unease. Roselind was herself unhappy, but no less so than her aunt or her brother. Bertie was so miserable, so torn between anger and impotence, that he would not look at her, nor for that matter at anyone else. Lady Agatha would have noticed his silences more had she not been so taken up with thinking of her niece, for it was evident to her, as indeed it was to the whole world, that if an offer had not been made already, it would be soon. Mr. Darnley, in fact, hardly ever came to the house in Pulteney Street, so his absence today was no sign of anything. He seemed conscious that he was not welcome there, and though he made a great point of making light of Lady Agatha's dislike of him to Lady Roselind, he never came to the house unless it was impossible to avoid it. His meetings with the young lady were planned ahead of time or contrived by one of them to seem an accident.

But Agatha Banforth had seen them together the night before, and the sight had been so unpleasant that she had done everything she could to avoid looking. She had seen Darnley, with his artificial smiles and exaggerated courtesies, his arrogant drawl and faintly disguised contempt of those he deemed beneath him, and she had seen how Roselind, looking like a small, sprightly queen, had seen it, too. The distress she read in Roselind's eyes today, if anything, only increased her own concern. As much as she had hated the idea of the match before, at least she had been able to delude herself that Roselind welcomed it. Today there was no getting around the fact that the child's eyes were at last opened. She said as much to General Banforth, who was beginning to take the threat in earnest.

"But why," said that practical gentleman, "would she wish to tie herself for life to a man she hates?"

His wife wore her "deep look" as she said, "She wants to be a sacrificial lamb."

"Ah! If that is the case, perhaps it will make her happy. No, don't look like that, my dear! I am only teasing you." And the general had then looked very stern, which made his wife hopeful, until he shrugged and said, "Little as we may like it, my love, I do not see there is any way of getting out of it. If Rosie is determined to be miserable, it is her right. She has her own settlement after all, and is old enough to make up her own mind."

This did not comfort Lady Agatha much. She did not see, either, what could be done, and even her attempts to make Roselind confide in her were to no avail. The young lady always smiled and pretended not to understand, and left the room as soon as possible.

What troubled Agatha Banforth most was that she was unsure how far the affair had progressed between them. She might have been certain, six months before, of being the first to hear what had transpired, but Roselind had grown so strange and secretive of late that there was no way of knowing if the offer had been made, and accepted, or held off. She was only sure it had not been refused, and she was convinced it would not be. Something—an instinct—made her pray for time, and so every morning, and every afternoon, she scrutinized her niece's face and manner, and though she saw many subtle changes there, she never saw a certain sign. On the afternoon following the duchess's soiree, Lady Agatha was contemplating just these things, and wondering what had made Rosie rush up to her room that morning without a word, and Bertie, coming in some time later, do much the same, when the butler announced Mr. Grey.

Lady Agatha had been sitting in the morning room over a letter, which would not come out any faster than a dribble between bouts of worrying, when the gentleman was shown in. She put up her head and smiled—for she liked Mr. Grey very well—and told him that Bertie was upstairs.

"I came to see you, my lady," said the gentleman, and, a little surprised, Lady Agatha bid him sit down.

Mr. Grey seemed troubled, and at the same time excited, and it was a while before he came to the point. Twice he opened his mouth, and closed it again, and at last he rose to his feet and went to the window, where he stood looking out for some minutes before he spoke.

"I suppose you think I am behaving very strangely," he said at last.

Lady Agatha smiled, and said it made no difference. She preferred Mr. Grey, at his strangest and most awkward, to many other gentlemen at their most charming. It had even crossed her mind more than once—in moments of weakness and optimism—that Mr. Grey was exactly the sort of man who would have suited Roselind, had she been free. The idea had always been suppressed, because it was impossible, but enough of it lingered to make her wonder whether this particular strangeness did not have some connection to her niece. She had seen Mr. Grey staring at Roselind many times, and though his expression was often angry, it had struck her that it might be jealous anger. The tenderness in his looks, sometimes, was not lost on her either.

"You may say anything to me, Mr. Grey," she said after another moment's silence. But Mr. Grey only smiled gently and shook his head.

"In any other case, ma'am, you would be the first to hear my confidences. But now I am thinking of your family's happiness, and not my own."

Lady Agatha looked startled.

"Why, is there anything amiss, sir?"

"Not yet, I hope. And yet ... and yet I fear there may be going to be."

Another moment's hesitation saw the end of Lady Agatha's patience. She could wait hours for a confession of love, but not for news of her family.

"If you have something to say to me about my family, sir," she said quietly, "you had better say it now."

Mr. Grey nodded, and came back to his chair.

"I wish I could say more, your ladyship, that would be helpful. I think perhaps in a day or two ... in a day, I hope, I *shall* be able to say more, but at the moment, I am tied, not only by fear, but by uncertainty. Only I must say it!" Mr. Grey got up again and walked about in agitation. "I bear you too much goodwill to risk seeing you hurt, if it is in my power to avoid it." Mr. Grey paused for a moment. "How much do you know about Reginald Darn-ley?" he asked at last.

Lady Agatha was now leaning forward in her chair. "Why, only what everyone else knows," she replied. "Only ... I do not like him as well as anyone else, I think."

"And yet well enough to see him become your niece's husband? I mean, you have no greater objection to him than dislike?"

"It is objection enough, I think, where the happiness of one so dear to me is concerned."

"But why do you say nothing? Surely you are influential to your niece's choice? A word from you—it might do wonders!"

Lady Agatha shook her head sadly.

"I am afraid that is not the case, sir. A word from me would only increase everyone's distress."

Mr. Grey turned away in disgust. "Why, is she such a head-strong creature as that, that she will not listen to her aunt's sense?" he demanded curtly.

Lady Agatha bridled a little. She could hear no ill spoken of Roselind.

"You do not know her, sir. Roselind is the last creature in the world to call headstrong."

"And yet she is determined to marry a man her relations do not approve? That seems very like headstrong to me! It seems like rank stubbornness!"

"Oh, yes, she is very stubborn. Where the happiness of some-one else is concerned, she is very stubborn. You would not be-lieve it, sir, to look at that little upright figure, that sweet, gentle face . . . but my niece has the courage of a general! She is a little soldier, Mr. Grey, and with the sort of bravery one does not see much. It is not the sort which flaunts itself on the field of battle, with cannon fire and prancing horses, and which everyone loves to applaud. It is the kind hardly ever guessed at, and which demands more real strength of character than anything you are likely to see in wartime, for it demands utter constancy and unflagging energy. It shows itself in unexpected places—in drawing rooms and ballrooms, at the dinner table, and even in sleep. It is so quiet and draws so little attention to itself that it hardly ever is recognized. You look astonished, sir, to hear me speak this way of my niece. Doubtless you think I am exaggerating out of a prejudiced view, a dim-witted, female tenderness, but it is not so. How could you guess what is really the case?"

Mr. Grey had sat down again.

"It is certainly amazing to hear you talk thus, my lady. And yet, no matter how great my respect for you, I cannot really believe you!"

"No?" Lady Agatha had fire in her eyes, a most unusual condition for that soft-mannered lady. "Then let me tell you what will astonish you still more. You will see why I have said nothing to Roselind in these last weeks, although I dislike Mr. Darnley—nay, despise him!—in a way that makes me long to forbid the match! You will see why I can speak as I do of that child, and still not exaggerate, still not approach the whole truth!

"My brother, Mr. Grey, was a man much loved and admired in this country. He was thought highly of—by the same people who crawl at Darnley's feet—because he was handsome, and rich, and titled, and because he had no concern whatever for anyone besides himself. He was married for ten years to a woman who was really an angel, and until she died, I think he was capable of suppressing his natural dispositions, which were to drink too much, gamble to excess, dress himself with the foppery of a dandy, and

take pleasure in anything which appeased his immediate appe-
tites, to the exclusion of any serious ambition. He could have
been a great political figure in England, for he possessed a seat
in the House, and was by no means stupid, and blessed with that
elusive quality of charm which is capable of making men go to
their deaths. But instead, he chose to lead a life of utter deprav-
ity and sloth. His two children, Roselind and Albert, were left
to fend for themselves, cared for by a succession of tutors and
governesses, until Bertie was old enough to go away to Eton.

"No one thought much about his way of life—it was accounted, in this great society in which we live, perfectly normal.
For a man to live as he pleased, provided he was rich, did not
surprise anyone. And Iseleigh *was* rich—immensely so, by any
rational standard. He had lands in Scotland and the West Indies, as well as England, and these would have been inherited by
his son, providing ample wealth for many generations to come.
But Iseleigh neglected his holdings. He let them run to rack and
ruin, allowing for the inevitable dishonesty of his stewards to rob
him. He lived beyond even his income, and gambled furiously.
He cared as little for his own honor as for that of his children.
When he died, he left a legacy, not only of shame, but of poverty.
Bertie, Mr. Grey, will be of age in one year's time, and when he
comes into the 'vast Iseleigh holdings,' they will all have been
auctioned off at the block. My nephew is nearly penniless, sir.
Roselind wishes to marry Mr. Darnley to save her brother. It is
not, I think, a cowardly thing to do!"

Lady Agatha stopped speaking, as much to catch her breath as
anything. She sat staring at Mr. Grey, who was plainly speechless.

"What do you say now, sir? That she is a headstrong wretch,

a stubborn, spoilt girl? Or that she has more real courage than many men?"

Mr. Grey could not speak for a moment, but at last murmured, "My God! If I had only known! That is the only reason she wishes to marry him?"

Lady Agatha let out a short laugh.

"I think it is enough! But no—I do not think she would have contemplated it otherwise. At least ... at least not now. I am convinced she has got over her first infatuation with him. It was quite natural, I think, for a girl as sheltered as she has been, to have been a little swept away by his grand way of life."

A deep sigh escaped Mr. Grey's throat. He leaned back in his chair and passed one tanned hand across his eyes, and then shook his head a little, as if to shake off some long-held conviction.

"Poor child!" he murmured at last. "I suppose she is what you say. A little soldier, indeed! A very saint! And ... I believe you are right. She does not love him, really. It is a great weight off my mind."

Perplexed at this peculiar reaction to the intelligence, which, in truth, had not lightened Lady Agatha's burden one whit by communicating it, that lady gazed at him in confusion.

"May I ask what is a weight off your mind, sir?"

Mr. Grey looked startled, as though he had forgotten there was anyone else in the room.

"Why, that she is very brave, your ladyship! She may need all her courage, I think! But I am very late for an appointment. I am sorry to rush off in this fashion."

And with these words Mr. Grey bowed quickly and walked out. Lady Agatha sat quietly for several moments after he had gone, wondering at his peculiar behavior. Something very odd had struck her about Mr. Grey almost from the first moment she had seen him; it had been a peculiar trick of the eyebrows, when he talked, and something in the width and fullness of the mouth. She had not known at first what it was, although her subconscious mind must have been working at it, for all at once it came home to her.

"Good Lord!" she murmured with a sharp little intake of breath. "I wonder . . . But it is impossible! And yet . . . and yet perhaps it is not, perhaps not just what it*seems* to be."

The words would have meant nothing to any listener, save perhaps one. But to Lady Agatha, sitting very straight behind her desk, a missing piece suddenly fit into a puzzle. She had not even known it was a puzzle until just now, or not, at any rate, one that could ever be resolved. But now she sat mentally calculating the number of pieces needed to complete the design. It was an old pattern, much obscured by weather and talk, and yet it was one. How much it might affect the fate of an old friend, and of a dear relative, she was unsure, but it made her very still, and rather frightened.

16

There was a concert held in the evening in the upper rooms, which everyone attended, or so it seemed at first. The Banforths went, with their niece and nephew, and Georgina Devonshire came in a moment before the music started, with her little entourage. Reginald Darnley was there, and Mrs. Hogarth, who hovered over everyone, with hints about her great friend Lady Roselind and the match which she had single-handedly arranged. Even Sir Walter and Lady Chumley, who had been little glimpsed since they had lost a prospective son-in-law, were among the audience. Miss Clarissa Chumley was more radiant than ever, for she had at last convinced her mama that marrying a poor captain whom she dearly loved was better than not marrying at all. She sat gazing gently up into the captain's face with her huge blue eyes; and with her froth of pale blue lace, her lovely flaxen waves, and the obvious adoration she bore the young man, she seemed like a soft cloud. The sight did Roselind, preoccupied with other worries, a little good, for she had always hoped Miss Chumley had not been hurt by Mr. Darnley's desertion.

But other thoughts came flooding in on her a moment later.

Mr. Darnley took a place just behind her, leaning forward now and again to murmur some comment on the music, and to wonder, more often than he needed to, if she was well-placed, if she had a clear view of the orchestra, and if she were not too warm. Glancing about, she could not help but wonder at the absence of Mr. Grey. He had been used to accompanying them to many of their evening entertainments, but now he was nowhere to be seen.

The interlude came, and she walked out into the marble foyer behind her aunt and uncle. Mr. Darnley stepped behind *her*. His presence was impossible to forget. She felt it about her like a kind of heavy weight, and yet the weight was not reassuring, as it ought to have been.

"Do you enjoy the music?" he asked as soon as they had positioned themselves in a space between two pillars that was out of the way of the crowd. She replied that she did, and attempted a little desultory conversation on the virtues of Bach's preludes. But the subject could not hold her attention. She found her eyes wandering repeatedly about the room, and returning with a little sinking, hollow feeling to her companion. Her smiles to him were all forced, but he seemed not to notice. Mr. Darnley was regarding her with one of his deep, penetrating looks, which had once had the power to make her heart beat faster. Now she could only manage to see it without looking immediately away; it was so false, so devoid of any real warmth! And still she could not help longing for a glimpse of another face....

"I have a concert room in Derbyshire," he was saying now. "It has been vacant too long, but if a great lover of music would wish me to open it up again ... it is a pity to have it go to waste."

"Do not you like music, sir?"

"Oh, yes. One must like music. It is like painting and sculpture. One needs it about one, in order to be civilized."

"I never thought of it that way!" declared Roselind. "I always considered music one of the great joys of life. If it were only civilized, it would be no better than a piece of flatware—a dish to keep one's meal from falling everywhere. But it must be more than that, indeed it must! Why does it make one's heart leap up so, to hear it, if it is not stronger and deeper than anything else? What gives it so much power over the mind and reason, and makes it affect the heart and spirit as it does?"

Mr. Darnley looked at her in amusement.

"What a passionate little creature you are," he drawled. "I never knew you had such spirit." But it sounded more, to Roselind's ears, like a criticism than a compliment. She had spoken with rather too much energy, she was aware, and now flushed and grew silent.

"It is only," she mumbled, "that I am very fond of music."

"And so you should be," said Mr. Darnley, smiling down at her. In a quieter tone he added, "It will be a great excuse for me to give concerts in Derbyshire. Do you know that district?"

"I was there once with my aunt," said Roselind, "but it was only a short visit."

"A beautiful countryside, but unfortunately I have not spent much time there in these past years. It seems very foolish for a bachelor to go all alone to the country, unless he has a party of guests. Of course, it is a different thing altogether for a married man...."

Roselind looked up. The tone, the expression on her companion's face, was unmistakable. She knew suddenly that the moment she had waited for, prayed for even, had arrived. But the

situation was so altogether different from the way she had imagined it. Even the room full of people was the exact opposite of the
scene she had envisioned for a proposal. That scene, rehearsed in
her imagination so many times, had always taken place in a quiet
arbor, with no sound but the singing of birds and the voice of
her lover. What could have been more different than this grand
hallway, crowded with fashionable people—the very essence of
Reginald Darnley's world? It was the world he was at home in,
and the one she should have to make hers. There would be no
more secluded walks in the country, no more leisure to read, and
think, and choose her own friends. She would be Lady Roselind
Darnley, fretted over by the ton, made much of by hostesses, and
as much a prisoner of their affections as if she had been a crim-
inal instead of a wife.

The declaration came in due time. It came with all the accompanying looks, and smiles, and meaningful changes in tone
required of a proposal of marriage, and yet it seemed as empty
as the wind to Roselind.

Mr. Darnley took her hand very lightly in his own broad brown
one, but yet out of sight of any of the crowd, and murmured, "My
lady, I have hoped for some time to tell you that of all the women
in the world, you are the dearest to me. Your smiles and laughter
are my joy, your sudden frowns and sadness my damnation. If
you will consent to be my wife, I shall be the happiest man in
the world, and if you refuse … But there, I cannot think of that!"

This last was spoken with a sudden clutching at his chest, as
if a pain had already asserted itself in that strong bosom at the
mere suggestion. Roselind was for the moment unable to speak,
and Mr. Darnley, evidently thinking some further elaboration
was required, proceeded. "I knew at once, when I first saw you in

Devonshire, at your father's house, that you were the only woman in the world I could ever admire. Even then, when you were silent and untamed as a young deer, I knew my fate was marked. And then to have seen you again—what a fortunate stroke brought me to Bath this summer!"

"Sir!" Roselind broke in, her panic at last giving way to urgency and the need to speak. "I beg you will listen to me for a while before you proceed!"

Mr. Darnley seemed rather startled by this interruption, and stared at her.

"I cannot allow you to do me so much honor, sir, without telling you . . . Indeed, I hardly know how to begin. But," she began again with a resolute look, "tell you I must. I am afraid I have misrepresented myself to you. I have seemed what I am not."

Mr. Darnley looked very startled indeed. In a cold voice he demanded to know what Lady Roselind was talking about.

"Only," said Roselind miserably, unable, now that the matter was at hand, to think clearly, "only that I am not what I seem. You think I am Lady Roselind Arden, brother of a rich earl, daughter of another, and able to bring to you not only titles and honors, but wealth. And yet I am not this lucky creature, but something else altogether. I know it is my own fault that you have been deceived. I should have told you long ago what I am, and yet . . . the happiness of my brother has depended on my not doing so. The whole world has been deluded as to our position in the world—"

"Are you not Lady Roselind Arden, then?" demanded Darnley very sharply. A look of disgust and contempt came over his face, which had the effect of making his mouth form itself into a hard, cold line, almost a cruel expression.

"Oh, yes! Of course I am, but . . . how can I say it? My father died a year ago, leaving a heritage of poverty! My brother has hardly any of the fortune that was his by right. I have my own settlement intact, but that must go to him, of course—"

Mr. Darnley put back his head and laughed.

"Is that all?" he demanded. "I should have known Iseleigh would run through his money, at the rate he was going! By Jove, you nearly put me in a panic! I thought you were going to say you weren't his daughter by birth!" he laughed delightedly.

Roselind was rather shocked at this suggestion.

"Of course I am his daughter, sir! What did you think? But about the money, you see . . . Bertie shall be poverty-struck, and I must help him—"

"Needs a bit of blunt, does he?" said Darnley, eyeing the lady he loved with a mildly calculating expression. "I always suspected your papa would run into trouble at the rate he was going. I told him, in fact, a dozen times, to have a care. These West India properties don't run themselves, and stewards are very prone to stealing anything they can lay their hands on. Let me see, I believe the chief estate—Windham—is worth about a hundred thousand pounds, is it not?"

"I am not sure, but I believe a great deal of money is needed to save it—"

"Aye. Still, I warrant most of the problem is lodged in poor management. And so that is the only trouble?"

Roselind was aghast. It seemed like enough trouble to her! "Yes." She nodded.

"And you are still Lady Roselind?"

"Yes."

"Well, you see, there is no problem at all. All you must say is, you will be my wife."

"I am deeply honored by your offer, sir," said Roselind, feeling somehow that matters had left her own hands, and unsure whether to laugh or cry at the ease with which it had all been settled. "Still, I should like a day to think it over. I am not ... I am not perfectly convinced that you are not only being too gallant. Perhaps you had better consider the matter more deeply . . ."

Darnley smiled sardonically.

"I assure you, my lady, I seldom do anything without thinking it over very carefully indeed. I have planned this—indeed, it is not the decision of a moment."

The bell rang, and before anything more could be said, the crowd swept them up on its way back into the concert room. Roselind sat through the remainder of the program without any thought to the music. Not all her love of Bach could raise her spirits, which had sunk unaccountably low. Her lectures to herself were to no avail, nor did the sight of Bertie, sitting tight-lipped beside her, help. "Now I have got all I want," she said to herself. "Mr. Darnley has been more than gallant! He is willing to do everything, and Bertie will never, I hope, know the difference. He and his Miss Quimby will live happily ever after...."

But what would her own life be like? The sight, a moment later, of Mr. Grey slipping quietly into the hall and taking a seat near the corridor, answered her question. There could be no happiness without his regard! Indeed, it had never been so clear. All in a rush, Roselind understood her own feelings. It had taken the fulfillment of all her previous wishes to make her see her one real desire. When the word "husband" came into her head, only one face flashed before her. It was not a dark face, with black hair and eyes, but a countenance all light and shadow, with blue eyes which could be merrier than any others in the world, and a glance which, when it was critical, had the power to reduce her to misery. In vain did she combat the image of that censoring look, and yet she could not get it out of her mind. Behind her, Reginald Darnley was smiling to himself.

17

Roselind lay awake that night long after the last of the household had drifted into sleep. The house was silent, and seemed to echo with her thoughts. Through her window floated the mingled sounds of a summer evening—a herd of crickets, and the lonely song of a nightingale fluting in a mimosa tree no more than a dozen yards from her bed, which lay in a stream of moonlight near the window. It was as though she were a prisoner, kept by force from the happy world outside; that she had imprisoned herself by choice only made her heart ache a little more.

No matter how she tried, she could not erase from her mind's eye the sight of that one face, the face of Mr. Grey, as he had given her one long, deep look as he came into the concert hall. How she longed to impute every kind of feeling to that look! How she would have loved to think that in those eloquent blue eyes there had been some longing, just as there had been in her own! But even if she could—and as it happened, she was too honest to think there had been anything but curiosity in his look—it would be to no avail. She was as good as promised now, to a man whom, if she did not loathe, she knew she could never love.

Still, Mr. Darnley had been more than kind. It was, in fact, the very method of his kindness which bothered her. He had nearly leaped at the idea of salvaging Bertie from poverty. Indeed, so ready had he been that he might have planned it all along. Certainly he had shown no signs of surprise at the fate of the Iseleigh fortunes. As Roselind turned over all of this in her mind, as her legs searched out some cool, soothing spot in the sheets, she wondered how she could tell her aunt what had transpired. She did not even know whether or not she was engaged—she had asked for a day or two, but Darnley had laughed it off. She wondered if she had any time left to break the news in her own way, or if, by the morning, everyone in Bath would be apprised of the engagement. There was one thing she must certainly do, which she had delayed doing for some days already, and that was to visit Miss Quimby, to tell her how glad she was of her brother's choice, and, as a future sister-in-law ought, to take her own tidings.

It sometimes happens between women at their first meeting (much more often, in fact, than between lovers) that an instant understanding is struck up between them. Something in the face or manner of each strikes a chord, which makes their future intimacy a certainty. This is exactly what had happened to Roselind on her first seeing Maude Quimby. Although she had seen her only once, and then for under an hour, she had no doubt about the other's character. She had known at once, even though she had never known anyone like Miss Quimby before, that they would be good friends. Roselind had never had a great female confidante before, save her aunt, and she had really longed for one. It was a great comfort to have a friend to whom one could pour out one's soul, and all the little troubles in one's life, and with whom one could share the great joys and sorrows, as well as the small ones. It was as much, therefore, out of a desire to share her thoughts just now, as to congratulate Bertie's betrothed, that she escaped from the breakfast table the next morning and asked for the carriage to go to Elizabeth Street. Lady Agatha looked more than pleased that she was not going anywhere where she might be likely to see Reginald Darnley, and instantly acquiesced.

Lady Agatha asked her to stop by the milliner's on her way, to see about a bonnet which was meant to be ready. The milliner was occupied with another lady when Roselind walked in, and then it took half an hour to determine that the bonnet was not finished, and so it was nearly eleven o'clock by the time Roselind started up the flight of dark, rickety stairs toward Miss Quimby's rooms. The place was very shabby, but its poverty did not affect her so much as it had done before. In the last weeks Roselind had experienced enough of human pain and suffering to look on the suffering of others with less horror and indignation than pity. She achieved the landing at last, and after a little searching about— for the candle which had been on the stairwell before had been extinguished—she found the door and knocked.

She did this before she heard that there were voices already inside. It was Miss Quimby's voice, and that of a gentleman, and when the knock sounded, the talking ceased. A scuffling sound ensued, and after a moment Miss Quimby's voice called out to know who it was.

"Roselind Arden," said she, and waited for another moment. There seemed to be a hesitation, and then Miss Quimby bid her come in.

The door opened onto a strange scene. The little room was as bright and cheerful as ever, with its scanty furnishings well dusted, and on the couch in the middle of the room, Maude Quimby was lying under her rug. But what struck Roselind instantly, and what, seeing it, nearly made her race out again, and down the stairs, was the figure of Mr. Grey, kneeling beside the sofa, with a look of inexpressible excitement in his eyes. The excitement would have been supportable, if it had not been mingled with joy—an expression of such immense happiness that it could not be mistaken. Roselind's entrance caused the expression to die a little, and Mr. Grey got hastily to his feet, but not before Roselind was so overcome with mortification that she hardly knew where to look. She glanced from one to the other of them, and saw that in Miss Quimby's eyes there were tears also, which seemed to be of happiness.

Now Roselind really wished to fly out of the room. It was quite clear what she had walked into. Here, if there ever was one, was a love scene. The idea made her first grow crimson and then white. And yet her first thoughts were not of Bertie's happiness and the deception which seemed to have been worked on him, but of her own! She could not bear to lift her eyes to Mr. Grey's, which seemed to be regarding her with curiosity. Her only desire was to get away instantly, and yet she was rooted to the spot.

"I ... I had better come back another time!" she blurted out, starting to turn around, but Mr. Grey cut in: "I was just going away in any case, my lady." If he had only looked her in the eye quite calmly, she might still have believed that there was some plausible excuse for this conduct! But Mr. Grey was as flustered as she was herself, and taking his hat up from the chair where he had dropped it, he raised Miss Quimby's hand to his lips, and walked out!

Now Roselind was left alone with the invalid, and she would

have been less human than she was if she had known what to say, or how, to the woman who seemed to be encouraging her brother's love, while all the time she had given her heart elsewhere. There was no time to understand the situation, but even in the moment in which Roselind stood, with her face quite white, before Miss Quimby, the idea occurred to her that they must have been lovers all along. "She must have used Bertie, thinking to marry him for his money!" she exclaimed to herself, looking in horror at that beautiful face, which even now was quite composed and gazing at her very fondly.

"I am so glad you have come, my lady," said Miss Quimby with shining eyes. "I have such news! Such an extraordinary degree of happiness in my heart!"

Was this the way to address the sister of the man she had just betrayed? Or was Miss Quimby so altogether heartless and cold that she could bear to smile even while she was breaking hearts?

Miss Quimby was holding out her hand, and Roselind, too bewildered to know what else to do, found herself taking it. Standing thus, with her hand in the hand of a woman she believed to be of all the creatures the cruelest in the world, she stared down at the exquisite face, so pure and seemingly incapable of calculation, and all her horror was in her eyes.

But Miss Quimby did not notice it at first. She was full of her own news, and some of it, at least, came out with a rush.

"You cannot imagine what I am feeling at this moment!" she exclaimed, squeezing Roselind's hand. "It is so much like happiness, I hardly know where to look! Oh, my dear, dear friend— you must excuse my calling you that, for indeed I felt at the first moment I saw you that you *were* my friend—I wish I could tell you everything! But I have promised to be discreet for another day or two—and yet, who knows? Perhaps even this afternoon I may be able to proclaim it to all the world! Oh, to have suffered so much, imagined so much evil, and at last to know that it may yet be a little better than it might have been—it nearly makes up for everything!"

Roselind did not understand a word.

"Where . . . where is my brother?" she stammered. "Where is Bertie?"

"Bertie?" Miss Quimby seemed to have forgotten *him*. "Oh, I believe he went off to do some errand. I do not know, in truth, exactly where he is! What a wonderful thing life is, to be sure, my lady!"

Roselind had at last managed to collect herself a little. Very firmly she withdrew her hand from Miss Quimby's and walked away to the window. She knew what she must do. If she had felt before like flying, now she wanted only to stay long enough to speak her mind and to determine exactly how much Miss Quimby had abused her brother. She was very angry now, very angry indeed, and she could barely control the emotion which threatened to overtake her. Her voice trembled with feeling as she asked, avoiding Miss Quimby's eyes. "How long have you known Mr. Grey?"

Miss Quimby laughed, a very innocent-sounding laugh.

"Good heavens! I believe I have known him forever—and yet I only just became acquainted with him! It is very odd, isn't it? I can barely acknowledge an hour when I have *not* known him! It seems to me that I have always hoped to know him. as I do now, even when there was no hope to hang onto!"

These riddles were driving Roselind mad.

"I mean," she said in a cold voice, and still looking away from the gay young lady on the sofa, "how long have you been . . . how long have you been intimate with him? When did you know you loved him?"

Miss Quimby's voice was very gentle as she said, "Oh, I have loved him forever! But in truth, how could anyone not love him? Even when I had only heard of his existence, and the love he was borne by those who knew him very well—even then, I must have loved him, if not for his own sake, for his brother's. In truth, I never knew what a wonderful man he was! How gentle and kind, and what a reserve of strength was in his character—how selfless he could be!"

This was too much for Roselind, and she burst out, "I am very glad to hear that you call his conduct selfless, Miss Quimby! I suppose you think it is selfless of you, too! Ah, yes, very selfless indeed—the very height of generosity! To accept the attentions of my brother, allowing him to think your heart was his, and his heart your own dear possession, when in fact you were making love all the time to his friend, to Mr. Grey!"

In the course of this speech Roselind had wheeled about, and now stood panting a little from her emotions, and staring very angrily at Miss Quimby.

This lady watched the scene in utter astonishment. She looked up at the pretty dark-haired girl, with her small, upright figure, and gray eyes ablaze with outraged innocence, and all she could say was, "Oh!"

"Is not this so, Miss Quimby? Do not tell me you have not done as I say. Do not tell me it was all a little charade, which only *happened* to look like love! I do not think men very often go on their knees to ladies they have only a passing acquaintance with!"

"Oh!" exclaimed Miss Quimby again, her eyes wide with astonishment. "I believe I see what you think!"

"Do you indeed?" inquired Roselind, and never before in that sweet, melodious voice had such a weight of sarcasm mingled with so cutting an edge. "Do you indeed? I am very glad for it! I could . . . indeed, I could even forgive you, for *you* are so unfortunate, and it is almost understandable how you might wish to take advantage of your friends—but Mr. Grey! Mr. Grey, who has lectured me about my wishing to marry for money, and who has never hesitated to be contemptuous of me, although my motives have all been to help my brother—how *he* could deceive us!" And with this Roselind burst into a flood of tears and sank into the nearest chair. All her heart was poured out in the stormy sobs which followed, and all the strength and resilience she had shown the world in these last weeks gave way to a flood of natural feeling. Poor thing, it was no wonder she had mistaken Mr. Grey's attitude for love, and Miss Quimby's for cruel dispassion! She had barely had three nights of undisturbed sleep in the last fortnight. When she had not been worrying over Mr. Darnley, she had been worrying about her brother, and when Mr. Darnley had begun to come around, she had started worrying about herself and her own heart. She had never had a moment's rest in all this time, and now the great hurricane of feeling which had been building up behind her brave little smile had no choice but to give way. For several moments she sat sobbing in this way, and while she sobbed, Miss Quimby watched her, torn between pity and understanding.

Miss Quimby did not interrupt the storm of tears, but let it subside as it could. She, too, had known some suffering in her time, and she, too, had sometimes let down the barriers of courage when she had been alone. And so it was with very, very kind eyes, and with no resentment whatever, that she said at last, when the worst of the sobs had died down a little to a faint hiccuping noise, "I see how it is, my dear friend. You are in love with him, aren't you?"

Roselind nodded blindly, incapable of any pretension.

"And you do not love Reginald Darnley?"

Roselind shook her head. "It is only ... it is only that Bertie has got no fortune, and I must try to help him," she murmured incoherently.

"Ah," said Miss Quimby, frowning, "I see. Bertie has got no fortune, and so you thought you would marry Reginald Darnley to save him. But meanwhile you fell in love with Mr. Grey, and that was not very good, was it? Because he is not so rich as Darnley, and you knew nothing about him. Nothing, I mean, except that he was very handsome and very kind."

"And that he hated me in any case," mumbled Roselind.

"But what made you think that?"

"Well, it is perfectly obvious! He is always looking at me in that angry way, and with that odious contemptuous look! But then, it does not matter in any case, does it? Because he loves you!"

Miss Quimby pushed the rug away from her legs and made to sit up. She tried, in fact, to do more, for she wanted to go and comfort her friend, but her legs were not up to the task, and so she only sat up very eagerly and said, "But that is not true, my dear! Not at all! I mean, Mr. Grey certainly does not love me, and, except insofar as I love anyone so capable of good as he is, I do not love him!"

Roselind looked up in disbelief.

"I don't believe you."

"But it is perfectly true! Oh, dear"—and Miss Quimby could not help laughing—"it must have looked very odd, walking in on us as you did! Quite like a lovers' *tête-à-tête!* Oh, dear! And I am forbidden to tell you what it really was! Oh, dear, I think really this is too bad!" But Miss Quimby was laughing delightedly, and not at all as if she were dismayed. "However," she said when she had calmed herself a little, "I think I may say this: Mr. Grey does not love me, nor I him. I love your brother, and, so far as I can understand, he wishes me to be his wife. Of course I shall not go that far until he is of age, for he may yet find some other lady he likes better, but I shall certainly consent if he offers again when he is twenty-one."

"And you do not mind," said Roselind doubtfully, "that he has no money? I mean, you did not count upon his being rich?"

Miss Quimby looked very startled.

"I hope," she said very seriously, "that you never thought it was his money I was in love with! I have been poor too long not to understand that happiness has very little to do with how many carriages one keeps!"

Now it was Roselind's turn to stare, and as she did so, she blushed to a deep shade of crimson.

"How will you ever forgive me!" she cried with all the warmth of feeling in her heart. "I have abused you so horribly, and now perhaps you will never really think kindly of me! Oh, my dearest Miss Quimby, my dear friend ... I am very, very happy for you! It is what I came to tell you in the first place, and what I should have done, instead of going on in this crazy way! Will you ever, do you think, be able to forgive me?"

Miss Quimby did not need half so much of an apology as this, and she nodded her head eagerly, and stretched out her hand, which Roselind took and pressed to her bosom, with great happiness. There followed a great many murmurs of mutual regard and esteem, and of course friendship, and the kind of mutual complimenting which so often takes place between new friends, which is very touching to hear, but perhaps a little tedious to those who are not directly concerned.

It was half an hour before either of the young ladies was capable of any really sensible remark, and by that time Roselind had got over the first of her relief at discovering that Mr. Grey and Miss Quimby were not really in love, and that her brother was after all still destined for happiness. It has been a great joy to discover that Miss Quimby was not the least distressed to hear about the Iseleigh fortunes, and yet the knowledge, while it assured Roselind of her future sister-in-law's generosity, could not comfort her own suspicions that, however much in love the two might be, they could not very well live on air. Air was very well for lovers, but it did not do married people much good. It did not feed them, or pay their servants, it had never been known to hire carriages and horses, or to pay the butcher, and no reputable tailor had ever taken it in for payment.

It was with this in mind that Roselind at last tore herself away from an embrace and said, "Well, I am very glad! But still, you know, I think you ought to have some money. I have got fifty thousand pounds of my own, which I will give you when I marry Mr. Darnley. I think . . . Indeed, he already intends doing something more for Bertie—"

"What!" cried Maude Quimby. "You are not going to marry Darnley, are you?"

Roselind did not look very happy as she said that it was nearly all arranged, but she did look determined not to be dissuaded.

"He did me the honor of asking me to be his wife last evening," she said, reminding herself of all the good intentions she had formed of behaving as if she really wanted to be his wife. "And I accepted him—at least, I gave him to understand that I would do so in a day or two's time."

Miss Quimby was looking even more determined than her new friend. "You really *must not* accept him, your ladyship," she said firmly. "I cannot begin to tell you how many are the reasons against your doing so—"

"It is really all arranged," said Roselind, smiling bravely, "and say what you will, you cannot live on air. Even were you content to do so, I could not let Bertie live like an impoverished peer. There are so many of them about, and they always are being laughed at. Besides, there are the children to think of, and your children's children. It is not only a question of *your* happiness. I am convinced," she said with a smile, "that you and my brother might be quite happy to be poor, with your cheerful natures, but there are my family's ancestral properties. They must not be allowed to go to ruin or to be auctioned off to anyone who can pay for them."

Miss Quimby looked very earnestly into Roselind's face and said, "I believe you, my dear friend, and I believe that you feel as strongly as you say, and, indeed, that you should. But only think—think what you are sacrificing! A real love, a husband you may feel proud of, and children born out of that mutual love and regard—the whole wealth of feeling and mature contentment which only a marriage founded on real devotion can provide! *Think what you are giving up!*"

"Yes," said Roselind, turning away, for she was really incapable of looking into those searching eyes again, "I have thought of all that, and, believe me, I am very well aware of what I am about! If there were any other way ... I hope you do not think I am capable of marrying only for mercenary reasons, for I assure you I could not! No, no, I have thought about it all a great deal, and although I do not love Mr. Darnley quite as I should perhaps like to, yet I am capable of feeling regard for him. He is at bottom an honorable man who has proved himself more than generous to his friends. Indeed, he has already been more than generous to me! I believe he expects to help my brother in a quite wonderfully generous way. So you see, I have at least some of those feelings which a wife must have for her husband, and what is wanting now, I am convinced I shall be able to give him before very long. A great part of love is rooted in habit, and that I want to love him is very sure! I shall be the best wife in the world to him, I promise—"

"Oh, I am very sure of that," said Maude Quimby. "I only wonder what he will do for you in return? A sum of money—is that all you expect? But what about tenderness, and companionship, what about understanding and love? Do those sentiments mean nothing to you?"

"They mean a great deal," said Roselind softly.

"Then I beg of you, give up the idea!" cried Maude. "There will be some other way, I am sure of it! Oh, if only I were at liberty to tell you all that I know! *Then* you should see how right I am! Only ... only, do not say anything yet, please! Give us another day before you tell him your answer! Do that for me, will you please?"

Roselind did not really see what good another day would do any of them, but Miss Quimby was so imploring in her looks, and really seemed to put so much store in the promised twenty-four hours, that at last she nodded.

"Very well," she said, "I shall try to hold him off. But he may urge me along, you know ... and then, I cannot risk losing him!"

Miss Quimby murmured her accord, and embraced her friend once more before the other left.

"Roselind," she said, just as that young lady was walking to the door, "if you see Mr. Grey, be kind to him! I know he does not hate you. You know ... it is only something else, something which I shall tell you tomorrow, perhaps, which has made him very strange of late, and taxed his good humor."

Roselind smiled, and nodded, and though she did not understand, she agreed that she would be kind to Mr. Grey. She wondered, as she walked down the stairs, if her kindness would mean anything to him. Once or twice, perhaps, she had thought she had detected a tenderness in his looks, but these moments had been so few, and had been so swallowed up by his cynical manner, that she thought really she had only imagined them. And yet she could not help feeling elated to know that he was not in love with another woman, after all. At least, not with Miss Quimby. The idea that there might be another lady engrossed her so much that she never saw, as she was stepping out into the sunlight of the street, the black lacquered phaeton of Mr. Darnley pull into an alleyway a little down the road from where her own carriage waited. Nor did she, as she waited to cross the street, notice a furtive figure creep up behind her. In a moment a strong arm had grasped her by the waist, and a hand was over her mouth. There was no one else in that section of the street, and her own coachman had fallen into a doze in the box. There was no one, therefore, to see Lady Roselind dragged into the same doorway from which she had just emerged a second before, followed by the sinister-looking figure of a broad-shouldered man with black eyes and hair, a cruel smile upon his swarthy face.

18

Mr. Grey had left Miss Quimby, as we have seen, in some confusion. It was true that the sudden appearance of Lady Roselind
Arden had thrown him, for a moment, off his guard, and although he had not, as that lady had at first presumed, been in the
act of making love to his friend's affianced, the two had been interrupted in the midst of a very moving scene. It had been a reconciliation of sorts, though neither one had ever met the other,
but only heard so much, through the same informant, that it was
as if they had been acquainted for years. The meeting, which had
taken place early in the morning in front of Lord Iseleigh, had
astonished no one more heartily than that young man. He had
stood back, after making his first introductions (somewhat tim-
idly, for he dearly hoped these two would like each other, being
each important personages in his own heart), and watched in
awe while Mr. Grey first stood perfectly still, then clapped a hand
to his forehead and cried out.

"By God!" he had exclaimed, incapable of any more eloquent
expression. And then "By God!" again. At last he had walked
very slowly to Miss Quimby's side (she, at first, had smiled in

a welcoming but not a recognizing fashion, but now her gentle face began to show signs of disbelief, and then astonishment) and looked her keenly in the face, as if he had been examining some rare art work. After a moment more of this he had taken out a little gold locket from his pocket-book—the very same object he had been examining that day in the park at Laura Place when Lady Roselind had surprised him—and held it up, as if to compare the little image painted there to the magnificent countenance of flesh and blood beside it.

The comparison was all favorable, it seemed—although even Mr. Grey, who had not known Miss Quimby when the miniature was taken, had been forced to admit the live girl had lost much of her color and plumpness in the intervening years. And yet the real face, if it was thin, and pale, and marked a little by hardship and sickness, had gained more than it had lost. There was a delicacy of feature, a gentle wisdom in the immense brown eyes, and overall the softening which suffering and time sometimes give a face, which, when the owner of the face is as beautiful in her soul as in the regularity of cheek, nose, and brow, can often add to its loveliness. Mr. Grey had fallen in love with the little painted image long ago—what seemed now like aeons ago—in a savage hut many miles away from civilization. His first glimpse of it had come in the midst of the most emotional moment of his life, what had been both a reconciliation with and a final parting from the one person he had loved, admired, and longed to emulate more than any other in the world. And so it had been some days before he had taken out the locket again and perused it at length. Even then the gentle gaze, the noble, delicate features, surrounded by their cloud of pale curls, had moved him. The direct look, so innocent and happy, could have torn his heart in two even if he had not known that face to be the one most loved by his own beloved brother. In the next weeks, aboard the frigate which had brought him at last to the shores of his own country, he had studied that face until he knew it better than his own. The face had come to be, for him, a kind of legend, and a goal. All through the homeward journey, and even after he had landed, on the hard ride from Southampton to London, and from London to Bath, the face had moved before him in the air. Only two things—that face and his brother's dying words—had kept him alive, he felt, since then.

"Find her, my dear Peter, take care of her, if you love me!" had driven him homeward, kept him through nights deprived of sleep, through days without food, and weeks without tranquillity, and had only given place to the last words: "But beware of Darnley." And so Peter had ridden at once to Bath, which had been the last place his brother had been seen in, and where he hoped he might find the owner of that face. For weeks he had scoured every part of the city, but without any glimpse of her. And now—now, through the sheerest piece of luck—he had been conducted to her very side!

"*You* are Maude Quimby?" he had gasped, and held up the locket.

Miss Quimby had been so stunned by the sight she had not known what to do. She nodded her head, and blinked, and tears sprang to her eyes, and she tried to say something, but it would not come out. Her first glimpse of Mr. Grey had told her nothing. The tall, slender, beautifully formed figure, with the hair so blond, the eyes so blue, had at first struck her only as pleasing. But almost at once she had noticed something else, something so ephemeral that it might never have been noticed by one who did not know another face and figure so well. In fact, feature and figure had little to do with the resemblance, for in truth Peter hardly bore any trace of Roderick's looks. But it had been inescapable, nevertheless. No other pair of eyes could twinkle like those boys', no smile ever curled a set of lips in a more endearing manner, no dimple ever appeared just in the cleft of the chin just so. And gradually, as Mr. Grey had spoken, the resemblance became so strong it nearly made her cry out. His voice, his habit of smiling on one side of his face more than on the other, the artless sincerity in his look, made her feel for a moment that a dead man had sprung back to life.

It had been some minutes before Bertie, between all the cries, and beginnings of confessions made by his friends, could begin to understand what was going forward. But at last Miss Quimby had broken off her questions—for she had a great many to ask—and held out her hand to him to join them.

"Bertie," she had said with shining eyes, "your Mr. Grey is a very wonder! I have made up my mind already to love him!"

Mr. Grey, at this, had put back his head and laughed, and exclaimed, "No more than I adore your fiancée, my lord! And now, if you will pardon me, perhaps I had better tell you who I am."

Bertie had been all wonderment as he heard the tale told, but after many assurances that this was all true, and that Mr. Grey had been forced into deception in order to avenge his brother's death, he rallied his forces and grew solemn.

"But if this is true, Grey—I mean to say, Peter—what is to be done about Darnley?"

And then he had looked at Maude Quimby, whose face grew equally serious with these words, and suggested she tell the story of that man.

Mr. Grey heard it all, and a great scowl began to darken his eyes. At the end of it, and after he had put one or two keen questions, he leaned back in his chair and was silent for a minute or two. His companions watched him eagerly, for there was that in the fair-headed man's presence which spoke of authority.

After a while he had said, "I know, and have known all along, that Darnley was the villain in all of this. And yet I have had nothing to go by. I still, except for this testimony, have no absolute proof, and yet it helps me know where to look." After a moment he had added, "Iseleigh, are you up to a little difficult maneuvering?"

Bertie had nodded his head very eagerly, and Peter said, "Very well. I think we have got precious little time. Where did you say your brother was at work, Miss Quimby? Ah, yes—in Cheap Street. Go you, then, Iseleigh, to Cheap Street, and wait for him to come out. Take your groom, or a servant, and keep him well in view, but send the servant to me as soon as you see where he is going. I do not want to surprise him and make him rush off. If he does not know who we are, he will certainly take to his heels, for I think he is living in deadly fear of Darnley and all of Darnley's people. Send for me at Pulteney Street, where I have an errand to do, and then I shall tell you what is next."

Bertie had gone off immediately, only promising his beloved that he would take great care of himself, which he agreed to do with some reluctance, and his friend and Maude Quimby were left alone for another moment, to assure themselves that they had not been dreaming. Peter Montague had gone down upon his knees, and kissed Maude Quimby's hand, and told her a little of what had been in his heart these last six months, since he had seen his brother die. He had sworn to avenge that brother's death

once more, and kissing her hand again, and swearing that everything would come out right in the end, so help him, God, he had
been about to leave when Lady Roselind had burst in.

The sight of the young lady had brought another subject to
the gentleman's mind. It had been one which had begun to take
up his heart increasingly in the last weeks, and which he had
tried to put aside with little success. The obvious dismay in her
eyes when she had seen them together had done more to cheer
him than anything. It had been a kind of glimmer, which she
had never shown him before, that he might mean more to her
than he had ever dared to hope. It is true he had been confused
at being found out in that awkward position—which indeed
looked very suspicious, if the observer were looking for suspicious conduct—but he never suspected what she had guessed.
Indeed, all he had seen had been a shocked look, a blush, and
then a pallor which might almost have meant anything. But the
long, deep, questioning look she had given him could not be interpreted many ways. The hurt in her eyes was clear, and yet it
raised his hopes—although Peter was not a man to take comfort
from inflicting pain on a lady he had been learning to regard very
tenderly of late. Still, a sudden shock may often reveal feelings
which have hitherto been kept well hidden, and in that moment
of embarrassment Peter had taken some hope from the look on
Roselind's face.

The idea made his heart leap up, but he quelled the sensation
instantly. "There is much to be done before I am free to think of
the future," he told himself. "So much of the past to be dug up,
and given a decent burial, before I shall be able to think of *that!*"
And the future was still very muddy, nearly as muddy as the past.

Peter went directly from Miss Quimby's rooms to Pulteney

Street, where he intended to do something he had been putting off a great while too long. He found Lady Agatha Banforth in the morning room, working at her letters. She looked up when he came in, and welcomed him.

"My dear Mr. Grey! I am very glad to see you, but I think Bertie is away this morning."

"I came to call upon you, your ladyship," said Peter, walking over to a chair, and then, changing his mind, moving to the window. "I came, in fact, to tell you something I have put off doing far too long. I cannot help feeling that, although I have received nothing but kindness from you, it has been repaid only by deceit. And so I have come to bare my soul, with the very real wish that you will not judge me too harshly when you see what made me pretend to be what I was not."

Lady Agatha looked very surprised indeed, and begged him to go on.

"It is very simple, my lady," said Peter from the window. "Only that I am not what I have pretended to be. My name is not Grey at all, and everything I have told you about myself has been false."

The young man stole a glance at his friend, and his eyes had a pleading look as he said, "I could hardly blame you for despising me at this moment, if that is what you feel. To have been so kindly treated, so generously brought in to the very bosom of your family! And then to be forced to admit that I have done nothing but deceive you since the first day we met. To be able to avoid this moment, this odious confession, I would give a great deal! And yet I pray that when you have heard my story, you will not think too unkindly of me."

The look of horror that had first been upon Lady Agatha's face when she heard Peter's words, the natural revulsion of feeling of a woman who has been lied to by one she has learned to respect and like, was soon replaced by an altogether different expression. Once, before, that face had reminded her of someone she had known and held dear. Now all at once the truth began to dawn on her, though it was not until Peter had talked for a little longer that she began to understand how and why those features had struck her as so familiar.

"I am not Grey at all," said Peter, forcing himself to look straight into Lady Agatha's eyes, "nor am I the devil-may-care, light-hearted fellow I have seemed to be. You cannot guess how much *that* deceit has cost me! To seem to care for nothing, when all the time my heart has been burthened with a misery indescribable in its weight—to seem to laugh always when inwardly I could do little but weep! Oh, I have deceived you, ma'am, but not from any motive crueller than the protection of a secret whose discovery might have harmed one I hold dear more than he has already been injured."

After a moment, for Peter's emotions were too strong to allow for further speech at once, he continued: "I was not in India for my pleasure but because of a great tragedy which overtook my family some five years ago. You have heard, I think, of the Montague scandal? The disgrace of Duke Hamilton's elder son?"

Lady Agatha nodded, bewildered. And yet the bewilderment quickly cleared away. She was less astonished than some others would have been at what she heard next.

"Well," said Peter, smiling, "Roderick Montague was my brother. My name is not Grey, but Montague, like his." He held up his hand, seeing that Lady Agatha would have interrupted, and went on.

"Five years ago, when my brother was disgraced, I was in my

third year at Oxford. Roderick was my senior by six years, being then twenty-eight, and several years out of university. He was living in town, at my father's establishment, and I saw him very little. We were not," said Peter, averting his eyes a little, "very close at that time. There were reasons for it—Roderick had always been my father's best-loved son, and in the absence of a mother, I found that I was often neglected. My father was a fierce old man, with very little softness in him, and what there was had all been directed to his elder son. Roderick was in every way the perfect young man—handsome, charming, and amusing, with a heart full of tenderness and a love of life which Papa could not but have found irresistible, as his own nature was so much the opposite. He reposed all his hopes in my brother, and neglected me. I should have seen how it was, for it is very natural for a father to prefer his eldest, and Roderick was in line for the title, but I was young, and stubborn, and my feelings had been hurt. I adored Roderick—if I had not, perhaps I should have been less blind later—but I envied him. Not to the detriment of all my brotherly feelings, you understand, but enough to make me think that, next to him, I was nothing. His career at Oxford had been famous. My own was nothing in its wake. Where he had been admired and petted by everyone, I was only accepted. By my third year I had grown so sick of always being compared to him, of gaining my identity only through a relationship to him, that I avoided seeing him. I know that in those years he understood a little of what I was feeling, and to compensate, he was always trying to bring me up to town, to introduce me to his friends and show me off (for he was really proud to have a brother, and not all my ill humor could erase it), but I always refused. Once I went and after looking me over quickly, everyone drifted back to him. He was always like that—a kind of magnet of humanity. People loved to be in the same room with him. His proximity was enough to make people feel happier, to laugh more heartily, and to be more at ease with themselves. But he had the opposite effect on me. I became more surly, more detached, and at last would not see him at all. I went back to school and buried myself in books, eschewing every friendship. I never went home, to Lancashire—there was my father, always asking if I had any news of Roderick, and wondering how life was going with him, always saying, 'I suppose Roderick will be one of our great statesmen one of these days,' or, 'When Roderick marries, then we shall have a dukedom! All the ladies are half-mad for him, I hear. I wonder whom he'll choose, at last?' And the questions drove me frantic. I wished desperately for my father's regard, and yet he seemed always to deny it me. At last I withdrew even from my own home and family, and became a sort of hermit, surrounded by scholars and books.

"I soon lost touch with Roderick, and perhaps might have been estranged from him forever, had it not been for what happened to him.

"One day I was in my study at Oxford, poring over a history book, when one of my father's servants rushed in. 'Your father has sent for you, my lord,' he said, and without any further explanation, but with a great deal of urgency, he pressed my cloak about my shoulders, and only calling out to my own valet to ready a valise, ran down the steps ahead of me. We made the journey in record time, without pausing to sleep or take any nourishment, and reached Hamilton Castle late on the following day. I knew enough not to rush in to my father's apartments—he hated to see anyone he had not sent for—and so spent the time pacing up and down in the corridor. I knew something was afoot, but no one would give me any information. At last the servant came, and I went in.

"My father was lying in his bed—for he had grown very weak in the last years, and hardly ever left it. His stern old face was turned to the wall as I came in, and never looked up throughout the whole interview. He watched that stone wall with so much fierceness that I believe he would have made a hole in it in half an hour, but the interview was very short.

"'Roderick has disgraced us all,' was nearly all he said. I could not believe it, and waited for particulars, but none came. He went on a little, saying he would never look at his son again—he seemed to have forgotten I was his son, too—and that whatever the law, he would disinherit him.

"'Let him have the title,' he growled, 'but I'll be damned if he has a penny from me!' And then he was silent again, and at last I left him, utterly perplexed, and hurt beyond all description that he would not confide in me. I waited for another summons, but none came. The lawyers were all there, going in and out of rooms, tiptoeing about, and at last I gathered, by degrees, what had occurred. Needless to say, I could not believe it. Even I, envying Roderick, could not believe what was imputed to him! And yet I believe a part of me wished to think it was true. Can you . . . can you comprehend that, my lady?" asked Peter with a miserable look, passing his hand over his forehead.

Lady Agatha nodded dumbly. She was very much moved by this narration, and would have gone to comfort the teller, for her heart really went out to him, but he turned a little away and went on.

"In any case, there was no doubt in anyone else's mind! No one ever doubted it! No matter how I try, I cannot understand why none of his friends, none of the people who had so eagerly gathered about him all his life, would not stand up and defend him! I returned to Oxford after a week, and everywhere the news was about. 'Montague disgraced' was on every tongue—I could not get away from it! And where, before, I had been selfish and proud about being held up to him, now it was all I could do to sit calmly in a lecture. Every eye in the place was on me. A day or two passed, and it was insupportable. I could not return home, to the comfort of a family, and the world seemed to hold us all in contempt. I joined a regiment which was going over to France, and by the time my father died, a month later, I was living in that country.

"I stayed in France for nearly a year, never communicating with anyone—indeed, I had no friends—and quite utterly lost in my heart. The only friend I ever had, who was Roderick, had disappeared from the face of the earth. My greatest misery was that I had deserted him when he needed me. Indeed, I do not know what I could have done—he had left the country by the time I had the news—but I had an idea. I thought at first I might find him fighting with our army, and to that end I searched high and low for him, or at any rate, as much as my duties would allow. But no one had heard of him, and then something struck me, something he had often referred to laughingly as a great desire of his. 'If ever I were tired of our old England,' he once said, 'I should go to India. There is a place to get lost in! Wild and savage, and yet I have heard it is more civilized, and its civilization more ordered and ancient, than anything we have here.'

"It was nothing but an idea, but I had no other one to go upon. I left my regiment and embarked on the next vessel for Calcutta. For four years I searched, visiting every outpost and encampment—or so I thought—in the jungle. I began to live in a kind of fever, which carried me through what otherwise I suppose I could not have borne. I had no notion if I should ever find him, if he were alive, or what, indeed, I could do if I did find him. I was living in a half-mad state, without any grasp of reason, and yet I could not give up the idea that he was somewhere in that wild country. At last, when I thought I had covered every inch of ground, I stumbled upon a piece of information—no more than a word dropped casually at dinner by an old colonel of the Sixth Cavalry, which sent me rushing off again. The man had mentioned an Englishman—more a dog than an Englishman, he had said, laughingly—who had passed through some months before, so riddled with malaria and fever that he had been hallucinating. 'Fellow thought he was a duke!' said the colonel, guffawing, and in an instant I had found out everything there was to learn about him. The information put me onto the scent, and after several weeks I came upon a desolate little group of huts in the middle of the jungle. And there"—Peter paused a moment, and breathed deeply—"there was my brother, lying in one of the huts, on a filthy old rag, and a half-devoured straw pallet beneath him, for a bed. I hardly knew who he was at first."

Peter closed his eyes and tried to push away the sight which immediately swelled up in him. Roderick, half-dead, with his cheeks so sunken and covered with filth that he had resembled some starving mongrel cur more than the dashing young duke he should have been, a beard covering the handsome lines of his cheek and chin, a mass of rags making very little semblance of a covering, and worst of all—so horrible that even his brother had had to look away in a second—the eyes, half-glazed and wild.

"He did not recognize me at first," continued Peter softly, "but at last, when I had sat by him for a day and a night, eagerly waiting for some sign of life, he mumbled my name, and then only two sentences. He searched for this locket, among his rags, and gave it to me"—Peter took out the little locket he had in his pocketbook—"and bid me take care of the lady painted there. He said, too, 'I am not guilty of disgracing you.' He said this two or three times, with a pleading look which nearly tore my heart in two, and then he added, just before he died, 'Beware of Darnley.'"

Peter paused for a moment to draw breath. Lady Agatha, meantime, had taken the locket from him, and even while the expression of horror had been on her face from the tale, a new expression came into her eyes.

"Lord!" she cried. "It is Maude Quimby!" and then their eyes met, and there was an immense understanding there.

"So ... he did it all for her?" murmured Lady Agatha at last.

"And for her brother, or that is what I believe," replied Peter, sitting wearily down. "I have just come from her, and she has told me what she knows. It is enough to make me believe that Reginald Darnley is the most infamous devil that ever lived, but whatever I think, it will not serve to convict him."

Lady Agatha stared in horror for several moments, for she was incapable of digesting so much all at once. The story had been told all in a rush, for Peter Montague, as he must now be called, had been incapable of stopping, once he had begun. The scenes had rushed through his mind as he spoke; it had been like a microcosmic hell, to tell it all again, and yet, as he sat now, very silent, and looking at his hands, it was as though an immense load had been lifted from his back. The confession of his own resentment of Roderick had been something even he had not been able to face for many months. The suspicion, which had often crossed his mind, that perhaps his brother had done all he was accused of, had weighed on him more heavily than a conviction of his own guilt could have done. He felt certain that Lady Agatha Banforth, for whom he had the greatest respect, and in whose eyes he wished desperately to read approval, must now be thinking very badly of him. And so he sat for several moments, when he had finished, before he dared to raise his eyes and look at her. What he saw then was the closest thing to heaven he had experienced in many years: it was a steady, gentle, all-comprehending gaze, which, even without words, told him all he wanted to know.

"You do not, then, think the worse of me for what I have told you?" he asked with an imploring look.

For answer Lady Agatha merely got to her feet and came over to him, laying a cool hand on his forehead. After a moment she said softly, "My poor boy, how could I? There is nothing more natural in all the world than to long to be loved by one's own parent. It will sometimes lead one into thought and actions which are regrettable, but what you have done—good Lord!—how could anyone call the penance you have made for a few moments of childish envy anything but monumental? No . . . no, don't say it. I think you have made up for any trace of guilt you might have borne, and that was only a small speck, compared to the evil in others. You must—poor man!—you must have been living in purgatory these last years!"

Peter nodded dumbly; it was all he was capable of, and a little drop of moisture appeared at the corner of his eye. With one heaving sob, which fairly tore Lady Agatha's heart, all the burden of that time was released. He put a hand to his brow, and mopped it, as if in doing so he could wipe away the pain of the last months, and then looked at her gravely.

"There," he said, with a little tremulous smile, "it is all done with. I thank you from the bottom of my heart, good lady, for hearing my tale without any rebuke."

Lady Agatha put up her hand and would have exclaimed at this, but he signaled her to be silent.

"And now," he said, looking once again like a man capable of anything, "there is much to do. I wonder if I may ask your help?"

Lady Agatha nodded eagerly, and then Peter told her the tale he had just heard from Miss Quimby. He recounted, somewhat more succinctly than Maude had done for Bertie, all the events which had led up to Roderick Montague's flight from England, including her own and her brother's part in it. Lady Agatha interrupted occasionally, for as she had heard the tale, she could not help but understand some things which had often perplexed her. She had herself been very well acquainted with Roderick, in the years past, and the story made her remember certain events and certain attitudes which had puzzled her then.

"Yes," she murmured when she heard that Roderick had been secretly engaged to Miss Quimby, "it was very odd, you know— for Roderick could have married any girl in London, they were all mad for him, and yet he always stayed apart. He used often to come and see me, and I once thought he was going to offer for my hand!" She let out a soft laugh. "Imagine my vanity, when all the while he was in love with Maude! She was always there, you know—she came to see me every day, and now I remember how pitiful she sometimes looked when Roderick did not come to call! Lord, I must have been blind! And now I recollect how they used to stay at opposite ends of the room, very careful to avoid speaking to each other, which was really very odd, you know, for it was a more telling sign that any number of little *tête-à-têtes* would have been! I suppose that was because your father would have disapproved the match?"

Peter nodded. "My father was dead set on a brilliant marriage for Roderick. I think he might have died on the spot if he had heard there was such an alliance already made—in that, you know, Roderick was very clever. He knew his own heart, and would not go against it even for my father, but neither would he break the old man's heart by marrying directly against his wishes."

"So he preferred to wait until the old duke died before making his engagement public? And then it was too late...."

"Yes, much too late," said Peter with a bitter smile. "By then he was already disgraced, and all for having taken pity on a poor fool who could not regulate his own debts."

And so the story was told, but when it came to the part about Reginald Darnley, Lady Agatha sat very silent and still, barely breathing, and with a look of utter contempt on her face. At last she burst out, "What! I can hardly believe it! Even of Darnley, whom I never liked. But even he should have been above such kind of evil! I only thought he was arrogant and vain, with too much concern for pomp and ceremony, and no idea of right. I never thought he was an outright devil!"

Peter looked at her keenly, waiting for the realization that must inevitably dawn on her. And so it did, with a great wash of pallor on her delicate complexion.

Lady Agatha sat speechless for a moment, gazing in utter horror at her companion. In a tiny voice she said at last, "And what... what of Roselind?"

"That is what I have been thinking of," replied Peter gently. "But I do not believe there is any cause for alarm just yet. I have got a plan. If you will help me, I think we shall yet be able to save her, not only from the marriage, but from any scandal."

But just as Peter was saying these words, the butler opened the door, and before he even had time to announce a visitor, Mrs. Hogarth swept past him into the room.

"My own dear Agatha!" cried Mrs. Hogarth, and if the joy had not been so clearly written on her face, it would have been visible through all the bobs and wags and tremors of her headgear. She had put on her very best visiting costume for this visit, which, as she was shortly to announce, she considered as marking a great victory in her career as a matchmaker.

"My own dear sister!" she cried, flying to that lady and embracing her with so much passion that for a moment Lady Agatha nearly lost her balance. Even the sight of her sister's visitor could not completely quell her ardor. She granted "Mr. Grey" a chilly nod and proceeded to unburden her bosom.

"I wished to be the very first to congratulate you, my dear!" she was exclaiming, her eyes brimming over with meaningful looks, "on the very great event which is so soon to take place!"

Lady Agatha smiled and wondered what that might be, but Mrs. Hogarth could not be put off so easily. With a scolding wag of her thin finger she exclaimed, "Naughty, naughty girl! You think you can deceive me, do you? Well, 'pon my word, I assure you I am not so blind! I have ears in my head, dear Agatha, and eyes to see lovers! Indeed I do!"

Lady Agatha's patience was beginning to be a little tried by all these effusive mysteries. She smiled again, very politely, but with a determination which anyone, save Mrs. Hogarth, could not have mistaken, and said, "I assure you, Clara, I have not the slightest idea what you are talking of! You must sit down and tell us quite calmly what it is."

Mrs. Hogarth would sit down, which she did with an infuriating degree of slowness, and a great many spreadings out of her crimson silk skirt, and patting of her numerous bows, but she would not tell "us" anything. She turned her back quite pointedly on Mr. Grey, whom she had never liked, and smiled very sweetly at her sister-in-law.

"I mean, my dear, exactly what you think I mean!" she said at last, with a wink. "I mean about our own dear Rosie being engaged at last! What a marvelous thing it is, to be sure! I knew it was going to happen in the end, you know—I flatter myself I had some little hand in the matter, after all—but to have it all come off so soon! Really, it is quite a charming start to the summer!"

Lady Agatha would not let her go on. She stood up and walked right over to Mrs. Hogarth and looked down at her very hard. "Clara," she said in a meaningful tone of voice, "you had better tell me what you know. I will not be teased in this manner. Have you got any real knowledge that Rosie is engaged?"

Mrs. Hogarth looked rather taken aback.

"Indeed, Agatha, I think you might be a little more trusting of me!" she said reproachfully. "You might have told *me*, you know, when you heard it was to happen! After all, I did help it all along, you know! I think it was quite horrid of you to leave me to find out from Louisa Chumley. It made me feel quite foolish, to be informed of my own brother's niece's engagement by a complete stranger!"

This was said with a pout, and Lady Agatha, seeing that she would get nowhere in this manner, went back to her chair, and glancing at Peter, who was frowning, said, "I suppose you are talking about Roselind and Darnley?"

"Why, of course I am! What did you think, you silly thing? Of course I was talking about them! Whoever else *should* I have been talking of? To be sure it is Darnley, my dear! And what a romantic thing, after all, to run off to Scotland and be married at once!"

"What?" Peter and Lady Agatha had spoken as one.

"Why, to be sure, my dear!" said Mrs. Hogarth with a giggle. "I always wanted to elope myself. Well, of course, this is not really an elopement. But I do think it was very sweet of Reginald"—Mrs. Hogarth had taken at once to using the gentleman's Christian name when she heard he was to be a member of the family—"awfully sweet of him, really, to be so impatient! He told Georgina Devonshire this very morning that he could not wait, and it was all arranged. Indeed, I am rather surprised to see *you* sitting about so quietly, when in truth you ought to be packing your things. I know it is only a preliminary ceremony, and only the immediate family to be present, but still, one wants one or two nice things about. But where are you going, my dear?" she inquired, for both Lady Agatha and Peter Montague had stood up.

"I … I hardly know what to think!" exclaimed Lady Agatha, with her hands on her heart. "Oh, dear, what am I to do?"

Mrs. Hogarth looked surprised, but she had no time to say anything. Peter Montague had reached her ladyship's side in an instant, and had taken a firm hold of her hand.

"Why," he said very calmly, and with a smile, "it is quite simple, your ladyship. I think you ought to go right up to your rooms and see about a valise. Mrs. Hogarth is right. There is no time for sitting about. Where is your husband?"

"He ... he is at his club," stammered her ladyship with a white face.

"Very well. I shall go and fetch him. I have another errand to do as well, but I shall be back before the hour is up. Go along, now, ma'am. It shall all come right in the end."

The last sentence had been spoken in a very soft voice, and Mrs. Hogarth, for all that she had ears as sharp as any knife, did not catch it. If the mood in the room was not quite so jolly as the imminence of a wedding ought to have made it, it was at least a good deal calmer than its occupants secretly felt. Mrs. Hogarth was a little stunned to find herself very soon alone in it, but she was not altogether unused to being deserted in this heartless fashion. With a little sigh of ill-usage, she gathered up her reticule and gloves and made to leave. As she walked out through the open door—left open in the urgency of the moment—she just muttered to herself, "Really! It is beyond everything! To be treated so by one's own family! They might, I think, at least have invited me to Scotland with them!"

Mrs. Hogarth had indeed entertained such sanguine hopes of being one of the party that she had not spared the expense of coming in a hansom cab, which now waited outside for her with all the bandboxes she had got ready against such an invitation. With a very low sensation she climbed in among them, and thought bitterly of the half-crown she might have spent on something better than a fruitless round trip to Pulteney Street from the bottom of Angel Place.

19

Lord Iseleigh had gone to Cheap Street, as he had said he would, and there he had been for nearly an hour by the time Mrs. Hogarth burst in on Lady Agatha with her alarming news. Most of the time had been spent by the earl dawdling in front of a printmaker's shop, pretending to be immersed in the delights of whaling boats in the New World and of racehorses at Ascot. Indeed, so complacent had the proprietor been on seeing this fine-looking young man show so much interest in his wares that he had sent out an assistant to better inform him of the type and style, the makers, and the artists of the prints. The assistant had been more than dedicated to his task, and had so exasperated Bertie with his hovering that the young earl had nearly cried out in annoyance. At last he had convinced the printmaker's assistant, however, that today he was only browsing, and had moved on down the street a little. But he soon found there were only milliners' and dressmakers' shops there, and having bought himself a pair of gloves which neither fit nor which he liked much, he was forced to return to the printmaker's, which afforded a very good prospect of Lucius Quimby's office.

After half an hour there was still no sign of Quimby, and Bertie was beginning to wonder if he were not on a wild-goose chase, or if Quimby might not be so taken up with his clerical work that he would not leave the building until the evening. Bertie had just been on the point of calling to his groom, who was standing a little way off with the curricle, when two things happened at once. The first thing, and by far the more important, was that the thin, twisted, furtive little figure of Quimby appeared in the opposite doorway, and having looked to left and right, made off quickly down the street. Just as Bertie was about to follow him, a hearty greeting sounded in his ear. In dismay the earl looked up to see Sir Walter Chumley bearing down upon him.

"Why, if it is not Iseleigh!" the baronet was crying, huffing up with a great beaming smile across his face. "I thought it might be you from a distance, and indeed, it was!"

Bertie smiled as politely as he could, and tried to think of some plausible excuse to get away. But the baronet would have none of it.

"What! Looking at these prints?" he inquired, squinting at the merchandise displayed in the window. "Oh, fancy that! There is a Bromley! I am devilish fond of Bromley myself! No one can draw a thoroughbred like 'im! Are you buying one, or just browsing?"

"Only browsing," said Bertie, casting a miserable glance in the direction of the corner, around which Quimby had just disappeared. He endeavored, through a series of peculiar squints and faces, to communicate to his groom the urgent need to follow the receding figure. But in one of those awful tricks of fate, the groom had chosen that precise moment to notice that one of the earl's grays had got something hanging from its hoof, and he was in the process of leaning over to detach the something—which was nothing more, as it happened, than a bit of a cobblestone—while his master was desperately making faces at him. It is doubtful whether the groom would have understood in any case, for although he was a perfectly satisfactory groom, he had none of that brilliancy of imagination which is so invaluable at such moments in life, and though his master had given him a minute description of the man they were looking for, and had urged upon him the importance of keeping the fellow in sight, the groom had received the information with a series of amiable grins which betokened more good nature than interest.

"Ah, indeed!" exclaimed Sir Walter. "Yes, yes, I am awfully fond of browsing about. As it happens, my wife is just gone into that dressmaker's down the street a ways—Madame Héloise Renault—for, you know, our little Clarissa is to be married in a month. They are gone looking for a trousseau, you know."

"Oh, really?" said Bertie, making a great effort to be civil.

"Yes, yes—Clarissa is to marry that young officer, Wedgeworth. Very good kind of fellow, too. Happy as a pair of skylarks, they are, though heaven knows what they are to live upon. Still, it is love makes the world go around, isn't it?" Sir Walter let out a nostalgic little sigh at this idea, although his own courtship, that period of tender billings and cooings before the nuptials, had lasted a mere second as compared to the eternity of henpecking which had followed it.

"Ah, well, love's all, is what I always say! And so, my good friend, I seem to be on my own for an hour or two. Great piece of luck to have run into you! In point of fact, I should have made a point of looking you up sooner, but the devil of it is, Louisa has always got something for me to do! Never a moment's peace in this world for those of us who are mated, is there? Heh, heh, but you know nothing of that, I suppose. How goes the farming?"

"The farming?" Bertie blinked a little. It had been some time since he had thought of farming. "Oh, you mean the farming! Well, to tell you the truth, I haven't really been thinking of that much lately." He noticed, out of the corner of his eye, that his groom was now erect, and grinning at him in a most idiotic fashion.

"No? Well, I have got a pamphlet here—let me see, I know I have it somewhere . . ." Sir Walter searched about the nether regions of his paunch for the elusive thing, and at last located it. "Yes, indeed, got it the other day. Most interesting piece of literature, I assure you ..."

Bertie was by now at the very limit of his patience. He was not much, in any case, for dissembling. He had tried once or twice, when still at Eton, to pretend he had read a passage in preparation for a class, which in fact he had not. His coloring, which was dreadfully prone to rise at any hint of embarrassment, had always given him away and made him so uncomfortable that at last he had vowed never to try to lie, or even to fib, again. Now his cheeks were grown quite ruddy, and his chest was heaving with exasperated sighs. Anyone but Sir Walter might have realized how little interested he was at this moment in agricultural reform, but the baronet was blissfully unaware that his company was superfluous. He proceeded to lecture the young man upon the contents of this new piece of propaganda, and at last grasped his young friend by the arm and proposed walking down the street to his club.

It was this very attitude in which Peter Montague happened upon him. Peter had come directly from Pulteney Street, in hopes of catching the earl before he went on to General Banforth's club. As we know very well, he had a piece of information to communicate which could not very well be transferred across the genial paunch of Sir Walter. His first instinct on seeing them thus seemingly happily immersed in conversation was to explode in anger, for he could not have known how unwillingly Bertie's company had been obtained by the baronet. He walked up quickly and took the earl firmly by the arm, hardly even nodding to Sir Walter. The look of absolute relief and mingled guilt which met him in the young man's gaze at once told him what had happened. But still he was in a quandary as, to how to get him away.

"By Jove!" Sir Walter cried at once. "If it is not the fellow who blasted Darnley so well in the highway! And how are you, sir? I must admit, I have long looked forward to shaking your hand . . ." But the baronet stopped at once, and almost blushed. "Dear me, I almost forgot. Darnley is to be your brother-in-law, isn't he, Iseleigh?"

It was thus that the vital piece of information was transmitted to the earl. The baronet had soon given away the whole story, repeating everything he had heard that morning from his wife about Darnley's eagerness to have the knot tied at once, and the plan to go to Scotland, and all the rest of it. He congratulated the young man effusively, and never noticed the meaningful looks and winks which were being sent back and forth between the other two.

"Great thing!" he said very heartily, although he did not himself think very highly of Reginald Darnley, but propriety made him ape joy at the engagement. "Great thing, indeed! Nothing like a great match, is there? And when do you all go to Scotland?"

"Immediately," put in Peter, thankful for an opportunity to get a word in. "That is why I have come looking for you, Bertie—your aunt has sent me for you. So, Sir Walter, I hope you will excuse our rushing off in this fashion, but the lovers mustn't be kept waiting, you know!"

"No, no, of course not!" The baronet laughed, and Bertie only gulped.

"I thought I should die if I did not get away from him!" exclaimed Bertie as soon as they were out of earshot. "But what's this about Scotland? Was it a ruse?"

Peter Montague looked grim. "Afraid not, my lad. We've a devil of a business ahead of us. But where's Quimby?"

"He just came out of the building, when Sir Walter accosted me. I'm afraid . . . I'm afraid he got away!"

"Never mind," said Peter shortly, and then, glancing at the curricle, he asked how fast it went.

"In a pinch, sixteen miles an hour!" replied the earl.

"Very well, then. There's no time to explain now, but let us go and rouse your uncle from the club, and then we're off to Elizabeth Street!"

"But what . . . what about Scotland?" demanded Bertie. "Has . . . ? Good God, has the fiend abducted her!"

"We'll know soon enough. In any case, let's not waste time standing about in the street. I'll tell you what has happened as we go along."

General Banforth was soon found, and roused out of a comfortable conversation with some old friends. His amiable smile, however, soon gave way to an incredulous look, and then a thunderous scowl.

"What?" he roared. "I don't believe you! But there—don't say it. I'll have your word for it, Grey," (for the general had not yet learned the true identity of his friend.) "You're not a man to pull my leg, I warrant. By God, Aggie was right, wasn't she? The man's a perfect fiend! But you don't suppose they've already embarked on the elopement, do you?"

"We'll soon know," said Peter with a grim face. "She was just at Elizabeth Street, visiting Miss Quimby. I left her there an hour ago."

Bertie had already climbed into the box of his curricle, and was whipping up the horses as these words were spoken. Within ten minutes the grim-faced trio had pulled into Elizabeth Street.

Peter was out of the vehicle before the horses had even stopped, and halfway up the flight of stairs. His visit took him no more than two minutes, after which he was down again, and saying, with a look which might have chilled even Banforth's battle-hardened heart, "He's taken her! They are ahead of us by forty-five minutes! Come along, now, Iseleigh, d'you think you can make these beasts compete with Darnley's team? They're said to be the fastest in half England!"

"I'll swear they can keep up—at any rate, we'll die trying!" replied the earl.

"Indeed, we may well do just that. General, you had best go home and take care of your wife. She needs you now more than anyone. Iseleigh and I are for Gretna Green!"

20

It is a question open to some speculation who suffers most in a crisis, those who may, by their own initiatives, influence the outcome, or those condemned to sit at home and wait for tidings of their loved ones. Certainly Lady Agatha, who was by now pacing up and down her sitting room, having heard nothing from anyone since Mr. Grey—or now, Peter Montague—had rushed out of her house an hour before, had already lived through the worst a dozen times. She had not even the comfort of knowing what had or had not as yet occurred, and visions of her niece being abducted in the middle of the city were continually appearing before her mind's eye. But Lady Agatha was not, by nature, given to melodrama. The idea that Roselind might have been treated harshly never really gained a stronghold in her thoughts. Imagine what she would about Darnley—and what she had recently been told by Peter Montague had surely thrown a new light on what kind of evil that man was capable of—she did not really imagine him to be equal to brutal abductions. As she was not much given to immersing herself in novels—*The Castle of Otranto* had lain untouched by her sitting-room sofa for six months before she had fingered it over and put it away again—she could not have understood the full flower of malediction of which the human spirit is capable.

But even without thoughts of chains and whips, harshly bound hands and feet, and caves alive with bat wings and the eerie cries of owls, there was enough horror in her imaginings to make her tremble. It was enough to think of her niece—however kindly she might be treated—undergoing the shame and fear of an elopement. The first part of her vigil, indeed, had been speckled with hope. She had expected at any moment to see her niece walk in, as cheerful as always, having returned from Miss Quimby's rooms with no other news than that of her friend's health. Roselind had gone in the carriage. That left her some hope. Surely the coachman, a faithful old retainer, would not let her fall into evil hands?

But even this idea made her fearful, for if Darnley had meant to elope with Roselind against the young lady's will, he would surely have used all his ingenuity and charm to persuade her. He might even have begun the journey under another guise; a drive, for instance, might have been suggested. Yes, he was quite capable of that! Perhaps he had contrived to meet her accidentally and offered to bring her home himself! He would surely not have dragged her off like a pirate! Yes, and having once got her in his phaeton, the rest would be easy. He might have suggested a drive to the Crescent, which lay in the same direction as the Northern Road. By the time she knew where they were, he might have worked all kinds of wiles!

As the seconds ticked away, the likelihood of seeing Roselind, unharmed and innocent, walk in grew more and more remote. The front door was thrown open, and Lady Agatha rushed to the top of the stairs. But there, standing in the hallway, instead of Roselind, was her husband. She had never seen him look so angry before. And in a second all her dearest hopes were shattered.

Lady Agatha heard the worst, and as she listened to General Banforth's account of what had passed, her worst suspicions against Darnley were confirmed. She wanted to cry out in rage and horror at a man who would take such vile measures against an innocent girl; but even as Lady Agatha heard the worst, and as she grew more and more determined that Darnley was a man without a heart, that gentleman was proving that, twisted and filthy as it was, there was still such an organ beating in his breast. The way it came out was very strange, and perhaps would not have impressed Lady Agatha much. But perhaps if she had been removed a little from the situation, if it had not been her own dear niece whose very life and reputation were in his hands, she might have been able to find a little something of pity in her heart for him.

For, strange as it may seem, and though he was indeed a villainous and blackhearted fellow, Reginald Darnley was not quite without any trace of emotion. Indeed, Darnley was a man full of passion, and, as everyone knows, wherever there is passion, there is also room for suffering and unhappiness, as well as vanity, and greed, and malice.

The story of Darnley's life might well merit an entire chronicle, but we are not concerned with that story here, except insofar as it may shed a little light on what had made him behave as he had done.

When Darnley had first set eyes upon Lady Roselind Arden, it had been in her father's house in Devonshire. Lord Iseleigh was apparently Darnley's great friend. They frequented the same clubs, moved in the same circles, invited each other to their separate lodgings, and looked to all the world like intimates. And yet Darnley was never really comfortable in Iseleigh's presence. He resented the earl's treatment of him, which, though certainly unconscious, could not help but betray a certain contempt which Iseleigh had felt toward his friend's parentage. Now, Darnley was a man whose very nerve endings were attuned to catch any such innuendos, no matter how slight or unintended. His father had been a brilliant man who had raised himself by his own fingernails from nothing to everything. Darnley's father's name had been Dooley, and Mr. Dooley had been the son of an ironmonger. But the ironmonger's son had discovered that through his own wits he could amass enough money to buy and sell whole kingdoms, and this he did by the time he was fifty.

But Dooley, although he was richer than anyone else in the kingdom, was not welcomed into its best drawing rooms. He grew used, as he grew older, to being scorned by peers who had not one ounce of his brains nor his wit, and yet who considered themselves vastly superior to him. He built a mansion off Grosvenor Square, to entice the aristocracy, but still they ignored him. As he grew older, Dooley grew more bitter, and he determined that his son should never be shunned in a public road by a penniless baronet.

To this end, Reginald was sent away from home to be educated, and under the tutelage of a whole string of elegant professors he mastered French and Italian, Latin and Greek. By twelve he was conversant in all of these, and knew, besides, the name of every river and hamlet in Europe, and what each region depended upon for its livelihood. He learned fencing, and dancing, appreciation of music and art; he learned, in short, all the gentlemanly arts, and besides all of this, he discovered the secret of the world. In fact, there were two: one was money, and the other was to be liked by those who made up the little, powerful world of society.

When Reginald went to Oxford to complete his education, he had his first and most severe confrontation with the wicked world. He discovered that although he was very, very rich, and very, very clever, yet he was not well-liked. On the other hand, Roderick Montague was generally loved. He, too, was rich, and although not so cunning as Darnley, he was clever. If Reginald had looked a little longer at what made Roderick so much admired, he might have seen that the other fellow had, besides, a wealth of good humor and an innate honorableness in his character. But Darnley saw only that the son of a duke was much admired and that the son of a merchant was not. He set himself, therefore, to have his revenge upon Roderick, and this he had plotted for some years. At last, however, the revenge was complete, and Darnley should have been happy, for he had schemed so well that he had contrived to make himself the object of everyone's admiration. But he was determined to secure his position for the future, and to this end he decided that what he must do was, he must marry a peer's daughter. That would give him rights he could never have on his own.

And so the first time he had glimpsed Roselind Arden, this had been greatly in his mind. But there were a great many belles in London already who were dying to marry him, and the soft, retiring, shy little girl hardly caught his attention. She had sat quietly at dinner, afraid to open her mouth, and then had rushed out into the shrubberies immediately afterward. He had hardly paid her any mind.

And yet other things worked inside of him. There was, for instance, the time his friend Iseleigh had spoken to him of his daughter's prospects. "Of course she has her own settlement," he had said, "so it doesn't matter much if the gentleman has any money or not." But it had mattered who the gentleman was—this Darnley felt very keenly, and he felt equally that *he* was not his friend's idea of a suitable husband. Perhaps it had been in that moment that he decided that he would marry Roselind Arden. When he had next glimpsed her, some years later, the desire was reborn. She was no longer a bashful little creature, and neither was she a sleek, lacquered femme fatale. But by now Darnley was grown very tired of lacquered women, and though it may be imputing too much feeling to a villain to say he felt genuine love, at least he knew something which seemed to him very like it. In any case, he was seized with the urge to make her his own. He could not look into those great limpid gray eyes without feeling something like a tremor. And besides, he discovered at about this time that he really needed her—more than he had ever suspected he might need anyone.

Now, there was only one human being who knew exactly what had transpired between Darnley and Roderick Montague five years before, and that was Lucius Quimby. Darnley was not afraid of *him*—he had already proved himself a spineless coward, and besides, Darnley gave him enough financial impetus, and enough warnings, to keep him quiet. But Darnley was a man with a hundred ears—or rather, he had a hundred ears in his employ, who were always eager to listen for him—and about this time he learned that Roselind's brother had become infatuated with Maude Quimby. He could not risk waiting another day. He awoke one morning in a cold sweat, and that evening proposed to Roselind. She had as good as accepted him, which gave him a great feeling of relief. But then he had panicked again, for his instinct told him he had something still to fear, and so he had gone that morning to Elizabeth Street, where he had seen first Mr. Grey and then Lady Roselind emerge.

He could wait no longer. Once he was married to Roselind, her family would be his protectors. No one would dare to discredit him in public then. He would be safe for as long as her happiness depended upon his good name.

The ruse had nearly worked itself. Roselind had been so surprised that Darnley's tiger, who had been instructed not to use much force, had barely exerted any effort. She had fainted dead away in a moment, and in another minute they were all inside the entryway.

Roselind's eyelids fluttered open, to see a shadowy figure hovering over her. She had forgotten where she was, and for a little while hardly recognized her savior—for that is what she thought him.

Darnley was leaning over her with a look of great concern, and even anger.

"Thank God you are safe!" he cried with just the proper trace of hoarseness in his voice.

"Where . . . where am I?"

Darnley ignored the question.

"Thank God I was passing by, my lady! I saw the heinous man take you by the waist! He must have meant to rob you!"

"Oh, dear!" cried Roselind, sitting up. "Did he get away with my reticule? I had my aunt's money purse in it!"

The reticule, which had been cleverly dropped on the street outside, was finally found and restored to its owner.

Missing from it were the little gold-link purse belonging to Lady Agatha and a jeweled comb of Roselind's own. Curiously, the thief had not got away with the silver smelling-salts box, which was now put to good use.

"Never mind about the money, my own darling!" cried Darnley in an outraged tone. "You might have been killed. Henry, did you see the man?"

Darnley's tiger blinked, and shook his head. He had been rehearsed, but not enough to make him open his mouth with any confidence. A shake of the head and a great deal of batting of his eyelids was all he was up to. But it was enough. Darnley had taken charge again.

"Never mind! We shall find him out later. Now, the thing to do, your ladyship, is to get you safely away from here! Your carriage is outside?"

Roselind nodded.

"Henry, you may tell the coachman that I shall attend Lady Roselind home myself."

And so the Iseleigh carriage had returned to its stable, and Roselind, thinking she had been saved from a fearful fate, went willingly along to the waiting phaeton. She was very grateful, indeed, to Mr. Darnley, and nearly forgot, in all the terror of the moment, and the aftereffects of dizziness and the pain in her arm, her former sentiments toward him. As for that gentleman, he was so immersed in attending her that he never glimpsed a furtive little masculine figure lurking in the shadows near at hand.

Lucious Quimby had seen it all, and by the time Roselind began to realize that she was being driven, not in the direction of Pulteney Street, but in a different one altogether, Mr. Quimby had raced up to his sister, reported to her his findings, and rushed off again. It was his intention to follow the phaeton in a separate vehicle, which he lost no time in procuring from a friend who ran a stable in High Street. And so the little cavalcade was formed: at the head of it was Darnley, with his superb chariot and his powerful team of blacks; then came Quimby, following in a rickety old curricle with two springs missing; and some ways behind, following on the Great North Road, were Lord Iseleigh and his friend Peter Montague.

But of course neither Roselind nor her abductor knew of this. For the first minutes of their journey Roselind was all gratitude and relief. She sat back in her seat and barely glanced at the way they were going; nor did she pay much heed to the look of closed determination in Darnley's face. Nothing was said for a while, except her occasional exclamations of thanks and bewilderment at what she had escaped. Darnley, with more than his usual terseness, replied that she was very lucky indeed. But when ten minutes had gone by, and Roselind saw that they were passing out of the central part of town in a new direction, she began to wonder. Darnley turned the phaeton into the Great North Road with no word of explanation, and she would have cried out that he was going the wrong way, but something in his expression made her stop.

Gradually light began to dawn on her. She could not at first believe it, but as the phaeton moved along, and the driver spoke not a word, terror began to creep over her heart like a chilly hand. She could not think clearly at first, although the sights and smells around her were clearer than usual. She saw, as if she had been watching it all from a great way off, the phaeton, and the team, and Darnley, and even herself, trundling along a smooth stretch of highway in the glaring heat of midday. Fields and farmhouses speckled the landscape, making a weird contrast of respectability and peace to what was really going forward. A farmer standing at the side of the road waiting to cross over with his hoe and rake gave them an admiring glance. What could be more pleasant, on a summer afternoon, than the sight of a dashing gentleman and a pretty young woman out for a drive in such an elegant vehicle? For one second Roselind was seized with an urge to cry out to the farmer, but in an instant they had passed him by, leaving him in a small cloud of dust.

For what seemed like an eternity they drove along like this, and neither one spoke. Time seemed to hang suspended in the brilliant sunlight, and at last Roselind began to feel quite dizzy. She was in no danger of fainting away again, but if she had, she could not have felt more removed from the scene. The thought occurred to her that this was all quite inevitable.

"Do not you wish to know where we are going?" Darnley said at last, looking straight ahead of him at the road. He had been driving very fast since they had left the city, and the horses were beginning to glisten with sweat.

"I suppose," said Roselind with a calmness which amazed her, "that you are taking me somewhere for a purpose of your own. Of course I shall find out in the end."

Darnley smiled. "It is no great secret, I assure you."

Roselind was silent. She felt that she would know very soon. She felt very little curiosity.

"We are going to Scotland," said Reginald Darnley, "where we shall be married. I have no wish to harm you."

"I am sure you do not. But I do not understand—why must we go to Scotland?"

"Because it is easier this way. It is imperative that we are married now. I cannot afford to wait any longer. In a week—perhaps even in a day—it will be too late."

"I am afraid I do not understand."

Darnley's face, as he spoke, had begun to take on an expression of anger. His usual calm, sardonic look began to break up.

"No, you wouldn't, I suppose. But what if I told you that in a week your family would forbid the marriage?" Suddenly Darnley looked at her very hard. His eyes were a little wild, and Roselind noticed this with a shudder. "Come, now," he exclaimed very sharply, "do not tell me you have not heard all about me from your friend?"

Roselind was too astonished to know what to make of this.

"Why, sir, I assure you I do not know what you are talking of!"

"Oh, come, now! Surely your Miss Quimby has told you all about her precious Montague?"

"Why, is there anything I should have been told?"

Darnley let out a strange sound, half laugh and half strangled cry.

"You cannot fool me! You despise me, I can see it in your face! But it does not matter anymore! By tomorrow we shall be man and wife, and your contempt will not be able to change it!"

Roselind's voice was very gentle as she said, "I assure you, Mr. Darnley, I do not condemn you. You have been more than generous with me. I wish to be your wife, and I am sure my family would never hate you. Only, this is a very strange way of going. We had much better go back quietly to Bath, and marry proudly before all the world. What will they think of us if they see we have run off together? Surely it will be much worse in every wise!"

"No, no, you do not understand!" Darnley's face had by now

lost any semblance of control. His eyes were wild, and on his lips was a strange, twisted smile. His voice had none of that slow drawling sarcasm of yore, but had taken on a piercing, high sound which frightened Roselind more than anything else. "You cannot understand! How could you, born into a title, with all the world to love you before you were five months old! *You* can have no conception of what it is to be scorned for what you have no power over!"

"People do not scorn you, sir. On the contrary, you are so much admired that . . . well, of course you know that in any case. Everyone admires you!"

"No, no, they only pretend it! They pretend because I am very rich, and they are all afraid of the power of money, and use me to their own advantage! They would never accept me if I were not wealthy!"

Now things had begun to go beyond anything Roselind had ever known. She had never seen anyone in such a state—never, in truth, known it was possible to come so unhinged. And yet she did not lose her own courage. On the contrary, in exact proportion to Darnley's increasing rage, she felt herself grow calmer. She spoke to him now in a soothing, quiet voice, which a mother might have used in speaking to a child awakened from a nightmare.

"You mustn't say that, sir! It is not true, indeed it is not. Everyone admires you, and I most of all."

Darnley cast her a disbelieving look.

"I don't believe you."

"But it is very true. And really, I *wish* to marry you . . . there is no need to carry me off in this way. We had much better go back to Bath."

For an instant Darnley seemed to soften. The young lady had spoken in a very coaxing tone, and really, he would much rather have done as he was bid. He was growing unaccountably tired, and the mere effort of keeping the reins in his hands was almost too much. But the instant passed, and he was himself again.

"No," he said in a cold, hard voice, "that is impossible. No shame will come to you—I've seen to that. I told them all we were running off to be married, but not to elope. They think we have only got impatient. I told Georgina we could not wait for a formal wedding, but were going off with your family to tie the knot at once."

This, at least, was a little comfort to Roselind, for her first fear, after she had got over her initial terror, had been that her aunt and uncle, besides being fearful for her safety, would be terrified for her reputation. She saw that Darnley had gained some control of his feelings again, and it eased her mind. She thought as long as he was collected, she could be, too. And so she sat back in silence, and, afraid to open her mouth again, lest he exhibit the same signs of craziness he had just done, said nothing. And so they rode along until the horses were exhausted, when they were forced to look up a posting house. Roselind climbed down with immense relief when they reached it. Her nerves had been unnaturally strained, and now all at once her legs began to quiver, and her hand would not hold still. She really did not know if she could bear any more.

21

The posting house was attached to an inn, which boasted a coffee shop. While Darnley's team of blacks was led away, lathered and heaving, from the phaeton, Roselind stood quietly by, afraid to suggest they might go in for some refreshment. She hardly knew from looking at his face if he would smile and say it was all right or if he would grow wild again. And so she stood in the dusty courtyard, with the sun beating down upon her bonnet, and did not stir a muscle. But gradually the heat began to do its work, and added to the exhaustion of her nerves and all the agitation of the morning, she found after a little that she was growing very dizzy. Darnley was busy giving directions to the ostler, but at last he came back to her side.

"Really," she said in a tremulous voice, "I think I must go inside. I think perhaps I will faint away again if I do not lie down upon a bed."

Darnley did not mean to hurt her, and when he saw that her face was really white and that there was perspiration on her brow, he at once agreed. A sitting room was instantly called for, and a bedroom, and the mistress of the establishment given charge of the young lady with many admonitions of care.

"My lady does not feel very strong," said Darnley to the inn-keeper's wife, a plump woman with a stern expression. "I think it is the heat of the journey. Put her to bed, and I shall order dinner, which we'll take in the sitting room."

The woman clucked, and peered into Roselind's face, and made some derogatory comments on men who would not hire a good covered carriage for a lady, and bustled inside, giving orders for the gentlefolk's rooms and dinner to be got ready. It was not a large place, but their hostess was a woman greatly given to organization, and when she had seen what kind of people she was dealing with, she at once ordered up the best sheets in the house to be laid upon the best bed, and puffed up the stairs herself, before she let them in, to see that everything was dusted as it should be.

"There, there, mum," she cooed when Roselind was safely tucked away, "there's nowt but a good rest needed to put you back in the pink, I'll warrant. I'll jest be fetching you up some good tasty broth in a minute or two, and then you'll see how quick you are yerself agin!"

Roselind demurred, and said all she really needed was a moment's rest, but her self-appointed nurse would have none of it. She bustled off, and in a moment bustled back, this time bearing a peculiar-looking tonic in a mug, and a cool pomade for Madame's brow. But neither the tonic nor the pomade had their desired effect. Peer at her as she might every moment, the good woman could see very little change in the young lady's pallor.

"Coo!" she breathed, laying a hand upon her brow. "Y'are like ice, noo!"

"I am only a little fatigued," murmured Roselind, but in truth she felt weaker than even her recent ordeal could account for. In half an hour she had grown ruddy and hot, and Darnley, who had been wandering in every five minutes to inquire nervously after his "wife's" health, became very agitated indeed.

"Now, don't ye go gettin' yerself caroused, sir," said the inn-keeper's lady with authority. "It's naught but a fever from the heat, it's not. Only give her a night's sleep and she'll be good as new!"

"A night's sleep!" cried Darnley. "But that's impossible! We must be on the road again in half an hour!"

"Now, sir, what can ye mean by that?" demanded the woman sternly. "Would ye have her expire, for all your hurryin'? Ye'd best sit down and calm yerself, sir, and let Matilda take care of 'er. These delicate ladies only need a bit of pamperin', they're not so hardy as the rest of us! What would you, go rushin' off, when she's sick and p'raps in danger? I ask you, sir—with respect—what's so urgent?"

And Darnley cast a miserable look at Roselind, who smiled weakly back, and then he sank into an armchair in the corner and seemed almost about to weep.

"Never mind," whispered Roselind—for she was capable of no greater effort than a whisper—"I shall come along now, if you like!"

"No, of course you shan't! You'll stay just where you are!"

And so the vigil was begun. Roselind sank lower and lower in the afternoon, and by evening she was growing delirious. Reginald Darnley was really beyond himself by now. He could not sit still, and the fear in his heart showed in his eyes. He wandered in and out of the little bedroom with the freedom of a husband, which of course he had said he was, and then would heave himself down upon an armchair in the adjoining sitting room and stare moodily into the fire. At last a doctor was sent for, and a stronger tonic administered. Roselind fell at last into an unquiet sleep, but her dreams were peopled with horrible faces and the noise of arguing voices. She awoke in a sweat sometime in the middle of the night. Her eyelids fluttered, and as she grew used to the dark of the bedroom, which was a little alleviated by a crack which had been left in the door into the sitting room, she realized that the argument she had been hearing in her dreams was really coming from the next room. She listened at first without any understanding of what she heard. But gradually it began to make some sense.

"I cannot bear it anymore!" a strange masculine voice exclaimed. "You may kill me if you like, Darnley, but I shall not live any longer like this! For five years I've been no better than an animal, continually living in fear of you, blind to my own conscience, and suffering the contempt of my own sister! What good is my life, when it is not my own? Only give up the lady, and then you may kill me!"

A low laugh was heard, which sent a chill down Roselind's spine, even before she knew it had come from Reginald Darnley.

"That I cannot do, my friend. You think you are the only one who has lived in fear these five years? Hah! You pathetic little worm, I daresay you never considered what has happened to me!"

"Never mind about that, Darnley." The strange voice, which had begun on rather a high note, seemed to deepen. As it did so, it gained in authority, and now it continued to speak, with a calm, low, almost fatalistic ring.

"Never mind about your own suffering, Darnley. You've put so many other people into a living hell, why should not you suffer? Only think what you did to Roderick Montague! I know that I had a great hand in that—if it had not been for my own weakness, I should have told the world long ago what you did to him! But that is all over. I shall never again lie awake all night, unable to sleep for the weight of my conscience."

"And what will you tell the world, Quimby?" came the sarcastic voice of Mr. Darnley. "Who will believe you? Who will believe the word of a legal clerk against that of Reginald Darnley?"

"I think there are those who may."

It had been said very quietly, and a short silence followed the remark. When Darnley next spoke, there was an edge of panic in his voice.

"Whom do you mean, man? Have you told anyone yet?"

"I told my sister some time ago, and I believe she has already confided in this lady's brother, in Lord Iseleigh. But what may interest you more is that Roderick's brother knows. Lord Peter Montague knows all about it! The world will believe him, if it will not believe me!"

"Montague! I thought he had died in France!"

"So everyone assumed, but it's not true. Peter Montague is in Bath at this very moment, and I believe your life is not worth much while you are both in England."

"Pshaw! I am not afraid of him! What can he prove against me? And besides, his brother was already disgraced. No one will put much credit in his word! And besides, I have got the lady. So long as Lady Roselind is my wife, no one will dare discredit me! Her uncle will see to that, I daresay!"

But at that moment the sound of a door being thrown open was heard, and another voice broke in.

"Thank God!" was all it cried at first. But it was enough. Roselind recognized the voice, even before a flood of relief washed over her. It seemed to her that there had never been a more beautiful arrangement of tones and rhythms than were mingled in those two words spoken by that voice.

"Thank God!" said Peter Montague again. "Where is she?" But now there was the sound of a table or some other piece of furniture being knocked over, and noise of feet and arms ensued.

"Never mind, Darnley, you had better not waste your energies," said Peter when there was a silence. "The word is out. By now there are at least a dozen people who know what you did to my brother five years ago. If you kill me, you only seal your fate forever. They know how you made Roderick sign away that deed of land, and then how you used it as evidence that it was he who had gambled, and not Quimby here! They know what you told my father—how you very nearly blackmailed him into discrediting his own son—and how, as a result, Roderick went willingly to his death. You killed him, Darnley," said Peter in a voice as cold as ice, "as surely as if you had run a dagger through him from the back!"

"I never meant to kill him," said Darnley in a low voice almost like a moan. "I only wanted him disgraced."

There was a moment's silence, and then Peter Montague said something in a low voice which was indistinguishable to Roselind. But the next thing she knew, the door which joined her room to the sitting room was thrust open and the beloved figure of her brother was silhouetted against the lighted doorway. "Rosie," he said in a querulous voice, "are you here?"

She just managed to respond, and in a moment they were in each other's arms.

"Oh, my dearest!" whispered Roselind. "I cannot believe it is you."

There followed many words of assurance and comfort before Bertie recollected where he was and what had happened and demanded to know if his sister had been harmed.

"No, no—he has been very kind to me," she protested. "Only I am very weak. I must have caught a chill or become taxed by the heat. At any rate, I care nothing for that now. Oh, my darling brother! You have no notion what it feels like to see you again!"

"Nor can you," said Bertie, "imagine the relief Montague and I experienced on seeing you had not overtaken us by much!"

Roselind looked up in surprise and saw that Mr. Grey was standing in the doorway with a smile upon his lips.

"So the scapegrace has not done your sister any injury, I see," he said.

"Oh, Rosie," exclaimed Bertie, remembering all at once, "I suppose you do not know—but Mr. Grey is really Peter Montague, in fact! He was masquerading so as to discover who had been responsible for his brother's flight from England."

Peter, still with a smile on his lips, made a bow. "I hope you will not hate me for having deceived you for so long, your ladyship," he said gravely.

Something made Roselind incapable of meeting those eyes, for her next words were spoken very softly. "Hate you!" she murmured. "I could never hate you."

It is doubtful whether Peter really heard these words, for he gave her a strange glance, and then turned from the room, saying over his shoulder to the earl that he would go and make preparations for their immediate departure. Roselind was still so weak that she had hardly any idea of what happened in the next hours.

There were intermittent moments of lucidity, and in these she remembered afterward that she had been aware of a chaise and four, and an endless stretch of highway in the moonlight, and at last that she had awoken, around dawn, in her own bed. But she was too ill for the next week to know much of what went on around her. Under the ministrations of Lady Agatha's physician she very gradually regained her strength, but still she slept nearly all the time, awakening at odd hours of the day and night to see a different face hovering over her, a different hand coaxing into her lips some sip of broth or tea or medicine. It seemed to her that often the face and hand belonged to Mr. Grey, but this she accounted to be a dream, for she had been full of strange fantasies, and her sleep was alive with his face, his eyes, and his hands.

On the seventh day of Roselind's convalescence, she sat up for the first time and took some nourishment. Lady Agatha was sitting beside her bed with a very happy expression.

"Well, my dear child," she said, "you have been very ill. You have no idea how worried we have all been. But I think you are beginning to look yourself again. It will be a week or two before you feel any stronger, but Dr. Sprague assures me you are over the worst."

Roselind began to remember patches of the events which had led up to her illness, and wondered what had happened since she had last been conscious.

"Reginald Darnley has left England," said Lady Agatha, "but I shall not tell you any more now. Tomorrow, if you are strong enough, we shall carry you downstairs and arrange you very comfortably on a sofa, with a rug and many pillows, and you shall hear it all. By the by, my dear," she said, as she was going out of the room a little later, "there is one friend who has been more anxious for you than anyone else—perhaps even more than myself. I hope you will send him a kind message."

Roselind's heart, even in her weakened condition, leaped up. "And who . . . who is it, Aggie?" she murmured, barely daring to hope.

"Why, it is Mr. Grey, my dear. But, of course, now we must call him his Grace, the Duke of Hamilton."

22

"*M*on *Dieu*, I can hardly believe it!" exclaimed Georgina Devonshire when she had heard the whole saga of Reginald Darnley's rise to consequence at the expense of Roderick Montague. "I wonder it has taken so long to come out!"

The duke smiled to himself. He had been standing with his back against the mantel in the Banforths' conservatory while he spoke.

"The truth," said Peter, "has no power to reveal itself without the help of human beings. Wherever there are people, there will be hypocrites, and little as we may like to think it, we are all of us sometimes guilty of that charge. We like to be comfortable, and truth is often unsettling; we like to think ourselves good, and yet not to exert ourselves in the effort to be so. The real villain in all of this, I am convinced at last, is not Reginald Darnley, but the machinery of human nature. If there is one culprit, it is society, and society's demand that however much there is of evil and unkindness in the world, we present an orderly front. I believe that even if Quimby had come forward at the time, he would have been ignored. No one wishes to admit that he has falsely accused an innocent man, and at the risk of sacrificing his own comfort, he will willingly send an innocent lamb to the slaughter."

Georgina gave a little shudder, and looked at Maude Quimby, who was lying on a little sofa near at hand. "At any rate, my dear Miss Quimby," she said, "it seems to have all worked out in the end. Even if we are all so evil as Peter is determined to make us, the truth has had its triumph after all."

Maude Quimby smiled at the duchess and said, "Your Grace is right. I think there is no gain in reveling in what has passed already. We had better look forward to the future, and determine we shall have more courage from now on."

"*You* have nothing to improve on that score, Maude!" put in Lucius Quimby, who was standing behind her sofa. "Through everything, you have been the very spirit of brave cheerfulness! It is I who must think of the future and try to do better."

"And yet," said Lady Agatha kindly, "you have already made up a great deal for your past weakness, Mr. Quimby. It took immense courage to go off after Darnley as you did. Imagine what could have happened to you had not Peter and my nephew happened to come in!"

Everyone agreed readily to this, and Roselind, who had taken up the sofa not in use by her future sister-in-law, was first and most eager in her expressions of gratitude.

"To think what might have happened if you had not come!" she exclaimed, and at the very thought, every face in the room took on a grave expression.

"But what are you to do now, Quimby?" demanded General Banforth. "I hope you shall not return to that position in Cheap Street! Now you have got friends, and I believe there are many among us who will vouch for you. You had better search out some more lucrative position. For you know," he added with a twinkle, "it will never do for the brother-in-law of an earl to be only a menial clerk in Cheap Street, when his sister is a countess!"

Bertie could not restrain himself at this.

"But that is all arranged, Uncle!" he protested. "Quimby is to oversee Windham while I am at Oxford, and to begin my program of agrarian reform. We have already had a consultation on the subject. It is all agreed."

"Are you to marry, then, before you come down from university?" demanded Georgina Devonshire. "I am so glad! It is a dreadful waste of time, I always think, for two young lovers to be kept apart by such a trivial business as age!"

Lord Iseleigh gave his fiancée a long, deep look, as if by surrendering himself to those eyes he could procure the secret of the universe.

"I could not bear to put it off," he said. "And Maude has very generously agreed to be the wife of a scholar for a few years. Besides, the physician I sent her has already had so much success with his new cure that I think by the time I am out of Oxford, Maude shall be cantering about with the best of us!"

"But this is wonderful indeed!" cried Georgina. "I never heard so many joyous tidings in all my life! Now, all I want is to hear that our sweet Roselind shall soon be on *her* pretty little feet, in time, at least, for her come-out ball. It would be a dreadful nuisance, you know"—this with a teasing grin at the young lady—"to be forced into sending back the gown I had ordered specially for it!"

"No danger of that, Georgina," said the general, smiling fondly at his niece. "Our Rosie is guaranteed to be herself within a week. That is Dr. Sprague's promise, and I shall hold him to it. But what

I should like to know," he went on, directing his gaze to Peter, "is what has become of Darnley. I know you convinced him to quit England, but is that all the punishment he shall have for all his misdeeds? If I had been you, I should have run him through on the spot!"

"But I am very glad you did not," interposed Roselind softly, looking at Peter a little shyly.

The young duke returned the look, and there was so much eloquence in it that Roselind, had she dared to keep her eyes upon him, might have laid to rest all the fears she had entertained since yesterday. "I could not bring myself to act as vengefully as he did," said Peter. "It should have proved nothing, except that I had learned naught from my brother's death."

"Well, you are a more forgiving man than I am," replied the general. "There are few people who could have acted as selflessly as you have done in these past years."

"I beg to differ with you there, sir," said Peter, with his eyes still upon Roselind. "There are some soldiers in the world who display more courage in an afternoon than we men, with all our pompous colors and plumes, could ever hope to emulate. What I did was done, at least at first, to redeem myself in my own eyes. But there are some others . . . Well, I hardly know if there is a way to praise them sufficiently!"

Georgina Devonshire cast an amused look between the lady, who had her head bent down and was perusing her fingers with every drop of attention in her being, and the gentleman, who, though still languishing against the mantel, might as well have been kneeling beside her on the rug, and said with a laugh, "Well, *I* shall not stand in the way of you anymore! I see there are perhaps five unnecessary mortals in this room, and shall make it my business to lead the way in exodus!"

It is very odd, but very true, that the one soul who was most concerned in the duchess's observation was the only one of all of them who did not take the hint. General Banforth shrugged and smiled, and followed his wife out of the room, and together Bertie and Lucius Quimby attended to Maude's removal to the carriage which had been summoned to take them home. In a very few minutes no one was left but Roselind, who seemed very surprised at the hasty retreat of everyone else, and Peter Montague, the Duke of Hamilton, who still leaned against the mantel looking increasingly self-conscious. It was some moments before either of them spoke. Roselind's silence owed chiefly, it is safe to say, to uncertainty, and very likely Peter, although he had rehearsed his speech more than once in the last week, found himself suddenly at a loss for words. But at last he collected himself sufficiently to mumble, "Thank God they have all gone away!"

And though this did not sound like much, it was enough to make Roselind glance up with her heart in her eyes.

"I am very glad, too, your Grace," she began tentatively, "for I have long wished to explain to you what was behind all my strange behavior since you have known me." Seeing that Peter was about to speak, she raised one little hand to stop him. "Please let me go on!" she said in a pleading voice, and then with many blushes and many worried glances at the gentleman, she confessed what had made her pursue Reginald Darnley for so long, and despite all his incivility, and the many occasions when she ought to have given off her pursuit of him, to continue. Peter let her finish, once she had begun, and when she was through, and had added, "And though I do not expect you to forgive my awful conduct toward you on that basis, I hope you will at least understand a little what made me act as I did!"

He was silent for a moment before responding. "I think I had better tell you, then," he said, "that I have known about all this for some time. Your aunt let me in on the secret of your brother's fortune nearly a fortnight since. And now it is *my* turn to apologize, for indeed I should have known instantly how hard it has been for you, without *my* helping you to feel worse! I confess"—and here Peter moved eagerly forward, as if to underline the urgency of his next words—"I did for some time persist in thinking that you really admired him. I was so torn between rage and jealousy and the real desire to warn you of his true character that for the moment I was incapable of any generous behavior! Every time I saw you together, I wished only to call him out, and I could not help crediting you with some of his coldheartedness. I thought at first that you really did love him, and in the desire to do only what was right, I did nothing but what was wrong. I was afraid to let my feelings toward you color my conduct toward him—to accuse him, perhaps, falsely—and so I waited, and waited, and as time went by, I lost any trace of sense in my head. I wonder ... I wonder you do not hate me for it!" he finished with a long, pleading look.

Roselind looked quickly up.

"Oh, I could never hate you, indeed I could not!"

There was so much passionate sincerity in her tone that it is a wonder Peter thought it necessary to say, after a moment, "But... could you ever love me a little?"

There was no response that could have been more clear, or more eloquent, or more loaded with feeling than the look which Roselind gave him then. All that was needed to seal their sentiments now was the cool, soft little hand, which she promptly offered him with the most trusting expression in the world, and which he took in his fine, large, slender tanned one with an infinite gratitude and devotion.

If there is anyone who cannot guess what happened next, then they deserve to be kept in ignorance of it. True love, when it has been tested and kept at bay even for a few brief weeks, must rush out into the sunlight, when it is allowed, with such a rejoicing and such speaking silences and tender looks that no one, save the two who live through it, can ever hope to describe it. Peter Montague and Roselind Arden could not have known that an hour had passed before they were aware of a whole world beyond those walls, and when they at last looked up from each other's eyes, Roselind had promised to be a duchess. There was only one question left to settle, and this was so easily arranged that it is amazing how much trouble it had caused in the first place.

"But," said Roselind, tearing herself away with some reluctance from her lover's arms, "there is still Bertie's future to be settled."

"Oh, that," said Peter with an impatient look. "I have already looked into it. I was in Devonshire for two days, consulting with your father's old steward. There has been a mass of mismanagement and a great deal of unnecessary expense, but the estates will survive quite well with a little organization. Your brother will not be the richest man in England, but he will be wealthy enough for a family of fifteen, if he likes. All round, I think he is a devilishly lucky fellow, for he has got the best lady in the world—except, of course, for me."

And then Peter laid his fingers over Roselind's lips so that she would say nothing until he had given her the longest and tenderest kiss that any duke ever forced upon his beloved.

www.ingramcontent.com/pod-product-compliance
Lightning Source LLC
Chambersburg PA
CBHW020718130726
47899CB00011B/387

* 9 7 8 0 7 8 6 7 5 5 0 6 6 *